Disciples of Priapus

By Donald Webb

STARbooks Press

Published in the United States by STARbooks Press, PO Box 711612, Herndon, VA 20171. Printed in the United States.

Many thanks to graphic artist John Nail for the cover design. Mr. Nail may be reached at: tojonail@bellsouth.net.

Herndon, VA

CONTENTS

CONTENTS

RUGBY BALLING

Billy and I were on our way home from an out-of- town rugby match. He was asleep and reclining on the passenger seat of my old sports car, while I drove. The shower-room at the field was closed for repairs, so we just drove home in our sweaty rugby outfits. The fact that it was hot and humid, and the air-conditioner wasn't working, didn't help matters. My cock was agonizingly hard, and it was all Billy's fault. He doesn't know it, but his body sends out some kind of pheromones that drive me crazy!

We are both big guys, which figures since we are both forwards on our rugby team. You have to be big and muscular to make it in the rugby league. We don't wear all that padded sissy-gear that footballers wear. The only protection we wear are jockstraps.

There wasn't much room for Billy's long muscular legs in the small car, so he had them widely splayed. The leg closest to me rested on the center console, the other rested against the door. He wasn't wearing much, just socks and shorts. His shorts were a mess. The side-seam, closest to me, was ripped from the hem to the waistband, so I had a great view of his bulging jockstrap and even some pubes. His muscular arms, extended above his head, framed his masculine face. His hairy armpits, and hairy chest, were close enough to touch.

I turned on the cruise control and rested my naked leg against his leg. There was no sign on his face that he was awake or aware of the contact, so I placed my hand on his thigh, gently shook his leg, and said, "Billy, you awake?" There was no response. I became bolder and slid my trembling hand down his thigh right onto the mound between his legs. His jock was warm and moist. His tumescent cock throbbed against my hand. I wanted to free his dick and stroke it, but I was too chicken. I knew that if he woke it would be the end of my rugby career, so I quickly withdrew my hand.

The guys on the team are always joking about "fags", so I always put on a straight act when I'm around them. I enjoy the body contact, and the rough and tumble of the game, especially when I'm in a scrum tightly surrounded by the other forwards. I often cop a feel of rear-ends, and baskets, in the heat of the play. It gives me something to think about during my jerk-off sessions.

I needed to take a whiz and my jock was feeling pretty crowded anyway, so I started looking for an area where I could pull off the highway. When I saw the rest stop sign ahead, I breathed a sigh of relief. The restrooms were closed for repairs, so I parked close to some bushes. There was only one other car parked at the far end of the rest area.

Since Billy was still asleep I quietly got out of the car, pulled off my jersey, dumped it on the hood, and then entered the thick bushes. When I was completely hidden, I pushed my shorts down my legs and freed my nearly-hard cock. It took a while before the piss started flowing. I watched as the thick stream of steaming piss soaked into the parched earth. As my bladder emptied, I scratched my swollen balls. It felt great to have them swinging free in the cool air. But I was feeling a lot more than that.

The thought of Billy, spread out in my car, brought on another hard-on. I ran my hand up and down my boner. My balls began to rise in their pouch as I jerked on my throbbing pole. I knew I needed to shoot my load before heading back to my car, and this was the perfect chance, so I started whacking. I was just getting into the swing of things when a twig snapped. I looked toward the noise and was startled to see a 30-something guy standing a few feet from me and staring at my hard dick.

Except for his black boots, he was stark-naked. A pair of shorts draped his shoulder. He was muscular and stood about five-ten and he was showing a good size boner himself. Dark hair emphasized his pale white skin, and there were intricate tattoos covering his arms and chest. One of his hands tugged at his nuts, while the other stroked his substantial piece.

When he saw I was cool, he took a few steps forward, dropped to his knees in front of me and licked the head of my dick. Just what I needed, I thought, a quick anonymous blowjob. I looked around, to make sure we were alone, then relaxed and let him go at it.

His lips slipped down my shaft, in one lunge, not stopping until they were pressed against my pubes. He grabbed my butt and pulled me against his face, trying to get all of my dick down his wide-open throat. He held me like that for a short while, his throat muscles working my shaft, then using my nuts as leverage, he bobbed his head up and down. He was a natural. If they had a Cocksuckers Hall of Fame, he would've had his picture up there.

Suddenly a warm hand rested on my shoulder. Billy was standing next to me watching the action. My heart missed a beat. I tried to get my rod out of the cocksucker's mouth, but the guy held onto my ass and continued his incredible deep-throating. I was in a panic. Being caught, with my cock in a guy's mouth, was my worst nightmare come true. Billy was probably disgusted, and it wouldn't be long before the whole team knew I was a fag. But I was wrong.

"I could do with some of that. I've been horny ever since you felt my dick in the car," Billy said.

I couldn't believe what I was hearing. Was he just testing me? He wasn't. He removed his shorts and jock and held his cock next mine. My dick is big – eight inches when I last measured, but he had me beat by at least two inches. I could see the ridge of his dick-head still encased in his smooth foreskin.

The cocksucker's mouth moved to Billy's dick. He chewed on Billy's pliable foreskin for a while and then he unsheathed the plum-shaped head and lapped up Billy's precum. As he slipped the head into his mouth, his violet eyes gazed up at Billy, as though he was looking for encouragement.

"Suck that dick, dude," Billy commanded. "All the way down. Show me what a good cocksucker you are."

The tattooed guy paused, and then slowly took Billy's huge dick all the way down, once again demonstrating his superb deep-throating ability.

"There we go ... I knew you could do it," Billy said.

I fumed as I watched Billy's long shaft sliding in and out of the cocksucker's mouth. I wanted to push him away and take over, but I didn't dare. I've wanted to do Billy for years, but have never had the courage. In the jock world men get blown, maybe sometimes by other guys, but they don't blow. But he said he knew I'd copped a feel in the car, so maybe he'd be cool with it if I dropped to my knees?

Billy moved the cocksucker's mouth back to my dick. It excited me to think that I was fucking the same hole as Billy. He placed one hand on my ass and the other behind the head of the cocksucker, watching as he gobbled on my dick, like it was the last one he'd ever see. Billy rubbed my asscheeks as his other hand moved from the cocksucker's head to my nuts. He briefly fondled them, and then held my shaft for the cocksucker, as though he was feeding him my dick.

"Oh yeah," Billy said. "Suck that big dick. Deep-throat that fucker."

Just when I thought I had seen and heard it all, Billy moved behind me and sank to his knees. His tongue began to lick my sweaty asscheeks and I could hear him groan in lust. He slowly moved toward the center of my ass, zeroing in on my pucker. His big hands spread my jock-framed mounds of flesh apart as his tongue dived into the crevice. He probed my hole and even nibbled at the sensitive crater. I looked back at him because I could hardly believe that it was really Billy on his knees behind me.

Next Billy was removing my shorts and jock. He spread my legs wider to give him greater access to my butthole, and then went back to rimming me. Meanwhile, the cocksucker had stopped briefly as my jockstrap was removed, but then he dived right back onto me as though he was scared I would get away. He wasn't a bad-looking guy but this must've been like a fantasy come true to him – two 20-something rugby jocks, right from a sweaty match, wanting him to suck them.

Billy stood up. His arms circled my torso. I could feel his hairy chest brush against my back. Then he pinched my nipples and rubbed his dick between my butt cheeks. Overcome with lust, I rested my head on his shoulder. He licked my neck and nibbled on my ear. I finally believed this was happening.

The cocksucker's mouth came off my dick. "Turn around. I want to taste your ass," he said.

I wondered what Billy would do when I turned around. I didn't have to wonder for long. He dropped to his knees and sucked me down to the root. He wasn't the straight dude I thought he was. I couldn't believe such a butch number would suck cock. His deep-throating actions brought me to the brink. Just when I thought I was ready to shoot my load, he backed off, stood up, and gave me a tongue bath. He licked the sweat off my chest, and dived into my armpits. Shit, I thought, at this rate I won't need a shower when I get home. Then he placed his hand behind my neck and pushed my head down to his throbbing dick. "Suck me," he said.

I couldn't wait. Not losing a precious second, I opened up wide and let Billy's dick-head move into my gaping mouth. I hung onto his hips to keep my balance, because the tattooed guy behind me was pulling my butt onto his face, and spearing my asshole with his agile tongue. My legs spread even wider as I crouched to open myself completely to him.

Billy grabbed my head and began to fuck my face, pushing his huge dick between my lips and sliding his shaft down my throat until I gagged. Then he pulled it back until just the head was left in my mouth, and then rammed it back into my throat. The two of them worked me between them, one in my mouth and the other at my ass.

After a while Billy pulled me up, turned me around, and started pushing fingers into my butthole. I was practically out of my mind with lust, pushing my ass back onto the probing digits, hoping he would delve deeper. He had unrestricted access to my asshole and let me tell you he took full advantage. I wanted him in my hungry hole. I whimpered when I felt his cock pushing at my butthole.

"Wait," the cocksucker said. He pulled a tube of lube out of his shorts and lubed my asshole and Billy's cock.

When Billy's dick once again probed my hole, I said, "Take it easy ... it's been a while since I've been fucked."

I gasped when his dickhead breached my tight assring. I'd never had anything that thick in me before. But there was no stopping him. His big boner shoved its way in to the hilt, almost lifting me off my feet when he hit home. He was touching areas that had never felt a cock, and it felt fantastic.

"Fuck that ass," the cocksucker commanded. "Give it to him." Then he lubricated his own asshole. He turned around and impaled himself on me, sinking my rod deep into his silky channel. There was just enough room for me to rock back and forth, sliding my ass back on Billy's rigid shaft, then planting my dick back into the cruiser.

Billy turned my face to his, planted his lips on mine, and sank his tongue into my mouth. I could taste my cock and ass juices in his mouth, but I didn't mind. The two of them allowed me to set the pace for a while, and then Billy took over. He grabbed my hips and pounded my ass as though there was no tomorrow, ramming deep in my hole. I didn't have to do anything. At the same time I got fucked, my cock slipped in and out of the cruiser's asshole as he jerked himself off.

I could feel Billy's hot breath as he whispered in my ear. "I can't hold back ... I'm gonna shoot my load in you."

5

When he started to cum, it was like a chain reaction. His pistoning rod seemed to push the cum right out of my balls, while my own cock fucked the cum out of the cruiser. I was gasping for air. My legs shook with fatigue, my heart pounded, and my asshole clenched around Billy's rod, milking out every drop of juice.

The tattooed cruiser got off my cock, slipped into his shorts and, without a word, walked away. Billy took me in his arms and hugged me. We kissed for a long time.

"Let's go home," he finally said. "I want to see what it feels like to be on the receiving end."

So that's what we did.

THE HUSTLER
GIVES UP HIS ASS

I'm sitting on a three-foot high wall – locally referred to as the meat-rack, near the intersection of two busy streets. I'm decked out in my cruising finery: A skimpy pair of cut-off jeans, with gaping legs and a rip up the one side, a well-worn white jock, and a pair of sandals. The top two buttons of my shorts are open, exposing the hair around my navel. My white T-shirt rests beside me.

Of course, I'm not just sitting twiddling my thumbs, I'm waiting for customers. I've been selling my body for years – ever since high school. It's the only way I know how to make money ... lots of it I might add, and tax-free.

I keep my blond hair short, and my chest and long legs smooth and buffed, ready for action. My sandal-clad feet are resting on the wall beside my butt, which I've pushed out to the edge of the wall, and my legs are widely splayed. My arms are resting on my knees and I'm leaning back against a wall taking in the rays. The packed pouch of my jock and part of my buttcrack are on display. I know because I've practiced different poses in front of the mirror.

Business is slower than normal. I haven't had a trick all day. None of my regulars has shown up. The temperature is rising, and I'm bored. Another hustler plies his trade a little further down the wall. He's a Goth-looking short young guy with a mop of curly black hair and a pale face. He's wearing an open, oversized black shirt, white T-shirt, baggy black pants and black boots. A skateboard leans against the wall. I know he's at least eighteen, because I've seen him up close. The Johns that pick him up are into young stuff, so we aren't competition. I bet he's good in bed; he must be, because he's very popular. I can imagine the act he puts on when they get him home; pretending innocence, making out like he's never sucked cock, and then squealing like a virgin when their big dicks forge their way into his tight pucker. The mental picture of him crawling around the bed, trying to dislodge a big dick, is giving me a hard-on.

I pick up my T-shirt, and wipe my moist chest and armpits. I bring the shirt to my nose and inhale deeply to make sure I smell okay. I don't use deodorants or colognes because my clients like me *au natural.* I look over at the other hustler. He's watching me. He nods, so I nod back.

He ambles over to me. "Slow ain't it?" he says in a surprisingly deep voice.

"Yeah, it's dead."

"You're Keanu, aren't you?" he asks.

I nod, "You're ...?"

"Gavin," he says, moving in closer so we can shake.

His obsidian eyes blink when he focuses on my crotch. "Wow, dude, that's quite a show you're putting on," he says.

"It pays the bills."

His hand feels cool when he reaches over and squeezes my calf muscle. "Nice legs ... you work out?"

"Every day."

He stares at me with his big eyes, like he's waiting for me to rebuff him, when I don't he runs his hand up and down my thigh. "Real smooth," he says.

I'm enjoying his attention – it's been years since I've let anyone touch me for free, so I don't object when he starts playing with the hair between my legs. He looks around. The place is deserted so he moves his finger to my pucker and gently probes.

"Whoa," I say. "That's virgin territory. I'm strictly top."

His face breaks into a smile. "Yeah, me, too."

He moves his hand up to his nose and sniffs his finger. "Nice," he says as he slowly licks the finger that had probed me. "I like the taste of a fresh butt."

I'm surprised at how turned on I am. The little stud is hot. He knows how to get a guy's juices flowing. He moves his hand into his pants to adjust his manhood, and then places his hand on the mound in my jock and gives me a squeeze. An older man is moving down the sidewalk towards us – I don't care if he sees us, but Gavin removes his hand and moves closer to block the view. I can feel his hard-on pressing against my leg.

"Fuck, it's hot," he says, lifting his T-shirt to wipe his brow.

I can see at least three inches of hard dick protruding above the waistband of his white briefs. As I watch, a bit of precum bubbles from the hole in his knob and, leaving a long silvery thread in its wake, sags towards the sidewalk. I'm tempted to reach over and rub my finger through his precum, but my ego wouldn't let me. He might get the wrong idea about me. I don't want him to think I'm gay. After all, I'm only hustling for the money. I look up at his face. He smiles again, like he's reading my mind. I'm disappointed when he drops his shirt.

"You thirsty?" Gavin asks.

"Yeah."

"Wanna come over to my place for a beer?"

"Sounds good to me," I say.

He tucks his skateboard under his arm and I follow him up a side street into the lobby of an old hotel. A huge black guy – who I've seen on the street a few times, is behind a grill at the desk. He's about 40, shirtless, with a shaved head. His huge deltoids, pecs and biceps, would be at home on any wrestler. You'd want him on your side in a brawl. He eyes open wide when he sees us, and his big smile reveals a perfect set of white teeth.

"Hang on a sec," Gavin says. "I have to talk to Mac."

He goes over, speaks to the guy, and then nods for me to follow him up the stairs. His room is small and hot. Sunlight streams through the open window. A twin bed takes up most of the space. The only other things in the room are a bedside table, a small bar-fridge, and a vanity.

I kick off my sandals, climb onto the bed, lean against the head-board, and resume my former trade position. Gavin pulls two cans of beer out of the fridge and tosses one to me. I run the cold can over my forehead, then pull the tab and take a long swallow. Just what I need.

He strips down to his briefs. I can't believe the tight little body that's been concealed under the baggy clothes. He's built like a dancer. He looks like he belongs on a catwalk modeling underwear. His body is smooth and hairless. The only hair I see is the tuft in his right armpit when he raises his arm to gulp down his can of beer. An intricate tattoo encircles his left bicep muscle and a small metal stud pierces his right nipple. He throws the empty can into the sink and then joins me on the bed.

His eyes lock on my basket. "I hear you're really well-hung," he says after a few moments.

I feel as though I'm back in school playing show-and-tell. "You wanna see?" I ask.

He nods. I place the can on the bedside table then remove my shorts and jock. My semi-hard dick flops onto my thigh. He picks up my jock, covers his nose and mouth with it, and takes a deep breath. "You smell real good, like a man should." After staring at my cock for a while he says, "How big is it when it's hard?"

"Why don't you see," I say.

He reaches over and grips my dick. I immediately harden. "Nice," he says as he strokes me. "About ten inches?" Right on I think. But I shrug. I don't want him to know that I've measured it. His dick is tenting out his shorts.

"You look pretty big too."

He stands and turns his back to me as he shucks his briefs. He has a star tattoo on his right cheek. It should've been five stars. When he turns to face me his big dick – that looks incongruous on his lithe form, sticks straight out from his body. He crawls between my legs. Ours nuts are pressed together when he takes our dicks in his fist. They are roughly the same length but the knob on his cock is huge, like a big ripe plum with a split down the middle. He retracts my foreskin and rubs our cock-heads together. I shudder when he smears his precum over my knob and strokes our dicks. He pushes my legs up to my chest, rests my butt on his knees, and gazes at my perineum. "Nice and hairy, just how I like them. I bet you taste good?"

"So I'm told."

"Fuck ... I gotta see for myself. You cool with that?"

I nod. I watch as he lowers his head and sniffs my bunghole. "You sure you're cool with this, dude?" he says. "You not thinking about asking me for some cash, are you?"

"As long as you're not thinking about getting paid?"

He smiles at me and then he buries his face between my legs. His tongue gently laps my hole, and then he becomes frenzied, like he hasn't tasted ass in years. Up and down he goes – driving me crazy, mashing his whole face between my legs, using his thumbs to pry me open then pushing his nose into me like an excited pig sniffing for truffles. He's a horny little fucker. His tongue slips into my channel when I bear down to open up. He continues eating me for some time, and then he looks up at me and says, "Your hole's ripe for fucking, dude."

10

I don't respond, so he crawls up between my legs and rubs the slick head of his dick over my dilated hole. I've never been fucked bare, but he has me so turned on, that I wonder how I'll react if he actually tries to stick it into me. He watches my face for a while, and then he quickly straddles my body, pins my legs to my torso, and rubs his dick over my lips. He pulls my head towards his body and holds his dick firmly against my lips. "Open up, dude," he says. "It's your turn to give me some pleasure." I open wide and let his smooth knob slip inside my mouth. I can taste my ass juices on his dick. He holds my head in place and fucks my mouth like I'm a whore. He's too big, and the angle is wrong, for me to swallow much of his hefty shaft, by I try valiantly to deep-throat him.

I'm gagging and choking on his meat when my peripheral vision picks up some movement. I turn my eyes in the direction of the movement, and am amazed to see Mac, the big black guy from the front desk, standing next to the bed. I try to free myself, but Gavin keeps pounding my throat. When I raise my eyes, I can see that Gavin is smiling at Mac. Mac disappears from view, and then I feel his hand on my dick.

"Nice piece," he says as he strokes me. I relax and go with the flow.

His hot mouth envelopes my dick and descends to my pubes. He holds me buried in his throat while his tongue laps at my nuts. His throat muscles milk my shaft. It's not too often I find someone who can deep throat me with such ease. He's a natural. Up and down, he goes bringing me to the brink of ejaculation. He must've sensed this because he backs off and starts playing with my hole. "His hole's nice and juicy, Gav ... you fuck him?"

"Nah, he says he's a virgin."

"Well, he won't be for long," Mac says as he uses two of his big fingers to open me up.

I try to resist, but my mouth is full of cock, and Gavin has me in a vise grip. It's only token resistance though; I don't want to protest too much because I'm enjoying being used as a sex slave.

"You got any safes, Gav?"

"Yeah, there's lube and safes in the drawer." I watch out of the corner of my eye as Mac comes around to the bedside table. He pulls some safes and lube out of the drawer. When he rolls a safe down his black dick, I let out a groan. Gavin and I have big dicks, but Mac has us beat by a few inches. I've secretly lusted after Mac ever since

I first saw him on the street, but I never thought it would come to fruition, because there was no way he'd pay for the privilege of fucking me. He watches my eyes as he lubes his shaft. The safe only covers the top half of his dick, so I know I'm going to get some bare backing.

He smiles at me. "You're dying to get this big black dick up your ass, aren't you, dude?"

The lube feels cold when he uses his fingers to prepare me for the fuck of my life. The mattress gives when he climbs onto the bed. I try to relax when I feel the head of his dick forcing its way into my chute, stretching me to the point of pain, not stopping until it's completely buried in me, opening me up wider and deeper than I'd ever been before.

"Yeah, baby, nice and tight. I told you he'd be a good fuck, Gav."

"Fuck, this I gotta see," Gavin says, "I can't believe you got your big rammer in him."

Gavin stands up on the bed, turns around, straddles me, and drops his bubble butt on my face. My tongue laps his tight hairless little orifice as he holds my legs in place. "He must like it," Gavin says as he grips my dick. "He's still rock hard."

"His hole's milking my shaft ... he knows what he's doing. He ain't no virgin," Mac says.

"Fuck his white ass with that big black dick. Give it to him."

Mac starts reaming my channel – in and out, in and out, like the piston on a steam engine, and I love every thrust. I try to slip a finger into Gavin, but he's having none of that. He slaps my hand away and says, "You can eat my ass, dude, but that's as far as you go."

"This is fucking awesome, Gav. Look at the way his asshole's clinging to my shaft."

"Shit, I gotta fuck someone," Gavin says.

"What you waiting for," Mac says. "Get behind me and give it to me."

Gavin jumps off the bed and rolls a condom down his shaft. Mac pauses briefly, allowing Gavin to enter him. "Oh yeah, baby. It's been a while. Give it to me. Fuck me with that big rammer."

I run my hands over the hard mounds of Mac's butt and hold Gavin's dick as it slips into Mac's hungry hole. I can't believe that such a little guy is fucking such a big dude. But he is. As soon as the head's in, he starts ramming in and out of Mac's hole like he can't hold back. Mac starts moving, sticking it to me, and then backing onto Gavin's rod. Back and forth he goes, like a pendulum. I run my hands over his smooth chest, marveling at the muscle definition.

"Shit I can't hold back any longer," Mac groans as the speed of his pistoning increases. "I'm gonna blow."

I grab my rod and start pounding. I'm so turned-on, that all it takes is a few strokes and I'm spewing cum over my chest and neck. I can hear Gavin grunting as he climaxes in Mac's chute. I grip Mac's shaft in my sheath and milk the cum from his big creamers.

We lie like that for a short while and then Mac says, "I don't know about you two ... but I have to get back to work."

We clean up, and I slip into my jock and shorts. As Mac's leaving the room he says, "Well I guess you won't have to pay rent again this month, Gav." The door closes.

"Hope you're not sore, dude?" Gavin says to me.

"I'll live."

We walk back to the meat-rack and get back to work. Freebies aren't going to pay the rent.

THE EXHIBITIONIST

I'm not ashamed to say I'm an exhibitionist. I don't mean I'm the kind of person who lets it all hang out in public. What I'm suggesting is, if the price is right, I'll strip – and do just about anything – for anyone, and everyone, if it comes down to it. I guess some people might say I'm a whore, but that's only because they're jealous of me.

I wasn't always so inclined. It started by accident, you might say, during my first year in college. I was feeling the pinch. Money was tight, and I'd already been told by my parents not to expect more from them. On the way to class one morning, I stopped at the bulletin board in the students' lounge to see if there were any part-time jobs advertised. In the bottom right hand corner of the board was a notice that read: *Are you broke? If you're between the ages of eighteen and twenty, and you're well-hung, you can make easy money.* A phone number was repeated about ten times across the bottom of the notice. The jagged edge indicated that three interested persons had already torn off phone numbers.

Well, both categories applied to me, so I tore off a phone number, stuffed it in my wallet, and headed for class. Later that evening when I was back in residence I pulled out the number. I wasn't sure if I really wanted to get involved, but when I reviewed my savings account book, and saw I was down to my last hundred bucks, I decided to go ahead.

I phoned the number. The man who answered told me he was looking for nude models. I'd never done anything like that before, but I had to admit to myself that I liked showing off my big dick. We set up an appointment for the following evening in his studio on Main Street.

During classes the next day my mind kept wandering away from the topic under discussion. What would it be like to take my clothes off in front of a camera? Would my dick shrivel up to nothing?

At the appointed hour I was outside the studio ringing for admission. I was surprised when a young guy opened the door. I hadn't really thought about it, but I guess I was expecting, let's say, a mature man.

"Matt?" he asked.

"Yeah," I said.

"Come on in ... I'm Jason," he said shaking my hand.

He locked the door and led the way down a long corridor into a brightly lit studio. "You ever done any modeling before?" he asked when we were seated.

"Nah. This is a first for me."

"Well ... I can tell you right off, you've certainly got the looks for a model, let's hope the rest of you measures up."

"How much can I make?"

"If you've got the right stuff the rate is one hundred an hour. If you're prepared to do some extra stuff the rate'll rise ... pardon the pun."

"How'd you mean?"

"Let's leave that for later. I'd like to see you naked now, to see if we can make a deal."

I stripped down to my briefs and stood waiting for directions.

"Nice body," he said. "You work out?"

I nodded.

"Okay ... off with the shorts."

It felt weird stripping in front of him. Lots of guys have seen me naked in the showers at the residence and in the gym, but this was the first time I was actually stripping so someone could check out my body. I hoped I'd measure up. I pulled my briefs off and stood with my hands on my hips.

"Nice," he said. "We're in business. Turn around so I can see all of you."

I did a three-sixty turn. I felt like a slave at an auction when he came close to examine me.

"Nice muscular butt," he said running his hand over my rear end. "I like the way the red hair peaks out between your cheeks, it'll show nicely in the colored photos. You've got a nice uncut piece," then weighing my nuts in the palm of his hand, "and nuts a bull would be proud of. Yeah, I'll definitely be able to do something with you."

I was strangely excited by his touch and his comments. I'd had sex with a few women, and they'd all told me I was well-hung, but this was the first time a guy had said it to me.

16

"I want to take a few stills first, and then we'll do some videos ... if that's okay with you?"

I nodded.

For the next thirty minutes he had me posing in every conceivable position; standing, bending, stretching, lying down, you name it. It felt strangely erotic when his hands touched me to move me into the desired positions, and I couldn't stop my dick from lengthening.

"Okay ... now for some more explicit shots," he said moving me over to a reclining chair.

After I was seated he said. "Move your ass to the edge of the seat and put your heels next to your butt."

I could feel my face reddening when he helped position me. I knew he could see my pucker, and I wondered what it looked like.

He moved in close with the camera. "That's great. That's a good shot. I like the way the red hair frames your asshole."

After adjusting the lights he said. "Hold your dick upright, so I can see what it looks like from this angle."

As soon as I touched my dick it became fully erect. I pushed it forward and held it in my fist.

"Yeah, great, great," he said taking shots from different angles.

I couldn't believe it when a glob of precum bubbled out of my dick and dripped onto my fingers. This guy's going to think I'm a homo, I thought, but I didn't care, I was enjoying myself and was getting more excited by the minute.

"I need to take some measurements for the record," he said. He removed my fist and laid a tape measure along the top of my dick. "Eleven inches," he said. He wrapped the flexible tape around my shaft. "And seven inches in circumference. I've never measured such a big dick. You could make a fortune with it."

He continued holding my dick, and I didn't object. Why would I when I'd never before felt so excited? "Does your foreskin slip right back?" he said as he ran my cock through his fist. "Ah, yes ... it does."

I was on the brink of shooting. I wasn't sure what to say. Should I tell him, or should I let things take their course? He moved his fist up and down my shaft. "Look at all the semen bubbling out of your dick. You must be really horny."

That was the final straw. Cum erupted from the hole in my dick like a dormant volcano coming to life. He kept pumping until I was drained. "What a load, I'm sorry I didn't get it on tape. Next time I'll have the video running."

He threw me a towel. When I was dressed he handed me two-hundred bucks. "Same time tomorrow?" he asked.

"Sure," I said. It was the easiest two-hundred I'd ever made, and it was the most exciting sex I'd ever had.

# # # # #

The next evening the photographer didn't waste any time with the initial posing. In record time he had me stripped with my legs widely splayed.

"Tonight I want you to play with your hole while I'm talking to you," he said.

"My hole?"

"Yeah, your asshole."

"My ... my asshole?"

"Yeah, don't worry about it, just the rim. You don't have to put anything inside."

While I thought about it he set up the video camera, and then moved a big mirror into place so I could actually see my hole.

"Nice view, huh?" he said.

I nodded. I did like the view. I'd never seen myself in that position before.

"Okay, get it hard."

I was already hard. I pushed my dick back through my thighs, and slowly stroked the full length.

"That's it," he said from behind the camera, which was connected to a huge HD monitor.

"Okay, tickle your hole."

I watched on the monitor as my finger slowly circled my crater.

"It looks a bit dry," he said. He knelt on the floor between my widely spread legs, lifted my nuts out of the way, and then sniffed my hole.

I could feel my face flush. Fuck, I hope I'm clean down there, flashed through my mind. "What you doing, dude?" I asked.

He looked up at me. "There's nothing like the smell of virgin ass. You ever smelt one?"

"No way, dude."

"Here let me show you how you smell."

He spat on a couple of fingers, ran them around my asshole, a couple of times, and then held them under my nose. I knew exactly how I smelt. I wasn't going to tell him, but I always played with my hole when I jerked off. I liked licking my fingers after they'd been in my hole.

"What do you think?" he asked.

"Yeah, I guess it smells good," I said.

He nodded. "Thought you'd like it. They say there's nothing like the taste of virgin butt. You ever tried it?"

"No way, dude! You forgetting I'm straight?"

"You mind if I have a taste?"

What the fuck! This dude is really weird, I was thinking. But I was also turned on by the thought of him doing me, so I said. "Go for it, dude."

I gasped when his moist tongue contacted my asshole. I couldn't believe how good it felt. I slowly stroked my dick and watched on the monitor when he opened my hole with his thumbs and licked inside. He mashed his face against my hole and ate my ass like it was the best thing he'd ever tasted. After a while he looked up at me and said, "You like that?"

I couldn't lie to him. "Yeah, I gotta admit, it felt great."

He ran his finger around my hole. "Your hole is still a little dry I think it needs a little lubricant." He poured some fluid onto some of his fingers and rubbed them around my pucker. "Push down," he said, "that'll loosen it up." When I did as he suggested two of his fingers slipped right into my chute. "Oops. Sorry about that," he said as he slowly twisted them and moved them in and out before completely withdrawing them.

I couldn't believe how good his fingers felt, but I wasn't about to tell him that. I didn't want him to think I was a fag.

A buzzer sounded.

"Oh, fuck, someone's at the door. I'll get rid of them. Don't move. Keep playing with your hole, but don't shoot your load." He passed me a tube of lubricant then left the room.

I squirted some lubricant onto my fingers, closed my eyes, and played with my hole. Now that it was lubricated it was easy to get a finger inside, in fact when I used two fingers they both slipped in. While he was gone, I continued fingering my hole, pushing my fingers in right to my palm, and slowly stroking my dick.

A noise in the room broke my reverie. I opened my eyes. Sean, one of my classmates, was standing in the room next to Jason.

I was stunned and paralyzed with shock. What could I do or say? I was reclining naked in a chair, bathed in high powered lights, with two fingers up my ass, and my stiff dick in my fist.

"Matt," Sean said, "I see you're also broke."

I started to move out of the chair.

"It's okay, Matt," Jason said. "I want to shoot some video tonight with simulated sex. You don't have to do anything to one another ... I know you're both straight. You'll both be getting three-hundred tonight."

Three-hundred tax free dollars, I thought. Bring it on!

I looked at Sean. He shrugged. "It's okay with me," he said. "I need the bread."

"What about you, Matt?" Jason asked.

"I guess it's okay ... as long as you don't want us to do any faggy stuff."

Jason nodded.

"Get ready, Sean," Jason said.

I watched Sean strip. He was tall and muscular and had a hairy chest. His dick, although soft, looked impressive.

"Okay, Matt, get back into position," Jason said.

I complied.

"Sean, kneel on the floor between Matt's legs."

Sean moved into place.

"I want you to pretend you're blowing Matt. Hold his dick up near your mouth and put your tongue out like you're licking him."

Sean looked at me and raised an eyebrow. I shrugged. He took hold of my dick and pumped it a few times. Precum oozed over his fist. His tongue was millimeters away from my dick-head. I couldn't help myself. I raised my hips and my dick brushed against his tongue.

He jerked away with a surprised look on his face.

20

"Sorry, Sean," I said. "I didn't mean to do that."

He nodded and moved back in.

"That's great guys. I'm getting some good footage," Jason said.

Sean pumped my dick. More precum bubbled out.

"Okay, Sean, keep holding his dick, but use your other hand to pretend you're fingering his asshole."

I watched on the monitor when Sean's finger hovered above my hole.

"I want Matt's hole to look wet, like he's had something inside. Use some of his semen on his hole."

I shivered in ecstasy when Sean used a finger to scoop up some of my precum and rub it around my rim. I pushed down and his finger slid all the way in.

"Oh, fuck. Sorry about that, Matt."

Before thinking I said, "You're good, buddy. It feels great."

"Good shot," Jason said. "Okay, Sean. I want you to stand on the chair above Matt and pretend he's sucking your dick."

Jason came over and positioned Sean. Sean's dick was fully hard, and boy, was it a whopper. I couldn't keep my eyes off it, not with it parked above my face. When I detected the erotic odor of his dick and balls, I took a deep breath. He smells just like me, I thought, as I breathed in his manly scent.

"Put some lube on Sean's dick, Matt. I want it to look like it's your spit on him," Jason said.

I put some lube in my hand and slid it up and down Matt's shaft. It was thick and long, just like mine. When precum oozed out of his dick and dripped onto my lips, I licked it up.

"Okay, Matt. Open your mouth wide. And, Sean, hold you dick next to his mouth."

Sean spread his legs and lowered his dick towards my gaping mouth. "I can't see Sean's asshole, Matt. Spread his cheeks with your hands." I placed a hand on each of Sean's muscular cheeks, and pulled them apart. I must've pulled too hard, because his feet slipped and his dick skidded between my lips and lodged in the back of my mouth. I couldn't help myself. Before I realized what I was doing I was sucking dick.

"Great, great," Jason said. "Keep it up. I'm getting some excellent footage."

21

I kept at it for a while, and Sean didn't seem to mind because he started fucking my face.

I was disappointed when Jason said, "Okay, enough of that. Let's try another position. Lift up your legs, Matt. I want it to look like Sean's fucking you."

I moved my thighs onto my chest and raised my butt.

"Put your dickhead against Matt's hole, Sean. Yeah, that's right. Hold it."

I looked at the monitor. Sean's legs were spread wide and his dick looked ready to impale me. I could hardly see his pucker in the lush bush between his legs, so I placed my hands on his buns, and once again pulled them apart. I must've pulled too hard again, because his big knob suddenly broke through my dilated sphincter and slipped into my chute. I could hardly believe it when I felt him in me, but when I checked the monitor I could see his shaft sinking into my hole. I should've stopped him but I couldn't. It felt too good.

"Great, great," Jason said. "Keep it in him, Sean. Fuck his ass."

And fuck me he did. I hooked my legs around his back and watched his big dick pounding in and out of my virgin hole. I grabbed my dick and jerked-off in time to his fucking. Something deep inside me responded to the pummeling. Before I knew what was happening, my load was spurting all over my chest and face, and Sean was pumping his load deep in my body.

"Great, great," Jason said. "Rest on top of him, Sean. I want to get some shots of your dick slipping out of his hole."

We rested for a while, then I felt his dick slip out of me.

"Look at the monitor, guys," Jason said.

A thick stream of cum was oozing out of my wide open pucker. Enough cum to impregnate the whole fucking campus I thought as I watched it drip to the chair.

"That was great, guys," Jason said. "Would you like to help me break in a new guy tomorrow, Matt?"

Try and keep me away I felt like saying, but I restrained myself and said, "Sure, as long as I get paid."

After Jason paid us we dressed and left the studio. "You wanna come to my room?" Sean asked on the way out. "I'd like to see what it feels like to get fucked by your big dick."

And that's how my life as an exhibitionist started.

FRENCHING 101

Being an avid cyclist, I was looking forward to some upcoming cross-country mountain bike races. Unfortunately an injured left wrist had sidelined me. I had taken a first-aid course, so I offered my services to the support-team.

The night before the event I received a telephone call from a guy named Terry, who informed me he would pick me up at seven the next morning. Terry, who turned out to be a good-looking brunette in his late twenties – with a body to die for, picked me up as scheduled, and drove through some back-roads to the halfway point of the 45 kilometer loop, located at the top of a mountain pass.

We spent about thirty minutes setting up our site. Terry placed two deck-chairs and a large umbrella at the side of the track then put two large coolers, loaded with bottled water, under the umbrella. We opened up the back of his van, unfolded a cot, and checked our emergency equipment. By the time we received a cellphone call informing us that the marathon was under-way we were sitting drinking coffee watching the sun rise over the rough terrain.

The forecast, for hot humid weather, turned out to be correct. By the time the first cyclist – in a cloud of dust, peddled by, the temperature had hit 80 degrees, and we were both sweating. Terry stripped off his jogging outfit then reclined in a brief pair of black silk shorts and a tight sleeveless T-shirt. I climbed into the back of the van and changed into shorts and Tank-top. As I walked back to the deck-chairs I could see his electric blue eyes checking me out. I had seen guys giving me the eye before – which I'd always ignored, but being alone with Terry in that isolated place made me uncomfortable because I could tell right away he was gay.

"You've got a good body," he said, "you must work out."

"Yeah, I do."

After I was seated he placed his hand on my knee. "How's the wrist doing?" he asked. "Still painful?"

I shook my head. "No, it's okay if I don't bend it."

A tingle ran through my body when his hand moved up my thigh. "Your legs are really smooth," he said. "You shave them?"

"Yeah, all the time. It's supposed to cut down on the drag, but I think it's a fallacy. Whadda you think?"

"Maybe ... but mine get really hairy when I don't shave."

He continued to stroke my thigh, and my rod was stiffening up. I should've worn a jock, I thought. If he doesn't take his hand off me he'll see my hard-on. I jumped up when I heard a cyclist grunting and groaning as he strained up the hill. I filled a paper cup with water and held it out to him. As he raced past, he grabbed the cup, swallowed the water and then threw the cup over his shoulder.

Other than handing out water to the dehydrated cyclists, picking up discarded containers, having sandwiches for lunch, and making small talk the day was pretty boring. We were informed by cell when the last group left the starting line, so we knew that after they passed our location we could pack up.

We were doing just that when I heard a loud voice. I looked out of the van. A cyclist lay on the side of the track. We rushed over to the supine cyclist, who turned out to be an irate Frenchman, swearing in his native tongue. It didn't take us long to realize that he couldn't speak English, and couldn't understand a word we said. After checking to make sure he had no obvious fractures, we helped him to his feet then assisted him into the back of the van where we eased him onto the cot.

While Terry checked his limbs I helped the Frenchman remove his helmet and shoes, then handed him a high-energy drink.

"Merci," he said taking a long swallow.

The top half of his muscular young body wasn't injured but I could see through the rips in his tight cycling pants that he had sustained bad abrasions to his right buttocks and left groin. Terry demonstrated to the guy that he wanted him to pull his pants down so that we could inspect the injuries. The Frenchman raised his hips, pulled his pants right off, then flopped back on the cot buck-naked from the waist down. I couldn't help staring at his thick uncut dick and heavy hanging nuts which were fully exposed between his well-developed cleanly shaved legs.

"Hey, dude," Terry said, "you didn't have to take them right off ... but I'm not complaining."

The Frenchman said, *"Je ne comprends pas."*

I couldn't remember much of my high school French, but I figured he was telling us he didn't understand.

Terry knelt on one side of the cot and I knelt on the other, then we gently rolled the cyclist onto his left side so that I could clean and dress the abrasion on his buttocks. His rounded white asscheeks, as taut as a drum, were divided by a deep cleft. The aroma of the heated sweating man wafted through the van when I parted his buttocks to check for injuries. As I tended to his wound my eyes kept straying to the hairy crevice. I had never touched a guy's ass and that was the first time I had ever really had a good look at that part of the anatomy. After my shaking hands had applied the dressing we rolled him onto his back again to attend to his other injury. I couldn't help staring at his dick – which had filled out considerably, now resting over the abrasion at his groin.

Terry unceremoniously pushed the Frenchman's dick out of the way and began to clean the wound. I watched fascinated as the oversized dick began to lengthen and stretch out as though it had a life of its own and, because of a natural tendency for it to curve to the left, watched as it moved back over the abrasion.

"Hold his dick out of the way so I can dress this abrasion," Terry said.

I looked at the reclining cyclist's face. His eyes were closed as though he were asleep. I slowly reached out and tentatively pulled his dick out of the way. Suddenly I realized that my own rod was fully-hard and that I was enjoying holding the Frenchman's dick. I watched mesmerized as he became fully hard. When his pliant foreskin slipped back to reveal part of the shiny head, a thin stream of semen oozed from his widely dilated meatus and covered my fingers. I looked up at the Frenchman's face. He was staring at me through his partly opened eyelids, and he had a wicked grin on his face which seemed to imply that he knew exactly what was going on in my mind. My hand jerked off his stiff rod as though I had been burned.

The dick, now free of restraint, bounced over onto Terry's hand. "Oh shit," Terry said as he took hold of the throbbing rod then looked into the highly aroused Frenchman's face. I could see that some kind of non-verbal communication was taking place between the two of them, then the Frenchman nodded. Terry's hand began sliding up and down the smooth shaft milking semen from the stud's big nuts.

"Ah, Oui." the Frenchman said. "C'est bon."

That I understood.

"Well," Terry said looking at me, "I don't know what your inclinations are ... but I'm not about to let this hunk go before I taste his cock."

I watched in shock as he lowered his head and began to tongue the Frenchman's dick. He used his thumbs to pry open the stud's dick-hole then pushed his tongue in so he could lap up the precum. I sat back on my haunches in a daze and watched him. I had always considered myself straight, and yet I couldn't deny that I was turned on by the erotic display. It was more exciting than any of the straight porn I'd watched.

After washing the knob with his tongue, Terry opened his mouth wide and the rod slipped inside. His head bounced up and down then with a final lunge he engulfed the whole rod, right down to the Frenchman's bush. I was flabbergasted by this blatant display of crude sexuality, but was also wishing that it was my cock that was in Terry's mouth.

After deep-throating the Frenchman for a while Terry moved his mouth to the bulging nuts, licking the guy's sac then sucking both orbs into his mouth. His hand stroked up and down the slick shaft as he rolled the nuts around in his mouth.

Hearing a loud "*Mon, Dieu.*" I looked up at the cyclist to see an ecstatic look of pleasure on his face. He winked at me then ran his hand down my back and slipped it into the gaping leg of my shorts so that he could rub my bare asscheeks and tickle the entrance to my virgin chute. I thought about rebuffing him, but I was enjoying his touch, so I let him continue.

After deep-throating the Frenchman's pole for a short while Terry suddenly stood up and shucked his shorts. His huge boner sprang into view as it was released from the tight confines of his briefs. The Frenchman's hand left my ass, came to the back of my head, and pushed my unresisting face towards his groin. His other hand held his rod to my lips. This was all the encouragement I needed. Without thinking I opened wide and sucked his dick-head into my watering mouth, marveling at the silky smooth texture of his manhood.

Terry straddled the cot then fed his dick to the reclining cyclist. As I sucked on the Frenchman's cock, he began to blow Terry. He placed his hands on Terry's ass-mounds and deep-throated his huge rod. As Terry fucked the Frenchman's throat the crevice between Terry's asscheeks opened wide revealing his tiny pink pucker. The cyclist's finger moved over to my sucking mouth where he gathered some saliva. My eyes were fixed on his finger as it moved to Terry's hole and entered with ease.

Terry wiggled his ass when the Frenchman starting finger-fucking him with two fingers, pushing them in right to the palm of his hand. The Frenchman removed his fingers and pushed Terry back towards the cock in my mouth.

Reaching over to his bag, Terry pulled out a condom and handed it to me. "Put it on his dick," he said as he lubed his asshole.

I opened the package and rolled the sheath down the Frenchman's dick. Holding it upright I watched in awe as it disappeared into Terry's slick chute. There was a look of pure pleasure on Terry's face when he wiggled his ass and settled on the muscular thighs of the injured cyclist.

I stood up and removed my shorts, stroking my long hard shaft as I watched Terry fuck himself on the Frenchman's dick. The whole scene was so new to me that I just didn't know what to do.

The Frenchman licked his lips and beckoned me with a hand.

I quickly straddled the cot and pushed my dick into his mouth, gasping in pleasure as he sucked the head of my cock. I had never felt anything so exquisite before.

"Oh fuck, his cock feels good," Terry said as he bounced up and down on the Frenchman's rod.

All of a sudden there was loud crack and the cot legs gave way. As we settled heavily on the van floor, I fell forward pushing my cock deeply into the cyclist's milking throat.

Garbled words emanated from the Frenchman as he tried to dislodge me. But I kept pushing until I was balls deep in his velvet throat. I couldn't hold back. Gulping sounds erupted from the Frenchman as my cum boiled to the surface and flooded his gullet.

Hot cum splashed against my back, in spurt after spurt, as Terry fisted his dick and fucked himself on the Frenchman's enormous endowment. Cum ran down the Frenchman's cheeks when I withdrew my cock. He pulled my head down and covered my lips with his, giving me my first taste of cum.

Terry rose up and removed the cum filled safe from the Frenchman's dick.

We cleaned ourselves with the medical supplies, dressed, and packed up. As I helped the cyclist dress I couldn't stop my fingers

27

from roaming over his muscular ass and into his sweaty crevice, wondering what it would be like to fuck him. We placed his cycle in the van then drove down to the finish line. As we unloaded him and his cycle we were surrounded by a chattering group of Frenchmen who were obviously pleased to see him safe and sound.

As Terry and I were preparing to leave, the injured cyclist limped over and gave us each a hug, kissed both of my cheeks, and whispered in my ear, "*Adieu, mon ami. Merci beaucoup.*"

"You're ... ah ... welcome," I said, hoping he understood.

He winked at me and walked off.

I quickly agreed when Terry suggested that we go to his place for a shower and a beer. My introduction to gay sex had been such a turn-on that I was anxious to broaden my horizon and attempt something different.

After handing me a cold beer, Terry went for a shower. I was enjoying the beer when he came back into the room with a towel wrapped around his hips.

"I would offer you a shower," he said, "but I don't want you clean. There's nothing I like more than the taste of a sweaty virgin."

He stripped my clothes off, pulled me down onto the rug, and gave me a tongue bath. First he licked my chest, paying particular attention to my hard nipples, and then he dived into my arm pits seeming to relish the taste. He rolled me onto my stomach so that he could do my back. His tongue gradually moved down my spine until he was licking my smooth ass-mounds. I gasped with surprise when his strong hands opened my crevice so that his tongue could enter my virgin valley. At first his tongue gently circled my crater then he concentrated on my hole, driving me crazy with lust.

After rimming me for a long time he rolled me over onto my back then attacked my cock and balls, deep-throating my shaft and chewing on my sensitive sac. My hand began to stroke his buttocks as he knelt beside me, my fingers straying to his manhole. I wet my finger with saliva probed his rear-end just like the Frenchman had done. His hole opened up allowing me to penetrate deeply into his hot silky chute.

"Oh yes," he groaned. "That feels so good. I want your cock inside me."

He got up and left the room for a minute then returned and threw a condom and lube at me. As I rolled the sheath down my shaft, he lay on his back, lifted his legs to his chest, and lubed his hole, opening himself for my invasion. I quickly knelt between his legs and sank my dick into his clinging channel, marveling at the ease with which he was able to take my boner. I grabbed his ankles then pounded my dick in and out of his asshole, enjoying my first man-on-man fuck.

"Fuck me. Fuck me," he kept saying as he pulled my cock deep into his chute. "Gimme me your load."

He grabbed his own rod and began to jerk-off in time to my fucking. "Oh yes," he bellowed as his huge load burst forth from his dick, spraying all over his chest. My own load followed soon after, jetting out of me while I was imbedded deep in his innards. His hands once again gripped my asscheeks pulling me into him as deeply as possible, while his tongue slipped into my gasping mouth. I lay on top of him for a long time until my breathing had returned to normal, and then gradually extracted my deflated dick.

"What a day," he said. "Hope you enjoyed yourself, Jared?"

"Yeah." Was all I managed to get out. But I knew that it had really been a monumental day for me.

It was a far different person who returned home that night than the one who had left in the morning. I can't wait for next year's marathon. Who knows ... maybe some unlucky Greek will need first-aid.

THE SANTA
FROM DOWN-UNDER

"You just made it," the bus driver says, as I hand him my ticket. "One more minute and you'd've been stuck here for another week." He gestures with his head, "There's two seats in back."

There's a loud grinding of gears, a sudden jerk, and we're pulling away from the Victoria Falls terminal. I grip seatbacks as I make my way through the hot humid interior of the dilapidated bus. I would've flown if I'd known the condition of the bus. It's going to be a long tiring journey to Johannesburg. I just know it's going to be my worst Christmas Eve ... ever.

The two spaces available are in the last row. One on each side. I opt for the one on the portside. I stow my bag on the overhead rack and drop onto the seat beside a young number. He's dressed in baggy black silk shorts with slits up the sides, a sleeveless white T-shirt, and an improbable Santa hat perched atop his shaggy blond tresses. He's probably about five-eight, has a compact gymnast's body, and looks to be about nineteen. His tanned hairy legs are widely splayed. He's not drop-dead gorgeous, but handsome in a rugged way. The small scar over his right cheek enhances his masculinity. I feel the old testosterone start coursing through my veins when he smiles and looks at me with his cerulean eyes. I've seen him before. Earlier that day we were both bungee jumping from the bridge over the Zambezi.

By the time the bus is bouncing down the potholed highway we're getting along like two old friends. He tells me, in his Aussie accent, that his name is Ryan and he's from Sydney. The twenty-something-year-old guy, across the aisle, is someone I wouldn't throw out of bed either. His tall lean body, topped with close-cropped dark-hair, sends pheromones across the aisle. He's leaning against the side of the bus with a bare foot propped up on the empty seat. Long legs are spread wide enough for me see a healthy bulge in the white underpants showing through the legs of his ragged denim shorts. The earring in his left earlobe, and the barbed wire tattoo around his left bicep, bring back memories of a night in San Francisco. He's absorbed in a book, and appears oblivious to his surroundings.

31

After the driver turns off the interior lights, Ryan yawns, lowers his seatback, and closes his eyes. I feel as though I'm in some kind of dark cocoon as we barrel along the perimeter of Hwange National Park. When Ryan slouches low in the seat, spreads his legs, and folds his arms behind his head, I can feel the hairs on his leg rubbing against my bare leg.

I'm hard and horny. I'll never be able to sleep with him sprawled out next to me – but I lower my own seat back and try to relax. When the temperature drops, I pull a blanket off the overhead rack and cover both of us. I turn onto my side to face him. My nose is only inches from his exposed armpit. I lie motionless for a while, breathing in his clean masculine aroma, and then I slowly move my hand until my palm is resting on his warm thigh.

My heart is beating rapidly, and I'm hardly breathing, as I await a response. When he doesn't move, or repel me, I allow the jolting of the bus to move my hand gradually towards his crotch. It seems to take forever, but I'm not in a hurry. I want it to seem natural. At last my hand slips into the wide-open leg of his shorts. I can feel the moist heat of his crotch as my hand moves closer and closer to his manhood. The elastic leg-band of the built-in briefs of his shorts has deteriorated, leaving him wide open to my assault.

I turn my hand over and a big set of moist nuts rests in my palm. I don't move for a moment or two, and then, unable to control myself, I grasp them in my fist. When I'm finished playing with his nuts, I move my hand further into his shorts, until it contacts his hard dick. He may be small in stature, but he sure has the dick of a full-sized man. It's thick and curves towards his abdomen. Just the right angle for playing havoc with my prostate when I'm flat on my back with my legs in the air. Believe me; I'm speaking from experience.

My fingers glide up to the tip of his dick. Suddenly the overhead lights go on. I jerk my hand out of Ryan's shorts and sit up.

"We're stopping for a while," the driver announces.

Ryan sits up and asks, "What's happening?"

"I guess it's a rest stop," I say.

We shuffle off the bus when it stops in front of a ramshackle thatched-roof building.

Ryan and I are on our second beer, when the bus driver announces there's a problem with the bus, and we'll be there until morning. "There's some cabins available," he adds. "If you can't get one, you can sleep on the bus."

There's a lineup at the desk by the time Ryan and I get to it. The brunette, who has the seat opposite us, is in front of Ryan. He gets a bed, and then it's Ryan's turn.

"You lucky one. Got last bed you, but you be sharing him cabin," she says pointing to the departing brunette.

Oh, fuck. Just my luck.

"I don't mind if you want to share the bed," Ryan says to me. He turns back to the clerk, "Is that okay, miss?"

"As long as he pay," she says.

We retrieve our bags from the bus and head for the cabin. It's small, just enough space for two twin beds and a bedside table between them. The brunette is curled up in bed when we enter the room. He raises an eyebrow, sneers at me, and then turns to face the wall.

Ryan shakes his head and stares at the guy. "Real friendly," he whispers in my ear.

The guy's jealous, goes through my mind. I would be too.

When we flop onto the bed, Ryan is closest to the wall. I turn off the bedside lamp. The ambient glow of the Christmas lights strung outside the window give the cabin a festive atmosphere. The distant roar of a lion sends shivers down my spine. I cover us with the sheet and snuggle up to Ryan.

If he asks what I'm doing, I'll tell him I'm scared.

I wait for a short time and when he doesn't deter my advances, I slip my hand into his shorts. His dick is already hard. I play with his pliable foreskin for a while, sheathing and unsheathing his big dickhead, spreading his precum over the knob with my thumb, and then I run my hand up and down the hefty shaft. I lick his exposed armpit. He hasn't used a deodorant, so I'm able to enjoy his natural male taste and aroma. I lower my zipper, release my aching boner, and fuck his naked thigh.

I continue licking his armpit as my hand moves over his abdomen and smooth chest. He sighs when I pinch his nipple. I lick his bicep muscle, then move over and chew on his ear. After running my tongue over the scar on his face, I gently lick his parted lips. When his tongue comes out to meet my tongue, I move my hand behind his head and cover his lips with mine. As we kiss, I run my hand back into his shorts, over his dick and balls, and into the warm area between his muscular thighs. His legs spread, allowing me access to his manhole. Using my middle finger, I gently probe the moist orifice. His hand moves down to stroke my rod.

We continue for a while, and then he raises his hips and shucks his shorts. I remove my own shorts and briefs then roll him onto his side so that I can feel his muscular butt. My hand rubs his mounds of flesh and then my fingers wanders back into his moist cleft. I lift his ass-cheek with one hand, and tickle his tiny orifice. He bends his legs up and pushes his tail back, as though offering himself to me. My finger slips into his hot hole, right to the knuckle. I can tell he's enjoying my probing when his manhole starts rotating on my finger.

I rub my cock-head over his moist butt-hole.

"Wait," he whispers in my ear.

He climbs over me, rummages through his bag, and then climbs back onto the bed with a fist full of condoms, and a container of lube. After opening a package, he hands me a safe. As I quickly roll it down my shaft, he lubricates himself. He lets out a loud groan when I place my knob at the entrance to his channel and gently push the head in. I put my hand over his mouth and whisper for him to be quiet. His hot chute clings to my rod like a second skin when he puts his hand on my rump and jerks me all the way inside. He wants it bad. He squeals when I start sliding my rammer in and out of his hole, slowly increasing my speed until I'm giving it to him like a jackhammer.

I'm so involved with the man from Oz that I've completely forgotten we have company. The sheet slips to the floor, exposing my naked ass, but I'm too far gone to stop pumping. My nuts are tightening up, getting ready for the final onslaught, when I feel a hand on my butt and a voice says, "Don't let him cum. I want a piece of his ass too."

I stop fucking. Ryan and I both turn our heads toward the voice. I can vaguely see the brunette in the gloomy room. He rubs his dick against my butt. It feels huge.

"You okay with this?" I ask Ryan.

"The more the merrier, mate," Ryan answers, and then he rolls onto his stomach, and spreads his legs.

Our roommate turns on the lamp.

I quickly resume my defiling of the guy from down-under, jerking my shaft in and out of his slippery chute. Our roommate straddles Ryan's back and rubs the head of his dick against my lips. I open wide and let him in. He's too thick and too long to deep-throat so I concentrate on the head. Ryan's ass wiggles when he feels me shooting my load deep in his luscious chute.

"Don't move," I say.

I reach for a safe and roll it down our roommate's dick. I run out of rubber before I reach the hilt. Lucky Ryan. I wish it were me about to be fucked by the monster. I'm tempted to offer my hole to the brunette, but before I can say anything, he's on top of Ryan.

I play with the hairs between his legs, and fondle his nuts, when he starts fucking the Aussie. I know he's plumbing depths that I had not reached. He fucks like a man who hasn't had a piece in ages. His dick pops out of Ryan when he comes to his knees. Before he can reinsert it, I move between his legs, strip the safe from his dick, plant my lips on his pucker, and jerk him off. Cum covers Ryan's butt when a massive load erupts from our roommate's pulsing dick.

My own cock is hard and my asshole is craving attention. The brunette moves out of the way. I run two fingers into Ryan's dilated hole and ask, "Did you cum yet?"

His shakes his head, "No, mate, not yet. You wanna blow me?"

This time I shake my head. "No, I want you to fuck me."

He reaches for a safe and covers his dick, and then, as though it's a second thought, he puts on the Santa hat. I lie on my back and pull my legs up to my chest. Our roommate sits next to me and runs his hand up and down my dick. He pours lube into his hand and fingers my hole, getting it ready for the Santa from down-under. Santa slaps my ass, and sinks a long finger into my chute. I groan when his finger twirls and massages my prostate.

The finger slips out of my aching fissure, and the mushroom shaped head of his dick forces my sphincter muscle. I take a deep breath and then shove back on the invader, opening myself completely. With one final push, Santa breaches my muscular ring, and plunges all the way in. I gasp as I feel him start to back out. I clamp down to keep him in my chute.

"Fuck me, Santa," I say, "Fuck me with your big cock."

He groans in my ear as his rod starts the age-old back and forth fucking movement. His warm breath makes my skin tingle when he plants his lips on mine and sucks my tongue into his mouth. Since he's been fucked twice, he's hot to trot. His dick pounds my rectum, rubbing against my prostate, just like I knew it would. I let out a long groan when I feel his dick pulsing in my chute.

Our roommate rolls another condom down his shaft, as though he's anxious to get back in the saddle. I think he wants a second go at Santa, who's still buried in my channel, but no, it's me he wants to fuck. He pulls Santa out of the way and then, before I can react, he's balls deep in my freshly fucked hole, and I'm in heaven. This second fuck is more prolonged. He probes me deep with his long organ, penetrating those areas which seldom get to feel a cock. My dick, still hard, is crying out for relief. I grab my shaft and start jerking-off. Santa crawls over to me and sinks my cock down his throat.

As Santa sucks me, our roommate increases his speed, ramming his rod in and out of my chute, plunging to even greater depths.

"I'm gonna cum," I say. Santa sits up and jerks me off.

I can feel our roommate's dick throbbing with life when my own dick sends volley after volley of thick cum over my face and chest. My hole feels open and abused when our roommate finally withdraws.

"Thanks, guys," our roommate says, turns off the light, and returns to his bed.

Ryan and I snuggle.

I'm glad I didn't take a plane. Santa would never've found me.

A TASTE FOR LEATHER

I've always been interested in motorcycles and bought one as soon as I could afford it. My interest in motorcycles probably started because my father and older brother were both bikers. As soon as I was old enough, and had enough money, I bought myself a secondhand Honda. Next I joined a motorcycle club, which I thoroughly enjoy. I always knew there was something different about me because I didn't feel the same need for chasing women as the other bikers in the club. My associations with women were always platonic, and I always seem to be the proverbial odd man out at biker bashes. I guess I wasn't ready to come to grips with my sexuality.

My life changed one day when I found a card lying on the sidewalk. The card was an invitation to a leather club located in the heart of the city. According to the card; membership was restricted to men wearing leather or denim, and the hours were from 11:00 P.M. to 5:00 A.M. on weekends only. The club seemed like the type of place that would be of interest to me, so I decided to check it out on the following Saturday. I thought about asking my best friend Kevin to accompany me, but was unable to contact him.

That Saturday night I went to one of the local bikers' hangouts, then at midnight rode downtown to the club. After parking my motorcycle on the sidewalk with the other bikes I went over to the club door. There were no markings on the door, only the street number. If I hadn't known about the club, I would never have guessed that there was one behind the door. After pushing the door open I entered a dark hallway containing a small cage. A guy in the cage was checking membership cards before admitting people. When I got to the cage he glanced at the invitation and then checked to see if I met the dress code.

"You have any cologne or after shave on?" he asked.

I shook my head. I try not to wear anything scent based, so if I did start sweating it was me I would smell, not something alien to my body.

"Have a ball," he said. Then he buzzed the door for me to gain access.

I entered a dark room that had a long bar down the one end, and two pool tables at the other. The place was packed with men in leather and denim. I pushed my way through the crowd up to the bar and, from a guy who was dressed in nothing but black leather pants and biker boots, ordered a Bud. The place was very warm, and I could feel sweat soaking my T-shirt as I leaned against the bar, enjoying the refreshing cold beer, slowly orienting myself to the place.

It took me a while to adjust to the dark environment, but I gradually became aware of the fact that the 40-something guy standing next to me was wearing a black leather vest and black chaps. But what really caught my eye was his muscular bare ass. He was wearing a jockstrap with the chaps and nothing else. As I stared at his rear-end a young guy came up to the bar for a beer. He too stared at the guy's ass, and as I watched, flabbergasted, he placed his hand on the uncovered butt and ran his finger into the deep cleft between the asscheeks. I was waiting for the guy to slug him, but the bare assed dude just kept drinking his beer as though nothing untoward was happening, then he bent further over as though offering himself to the young man. I couldn't believe it when the young man's finger slipped into the guy's asshole, right to the palm of his hand. Then he picked up his beer and walked off. It was right about then I realized I was in a gay bar. God, you're naïve, I thought. What took you so long? If I wasn't so dumb I would've known what kind of place it was by the invitation alone. I was shocked, but at the same time I was strangely intrigued. I felt as though I was an outsider looking in, and was not really affected by what was happening, as though I was watching TV. Rooted to the spot, I watched as two other men came up to the bar each probing the muscular guy's chute.

My mind was in a whirl, particularly when I realized that I was aroused by the blatant sexual display. I couldn't believe this was happening to me; after all, I was straight, wasn't I? Everyone else in the bar seemed unaffected by what was occurring, as they continued drinking beer and shooting pool. Being a writer, I rationalized that this was a unique opportunity for me to observe how the gay subculture lived and played, and decided to make the most of the opportunity. After buying a second beer I started circulating to check out the action.

I moved over to a darkened corner of the bar and sat at a small enclosed counter. A shirtless bald headed older guy, with a thick pelt of hair on his chest and back, looking like a grizzly bear, was sitting two seats away from me. As I drank my beer I slowly became aware of a sucking noise under the counter. Once my eyes adjusted to the darkened corner I could see that there was someone under the counter sucking the bear's cock. When I looked down I realized the bear's jeans were around his ankles. His enormous saliva-coated shaft was shining in the reflected light as it slipped in and out of a cocksucker's mouth. You can imagine my consternation when my own dick became fully hard.

The bear raised his glass to me. "You can have him next if you want," he said.

"No, it's okay," I said. "I'm getting ready to leave."

Since my bladder needed some release, I went looking for a toilet. I went through a door in the rear of the bar, then down a dimly lit corridor, eventually finding the restroom. It was a fairly large room with urinals down one wall, stalls down the other, and a large bathtub right out in the center of the room. I couldn't imagine what the bathtub was for. It appeared so incongruous sitting out there in the middle of the room. It was a very busy place with most of the urinals occupied, so I went into one of the stalls.

As I pissed I looked around the stall at all the graffiti on the walls. I couldn't help noticing that there were holes in both side walls of the stall, and realized almost at the same time what their purpose was. A finger came through the one wall and wiggled in my direction, obviously attempting to entice me. Boy, are there ever a lot of psychos in this place, I thought as I quickly stuffed my stiffening dick into my pants and left the toilet.

I decided that I had done enough research for one night, and that it was time to depart. I followed the corridor, looking for the exit, but instead ended up in a darkened room. My heart was pounding as I put my hand out to touch the wall. Scared at what might happen to me in the impenetrable darkness of the room. As I followed the wall around the room looking for an exit, I could hear movement, groans, and slurping noises coming out of the dark. The acrid aroma of some kind of incense made me dizzy. I bumped into a number of bodies as I circled the room, becoming more and more disoriented. By then I wasn't sure which direction I'd been moving in. Placing my back to the wall, I paused, attempting to determine my best course of action. As I stood leaning against the wall I could sense, rather than see, the presence of someone next to me. A hand ran over my chest and abdomen, checking my physique. My immediate reaction was to push the hand away, but instead I

39

decided to do some more research. Maybe you'll be able to write a story based on this experience? flashed through my mind.

The hand moved over my abdomen then down to my crotch, seeking my dick. I stood dead still as the stranger's hand began to rub my expanding dick through my shiny black leather pants. The person moved in front of me and dropped to his knees. The hand covering my now fully hardened dick was replaced by a hot mouth, which sucked me through the leather, breathing hot air onto my tingling skin. Hands came up and loosened my belt then gradually pulled my zipper down, exposing my bursting jockstrap. The mouth moved over the mound in my jock and began chewing me through the material. I wanted to push the mouth away but I couldn't, I was too turned on to move.

There was a loud groan from the guy on his knees when my throbbing dickhead popped out the side of my jock. My pants were lowered to my boot tops baring my ass then two warm hands clasped my asscheeks as the guy's mouth began to pull my jock down my legs. As my jock descended my pecker broke loose and slapped the guy in the face, making him groan even louder. I was so turned on by then I knew I had passed the point of just doing research, but I wanted this to happen. I was into it.

My cock was pulsating and I couldn't wait to feel it in the guy's hot mouth. He took the swollen shaft in his hand and began licking my sensitive cock-head then his mouth slipped over the head, and I could feel my dick sliding down his slick throat until his lips were wrapped around the root. I couldn't believe he'd managed to swallow my ten inches of meat, so I put my hand down and felt around. He had swallowed me. No wonder they call them cocksuckers, flashed through my mind.

The guy's hands moved under my T-shirt and grasped my hard nipples. I gasped with pain and pleasure as his strong fingers twisted and pinched the small nubbins of flesh, not realizing until that moment how sensitive my tits were. My hands went to the head nursing my dick, and I began to fuck the wide-open throat. My dick pounded in and out of the receptive cavity so aggressively that the sucker had to grab onto my asscheeks to keep his balance.

The cocksucker, obviously attempting to slow me down, came off of my swollen saliva coated dick and moved his mouth further down. He licked and sucked my balls, chewing on the sensitive orbs until it was my turn to groan in lust. Strong hands grabbed my hips and turned me around so that my ass was presented to the sucker's face. The mouth moved to my asshole and a tongue began exploring my virgin orifice. Hands spread my cheeks wide, giving his tongue access to my tight sphincter. My body was in a stooped position with my knees slightly bent so that my hole was totally exposed to his probing tongue. Teeth chewed at my sensitive fissure, driving me crazy with passion, while a hand pulled my rigid dick back through my legs and milked the shaft. His tongue licked my whole perineum, from cock-head to asshole, pausing in between to chew on my swollen balls.

Just when I thought I would explode, the cocksucker stood up and pulled me upright. He spun me around, took me in a crushing bear hug, then placed his lips on mine and kissed me. I wanted to resist, but then I thought, what the fuck, no one can see you, enjoy yourself you up-tight asshole. This is an opportunity for total experimentation without any repercussions, so I returned the kiss, hugging the muscular body, aware that I could taste my own cock and asshole in his mouth.

My hands moved down encasing two bare muscular cheeks. I gently probed the moist crevice between the mounds of flesh, marveling at how smooth the skin felt. My finger poked at the tight pucker then slipped all the way in. Well, you might as well go all the way while you're at it, I thought to myself, so I sank to my knees and began nuzzling his cock. The shaft was hot to touch and I could detect a distinct male aroma emanating from the well-endowed man standing before me.

I tentatively licked the leaking head, tasting my first cock, and then holding his free swinging balls; I brought the cock into my mouth and began sucking. Being a novice, I could only get a small amount of his enormous cock into my mouth, choking on the big head. Luckily he didn't try fucking my mouth in the same way I had fucked his. My hands continued to feel his muscular butt, fingering the tight hole between his asscheeks. As I fingered him, I realized that I wanted a taste of his asshole. My hands turned him until his ass was spread before my face.

My tongue probed the juicy hole that I had been fingering. I could feel a slight sprinkling of hair around the small aperture and wished that I could see, as well as feel, his hole. My thumbs pried the hole open enabling me to gain entrance. The taste was like an aphrodisiac to my senses and I knew that this is what I desired, what I had been denying since my first wet dream. I grabbed his dick and jerked it slowly as I continued with my oral invasion of his manhole. He bent over and, reaching through his legs, began stroking and lubricating my stiff dick with a cool balm.

I couldn't stand the stimulation anymore, realizing that I wanted to fuck this stud like I never wanted to fuck anyone before. I struggled to my feet and placed the head of my rod at the entrance to his chute. He reached behind and handed me a condom which I quickly rolled down the length of my throbbing shaft. I could feel him lubricating his hole, then he held his cheeks wide open to give me access to his pucker. My gentle, but determined, pushing slowly opened his orifice allowing my dick to slide into the hot channel. He gasped when my shaft followed the bulbous head of my dick into his tight chute.

We both rested for a moment. His invaded tunnel began to twitch around my deeply imbedded dick, and then he began to fuck himself, moving his ass back and forth until I took over the rhythm. I grabbed his hips and pounded my shaft in and out of his silky hole, sinking down to my nuts then pulling out until just the crown of my dick remained encased. I pulled him upright, and then fucked him standing up, jerking on his throbbing dick at the same time. I began building up speed until he was practically lifted off his feet with my pounding. He let out a long wail as his throbbing dick spewed out his seed, his gripping ass muscles bringing me off at the same time.

We stood there panting, for what seemed like a long time, until my dick slipped from his well-fucked hole. He turned around and embraced me in a passionate kiss. My hand covered his asshole as though to protect it, as he removed the loaded safe from my dick.

We leisurely dressed as our senses returned to normal then, not wanting to lose each other, held hands until we were out of the back-room.

Back in the corridor we were both still hungry for each other, so we stood there hugging and French kissing. I knew that if there was any way at all I wanted to continue this sexual relationship, since I had never before experienced such an incredible climax. We couldn't get enough of each other and I could feel him once again getting hard as I ran my hand into his jeans fingering his now familiar hole. I think we both gasped at the same time when someone opened a door throwing a shaft of light over our faces. I gazed in wonder at my best friend, Kevin, as he too gazed at me.

After the initial shock we both realized that it didn't make any difference, we were inextricably attracted to one another, and still are. We had shared some of the most intimate moments with each other and things would never be the same again.

As we left the club, the doorman stared at us and said, "What the fuck, Kevin. It didn't take you long to pick up the new meat. Maybe next time you'll save some for me. "

BORED IN SUBURBIA

It's the summer before my first year of college and I'm bored in suburbia, extremely bored. I haven't been able to find a summer job, and the ennui is driving me crazy. I seem to be the only nineteen year-old male in this part of the world. I could take public transportation into the city, but it's a real chore. My parents are on vacation, so I don't even have them to talk to. I spend most of my time reading, surfing the internet and, of course, jerking-off. To keep fit, I go out jogging every afternoon.

It's going on five. I've completed my usual three mile jog and, to cool down, I'm walking the last stretch. I've noticed a fifty-something hunk, who lives down the street from us, wheeling around in a 1965 Mustang convertible. Today, as I pass his place, the garage door is open and he's working around the raised hood of the Mustang. I slow down to take a look. I feel embarrassed when he straightens up and sees me looking. He waves, then – wiping his hands on a grease-stained rag, he walks toward me. I stop and wait for him. He's dressed in khaki shorts, white Tee, and scruffy sneakers. His salt-and-pepper hair is closely cropped, and he has a pronounced five-o'clock shadow. He's even more handsome up close I think, as he stops in front of me.

"Hi," he says. "You live up the street, don't you?"

"Yeah, at number ten."

"Thought so. Seen you 'round."

"I'm Parker," I say.

He sticks out his big mitt. "Nice to meet you, Parker ... I'm Cal."

Cal's hand is warm and rough when we shake. "Awesome wheels," I say. "Having trouble with it?"

"It needed a tune-up. I've had the cylinder heads resurfaced, so now I'm putting it back together. You wanna take a look at it?"

I'd love to take a look at it, goes through my mind, but of course, he's talking about the car. I nod then follow him into the two-car garage. A dusty old Toyota Corolla occupies the second space. The top is down on the Mustang. The white interior is spotless, and the metallic blue paint job is top notch. He walks around the front end of the Mustang to a workbench at the far end of the garage. He points to two objects on the bench. "Those're the reground heads," he says. I try to look impressed. "You know anything about engines?" he asks.

"Nope. The only thing I know is that when you turn the key and start them, they run. If they don't, you call a mechanic."

He guffaws. "I guess you're no different than most people. If you wanna learn something about them you could give me a hand with it."

At last, something to do flashes through my mind. "Yeah, I'd like that," I say. Of course it's got nothing to do with the fact he's a hunk.

"I'm usually home by four every day. You can join me if you want."

"Cool," I say. "I'll see you tomorrow." Then I walk home thinking about him. I wonder if he lives alone? I've never seen anyone else with him, or seen anyone else on the property. Is he a bachelor, widower, divorcee, or what?

The next afternoon on the way back from my jog, the garage door is raised and he's bent over the Mustang's right front fender. I walk into the garage, and we both say hi. I throw my sweaty Tee onto the back seat of the Mustang. He's only wearing shorts today. A pelt of graying hair covers his muscular chest. "I'll give you a general overview of the motor so you'll have some idea of what's happening," he says. "Stop me if you don't understand, or if I'm being too technical."

He makes room so I can lean into the motor well. My dick hardens when he leans over me, and his chest hair comes into contact with my naked back. I'm glad I'm wearing a jock, or my cock would be tenting out my shorts. He's pointing out various components to me, but it's all going over my head, because all I can think about is him. "So now what we have to do," he summarizes, "is put the heads together so we can reassemble the motor."

He walks back to the bench, I follow. "You can help me seat the valves," he says. He points at the heads. "These are the intake valves, and these are the exhaust valves." It's all foreign to me, but I try to look intelligent and nod my head. He demonstrates how to use grinding compound on the valve seats, then steps back so I can have a go. I'm rolling the tool between my hands like he'd shown me, when he presses against my back, puts his arms around me, places his hands on mine, and demonstrates the correct technique. His biceps feel big and smooth as they rub against my bare arms. His hairy chest is rubbing against me and his basket is pressed against my butt. I'm suddenly aware of the masculine aroma arising from his body. My stiff boner is threatening to rip the seam of my shorts, and I feel like leaning back and resting my head on his shoulder. I wonder what it would feel like if he rubbed his hands over my chest? He leaves me to continue with the grinding process, and begins work on the second head.

He keeps checking to see how I'm doing, each time leaning over me and commending me on my performance. It's going on six when he decides we've done enough for the day. "You wanna come in for a beer?" he asks as we use soft-soap to clean our hands.

I want to say yes, but I'm too scared he'll see my boner, so I say, "No thanks, I've got stuff to do."

"Okay," he says. "You be over tomorrow?"

"Yeah, it's been ... different."

"Great," he says.

I hold my Tee in front of me as I walk home. As soon as I'm in my bedroom, I remove my shorts and jock, flop on my bed, and jerk my rod. I can't believe how horny I am, and I can't get him out of my mind. I'm thinking about his hairy chest when my dick erupts and cum spurts over my chest and face. Still thinking about him, I dash into the shower. He's constantly on my mind. I try to visualize his dick. He's such a hunk, it must be big. I wonder if he's cut? I can't wait to see him again.

When I've finished my shower I wrap a towel around my middle and sit down at my computer. After checking a few gay porn sites on the internet, I place my feet on the edge of my desk and bend my knees. I smear Vaseline on my fingers, play with my hole, and yank on my dick as I watch the show. I'm thinking of him, wondering what it would feel like to have a cock up my ass, when I shoot a tremendous load.

The next three afternoons are pretty much a duplication of the first afternoon. At the end of the third day we have the heads fully assembled, so when we start work on the forth day they are ready for installation. I'm leaning over the fender when he leans over my back. He couldn't be any closer if he tried. I'm sure he's hard, crosses my mind when a solid chunk presses against my butt. I don't move. I close my eyes and visualize his dick sliding into my asshole. He keeps up the pressure. When he starts tightening the bolts his dick grinds between my butt-cheeks and I can't stop myself from pressing back against him. My boner slides against the smooth surface of the car and before I know what's happening, I'm shooting a load in my jock. When he backs away from me I straighten up and tell him I gotta go.

"Should be ready to take it for a spin tomorrow," he says to my departing back.

I dash home and climb into the shower. Even though I've just dropped a load I'm still hard and horny. I spread my legs and push two soapy fingers into my chute. It only takes a few soapy slides through my fist and I'm once again shooting. The next afternoon, I figure we won't be doing any more work on the car, so I shower before walking over to his place. When I enter his garage, he's got the whole motor assembled. "It's ready for a trial run," he says. "You up for it?" He lowers the hood and climbs into the driver's seat. After a couple of false starts the motor turns over and runs smoothly. He pats the passenger seat and says, "Let's go."

I climb in. He backs out of the drive and takes off down the street. The roar of the V8 sends shivers down my spine, and I'm proud I participated in the repairs. It doesn't take long before we're in the country. "You ever driven a stick-shift?" he asks. I shake my head. "You have a license?" I nod. "Well, it's time you learned then."

He pulls over, turns off the motor, we swap seats, and then he explains how the manual shift works. I start the motor, and immediately stall when I try to take off. I try a couple more times, but stall each time. On the forth go he places his palm on my left thigh and says, "Gently, gently, does it. Let the clutch out slowly." His hot hand is not exactly helping, but I manage to get under way. He leaves his hand on my thigh as I move, with a little grinding, through the gears. "I own some property out here," he says after we've covered a few miles. "I've got some beers in a cooler in the trunk, so we'll stop there for a brew." He points out the gateposts of his property to me. I turn in, and then we slowly make our way down a narrow lane to a small lake.

When I turn off the motor, he climbs out of the car, opens the trunk, and hands me a cold can of Bud. We remove our Tees, lower our seatbacks, and relax in the afternoon sun. I remove my sneakers and socks and put my bare feet on the dash. We're on our second beer when he runs his hand up my thigh. "You've got nice legs," he says. "The jogging's paying off." I'm immediately hard. Since we weren't going to be working on the car, I'd thought it would be safe not to wear my jock. I was wrong; I should've worn it, because now my cock is free to go any-which-way. "You're hard," he says covering my boner with his hand.

"Ah, fuck, I'm sorry," I say. "It's the beer and the sun."

"No problem," he says. "I'm hard too." He pushes his shorts down his thighs and the dick I've been dreaming about pops into the sunlight. He holds it in his fist and waves it around. It's big, probably ten inches I think as I stare at his uncut dick. "Take yours out," he says. "I wanna see it." I shove my shorts down my thighs and free my boner.

"Ah," he says. "Beautiful, just like I knew it'd be." I'm shaking when he slides his hand up and down my shaft. Precum bubbles out of my dickhead. I can't believe it when he leans over and licks it up. He tongues the head of my dick for a short while then his lips slide all the way down my shaft. He rolls his tongue around the base of my dick then he backs off, sits up, and licks his lips. "You wanna feel mine?" he says.

I don't answer him, but I lean over and fist his dick. I play with his skin for a few moments then, just like he did, I lick the head of his oozing dick. I try to suck him, but he's too big for me to get more than a few inches in my mouth.

"Take your shorts off and stand up over here," he says. I drop my shorts and place a foot on either side of his thighs. "Ah," he says again, and then he opens his mouth and swallows my boner, right down to the hilt. He places his hands on my butt and pulls me hard against his face, like he's trying to get all of me into his throat. The feeling is fantastic. He pulls back and then he chews on my skin. He rolls my nuts around in his hand and deep throats me again. I place my hand on his head. "Stop," I say, "or I'll cum in your mouth."

He sits back and smiles. "This your first time?"

I nod. "Yeah, I've never been blown."

"Turn 'round," he says. "I wanna taste your butt."

I turn around and lean on the top of the windshield. "Beautiful," he says as he spreads my butt cheeks with his hands. "The sun's shining on the blond hair in your crack." I can feel his day-old beard and his hot breath when he runs his tongue through my cleft. He licks my hole. I push back on his face. He spreads my hole with his thumbs and spears my chute with his tongue. He takes a breather. "You like that?" he asks.

"Awesome, dude," I say and wiggle my ass in his face.

He resumes licking me. After a few minutes he reaches into the glove compartment and pulls out a tube of lube. He's come prepared, goes through my mind. He's planned this outing. He spreads lube on his finger and pushes it into my chute. It feels fantastic so I push back against his probing finger. I know he's getting me ready so he can fuck me, and I want it to happen. A second finger slides into me, then a third. The fingers feel good, but I want his dick in me. "Fuck me," I say. "I want to see what it feels like."

I watch as he sheaths and lubes his big dick. I'm nervous. I've seen guys getting fucked on the porn sites, and they seemed to enjoy it, and I like playing with my hole, so I relax and let him take the lead. He holds his rod upright with one hand, and then pulls me down with the other. I stop dead when I feel his big knob at the entrance to my virgin hole. He pulls my head back, kisses me, and rubs my chest with his big hands. He licks my ear, then whispers, "Relax. It'll be okay. I'll take it easy. Take some deep breaths and push down." I do as he says, and let the weight of my body do the work. I gasp when I feel the pain of his dick breaching my sphincter. He holds still for a long moment, then he's sliding in and I'm resting on his thighs. The feeling of his dick boring into me is one of the best feelings I've ever had. I sit still for a while, and then he slowly lifts me up and lowers me again. My dick is still hard when I start riding him.

His arm comes around my waist and his lubed hand grabs my boner. As I ride his big dick my boner slips in and out of his fist. I'm getting close. I clamp my chute and ride faster. His hot breath sends tingles through my body when he says, "Shoot your load, I'm gonna cum." I'm there, having my best orgasm ever. My cum squirts over the dash and windshield. I can feel him unloading in my channel, way up inside of me where no man's been before.

We sit for a while until our breathing is back to normal. I can feel his heart beating against my back. I open the car door. We swivel around. His dick pops out of my ravished hole as I step outside. I turn around and watch him removed the loaded safe. I can't believe his huge dick has been in me, but it has, and I know I'll never be the same again. He smiles, gets rid of his shorts and sneakers, then stands up and takes me in his arms. "I've been wanting to do that to you since the day we met," he says. "And I've wanted you to," I say.

We kiss for a long time, and then he takes a couple of towels and some cleaning rags out of the trunk. He cleans my cum off the dash and windshield and then says, "Last one in's a chicken." He dashes into the lake. I'm right behind him. After a short swim in the freezing water, we towel dry and dress. When we arrive home he smiles and says, "Will I see you tomorrow? I still need to do a lot of fine tuning. Need to get the timing just right."

"I'll be back," I say like Arnold, then turn and head for home.

COMING OUT
IN THE SAUNA

I was always a very shy individual as a child and this shyness followed me into my teenage years. My first sexual experience took place on the night of my twenty-first birthday. I had decided to go out to a bar downtown and celebrate. I'm not very tall, have long blond hair, a compact gymnast's body and still look about sixteen years old, so I knew I would have trouble getting into a bar. That night I made sure I took my identification with me. Sure enough the doorman insisted on seeing my ID and then still needed some convincing that it was actually me.

The bar was a very raunchy place with strippers performing for the mainly male clientele. I guess I must have had a good deal to drink because at closing time I could hardly stand on my feet. I left the bar and started walking to the bus depot. When I arrived at the depot I was astonished to hear that the last bus had already left for the suburbs. My bladder was bursting so I went downstairs to the restroom. There was a sign over the urinals indicating that they were out of service so I went into one of the stalls.

As soon as I was in the stall I pulled out my dick in a hurry and proceeded to get rid of a couple of pints, all the time swaying back and forth. While I was pissing I started thinking about the strippers and began getting a hard-on. By the time I was milking the last drops of piss off the end of my cock it had expanded to a full erection. My cock is one thing I am really proud of. I know it's big because the guys at school always teased me about it. Some of them had even tried to talk me into circle jerks, but I wasn't into that – it seemed too queer for my liking.

Attempting to stuff my rod back into my pants only made it worse. I knew the only answer was to jerk-off and relieve the pressure so I spat in my hand and coated the head of my stiff cock with saliva. The feeling was sensational and I knew it wouldn't take long to shoot a big load.

As my hand started slipping up and down the shaft I was astounded to hear a voice saying, "Let me suck that big dick."

I glanced about and only then noticed the hole in the partition between the stalls. There was an eye peeping through the hole

53

watching my every move. My first instinct was to leave the restroom, but I still had the problem of my stiff cock.

"Go ahead," the voice pleaded, "give it to me. Let me suck you."

What surprised me most was that I didn't go soft and that I was really turned on by the prospect of getting my virgin cock sucked. The eye changed into a mouth and then a long pink tongue came poking through the hole. I couldn't resist the temptation so I stepped over and rubbed the head of my cock over the smooth tongue. There was a groan from the other side of the partition, the mouth opened wide, so I gently pushed my throbbing cock through the hole. The most incredible feeling followed. The mouth concentrated on the head of my cock and I could feel the semen being sucked out of the big hole in my shaft.

I grabbed the top of the partition and began pumping into the worshipping mouth. Suddenly there was a loud noise in the restroom, the hot mouth was withdrawn and I could feel the coolness of the air-conditioned room on my cock. I was just going to start swearing when a voice called out, "Okay, guys. I'm closing the restroom for cleaning. It's time to leave."

Fuck I thought, just my luck. After struggling for a short time I managed to get my aching boner back into my pants and then left the restroom thinking about the fucking faggot who had left me hornier than before. A jumble of thoughts went through my mind. What did he look like? Was he old or young? I had no idea, and realized it didn't make any difference, a mouth was a mouth.

I left the bus depot and headed down the street, intending to walk home. It soon became evident to me that I was not capable of this because I was staggering all over the sidewalk. I knew that I would have to find a place to sleep before I got picked up by the cops. It was then that I saw the sign advertising an all night sauna. Just what I needed. A cheap place where I could spend the night. There was a sign which indicated that the price of a room was twenty dollars, while a locker was only twelve. I decided I needed a room, so asked the man behind the desk for one.

He stood there looking at me for a few minutes then said, "How old are you, kid? We don't allow no chicken in here."

I pulled out my ID and convinced him that I was an adult. "Okay kid ... so you're twenty-one," he finally stated, then after looking at my ID card again added, "happy birthday – but we ain't got no rooms. You'll have to settle for a locker."

After paying for the locker and locking up my valuables, I was allowed through the door. He informed me that the lockers were on the first floor and that there were some bunk-beds on the third floor. I stripped my clothes off and wrapped a towel around my waist. After another good piss I headed for the third floor in search of a bunk. The bunkroom was pitch-dark so it took me a while to find a free bunk. It wasn't long before I literally passed out.

I don't know how long I was out. I was dreaming of the sucking that I had received in the restroom, when I slowly became aware of the fact that someone was once again sucking my cock. It was no dream. I was lying flat on my back, with my legs pushed up to my chest, and my butt resting on a pair of thighs. My cock was getting the sucking of its life and whoever was doing the sucking was a real pro. As I held my breath in shock, the mouth came off my rampant cock and descended to my cum filled balls. The mouth slavered around giving my nuts the best wash they'd had in ages. A hand encircled my balls and pulled them tight in my sac, while teeth gently nibbled on my sensitive scrotum.

This went on for sometime and then the mouth licked further down and started reaming my asshole. I was practically out of my mind. The experience was so new and thrilling that I gave myself up completely. Suddenly I felt a mouth on my chest which started licking my tits. My arms were raised above my head and the tongue began licking my armpits. The erotic sensations were driving me crazy with desire and I started moaning and twisting my body about begging for more.

While the tongue was still up my ass another mouth began chewing on my throbbing cock. I heard a voice saying, "What a whopper."

My balls were again being squeezed and I couldn't decide who was doing what. Teeth were chewing at my manhole and I felt as though I was on fire. I was suddenly turned onto my side, the mouth never left my rear-end, but I could feel someone moving around in front of me. Before I realized what was happening there was a thigh on either side of my head and a big cock was rubbing over my lips.

I was just about to object when a hot mouth sank all the way down my throbbing shaft. My mouth opened in a long groan of desire allowing the stiff cock to slip inside. It seemed a bit silly to start protesting so I began sucking the intruding cock. I was surprised at how smooth the cock felt and how much I enjoyed the sensation of it in my mouth. Soon I was sucking as though I had been doing it all my life.

The mouth that had been working on my manhole moved away and then I could feel a long finger up my chute, rooting away as though it was looking for something. Soon there were two fingers, then three, fucking my hole, opening my sphincter wide. The sensations were so overwhelming that at first I didn't realize someone was slowly slipping a hard cock up my virgin chute. I quickly reached down to check and then relaxed when I felt that the probe was covered with latex. I couldn't believe the incredible feeling. My asshole seemed to open up all on its own, welcoming the invader. The tissues in my tight chute were clinging to the long dick as though they were made for it and the pleasure increased when the hard cock began to slip in and out.

The mouth on my cock began to move up and down my shaft, deep-throating me on the down stroke while at the same time the cock in my mouth started pumping in and out of my throat. The cock up my dilated asshole began to piston in and out, faster and faster, massaging my tender prostate gland. I felt as though I had died and gone to sex heaven. Nothing could have prepared me for this erotic experience. All at once all three cocks started shooting their loads. The cock up my chute expanded and began firing load after load, while the cock in my mouth began pumping out a massive load, forcing me to swallow every drop. As soon as the two cocks began to unload into me my cock exploded. I could hear the guy gulping as he attempted to swallow my tremendous load of cum which had been building up all night.

We lay without moving for a short while. I could feel the cocks in my two orifices beginning to deflate and slip out of their respective holes. The two guys got up and left me lying there in the dark. Before I could move a hand took hold of my cock and a hot mouth swooped down on it, sucking out any remaining jism. Even though it felt great, I was a bit sensitive now that I had cum, so I had to push the guy away.

I slowly got to my feet, flexing my asshole, testing to see if there was any damage. After I was convinced that everything seemed intact I left the room and went looking for the showers. I couldn't believe all the activity going on in the place. When I had first come in my eyes were not adjusted to the dark so I had missed much of what had been going on. There must have been literally dozens of men parading around the corridors looking into the rooms. Most of the room doors were open with men lying on the beds in various positions. Feeling a little embarrassed I headed straight for the showers.

After giving myself a good scrubbing I entered the steam room. Steam was billowing around the room and it was difficult to see anything in the dim light. I soon realized that the steam room was built like a maze, with narrow passageways going in all directions. I found a small alcove with a white tiled bench and sat down. I hadn't been there very long before a young man with a fantastic body lay down on the bench close to me. I tried to look nonchalant, even though I could see that he had started playing with his substantial cock.

He ran his hand up and down the glistening shaft then bent his legs and slipped one of his fingers into his asshole. Even though it hadn't been long since my last sexual encounter, my cock began to expand to its previous proportions. I tried to hide it with my hands, but it was no good, the young man had seen the shaft sticking up between my thighs. He reached over and ran his hand up and down the throbbing tube of flesh. "Please," he said, "stick that big dick up my ass."

I was astounded. How could anyone be so gross? I was just about to leave when he leaned over and began sucking the head of my cock. It didn't take him very long to help me get rid of my inhibitions. He opened a safe, rolled it down my rod, lay down on his back and then lifted his legs in the air, exposing his small pucker. After he had lubricated his hole and my throbbing cock I took hold of his ankles and let him stick my dick into his welcoming orifice. The feelings were incredible. His asshole gripped every inch of me like a glove.

The strong muscles in his ass began to milk the cream right out of my hard cock. I was just about to start fucking him when I felt a hand on my ass. My cock rammed into the guy's channel with shock, causing him to cry out in delight. I turned around and saw a tall man on his knees behind me. As I looked at him he bent down and began licking my moist asscheeks. I relaxed my muscles, allowing him to place his tongue on my hole. The man under me pulled me down on top of him and started kissing me. At first I resisted but soon we were both sticking our tongues in one another's mouths.

Meanwhile the man behind me was loosing no time, rimming my ass like crazy and sticking his tongue up my tight chute.

Hearing a noise next to me. I raised myself up and noticed that, surrounding us, there were at least three other men. They were all starting to get into the act. The tongue in my asshole was replaced by a bulbous, condom encased cock-head, which slowly started to sink into the depths of my newly breached hole. The sensations were fantastic.

One of the other men knelt over the guy under me and shoved his big cock into the guy's mouth. He bent over giving me my first view off an anus. The sight made my mouth water. His fissure opened and closed as he fucked his cock in and out of the sucking mouth. I lowered my head and gently ran my tongue over the satin smooth hole, relishing the male aroma. As I gave my first rim job, I reached through his legs and played with his swollen nuts. The cock up my ass began pounding away driving my own cock in and out of the guy under me. Being sandwiched between two men was an experience I will never forget.

A fourth man got into the act. He straddled the guy in front of me and stuck his big cock into my mouth. By now I had lost all reason and attacked the cock in my mouth as though it would be my last. The cock slipped down my throat until I could feel pubic hairs on my upper lip. We were now all beginning that last rush to orgasm. I could feel my balls rubbing against the upturned ass and all at once my load burst from my swollen cock-head. My ass muscles spasmed, causing the guy up my tightening chute to pump out his cum, while the cock in my mouth spewed a load of man-juice, which I greedily swallowed like an old pro.

After a few minutes I managed to extricate myself from the group and once again headed for the showers. I was surprised to see that it was daylight and therefore quickly dressed and left the sauna. I spent a good part of that day sleeping and attempting to come to grips with my new found sexuality.

MEETING THE NEIGHBOR'S NEEDS

"Tony ... telephone," my mother yelled, waking me from a deep sleep.

"Hi," a male voice said when I picked up the extension. "It's Allan. Hope I'm not disturbing you?"

He didn't need to tell me who he was. I recognized the voice immediately as that of our rural neighbor. "No, I was just taking a nap."

"Sorry. Did you know that Rachael was in New York, and that I'm all alone in the house?" he asked.

"Yeah, my mom saw her leaving yesterday. She gone for long?" I said, wondering what his wife's being away had to do with me.

"Probably. I've been trying to get maid service in, but it's impossible. No one wants to come out to the country. I know you've been looking for a summer job, and wondered how you would feel about doing some chores for me."

Since I didn't know him all that well, I was a little surprised at his request. Our first meeting had taken place the month before. I'd missed my ride home from college, and was standing on the side of the road with my thumb out, when his motorcycle had pulled up next to me. I'd never been on a motorcycle before, so was a little apprehensive, but gladly accepted his offer of a ride home.

"Snuggle up against my back," he'd instructed, "and hold onto my hips."

I did as he suggested. I was kind of scared after he took off, so I rested against his back and held on tightly. We hadn't gone very far before I realized that my dick was bone hard and pressed against his rear-end. I was so horny when I got home that I had to rush into my room and jerk-off. A couple of days later I was once again standing on the side of the road when he pulled up. When he dropped me off he suggested that he pick me up every day. I quickly agreed to this. After a few days I got used to the motorcycle, but I still held on tightly, my hands circling his waist, and my face resting against his leather jacket. I always ended up in my room jerking-off.

Suddenly I was brought back from my daydream. "You still there?" he asked.

"Yeah. I was just thinking. I don't know whether – "

"Please, say you'll do it. I'll pay you the going rate. I wouldn't expect you to do it for free. I just need someone to keep the place tidy and to do the laundry and dishes."

I was still unsure about his offer. I was scared to be alone with him because he affected me in ways that no one else had ever done – but I did need the cash, so I finally agreed.

"Good. Could you start in the morning?"

"Yeah ... I'll be over about nine. Is that okay?"

"Sure ... and thanks. I'll leave the key under the mat."

The next morning I went over and let myself in. The place was already a mess. After cleaning the kitchen I went into the bedroom. The bed was all rumpled, and there were dirty clothes lying on the floor. As I pulled the linen off the bed, I noticed some blond pubic hairs, and a big wet stain on the sheet. It was obvious he'd either been jerking-off, or he'd had a wet dream. I put my nose to the wet spot and was overcome by the strong smell his cum. My dick immediately began to harden in my shorts as I thought about him beating his dick.

After making the bed I started collecting his dirty clothes. When I picked up his briefs I could detect his familiar masculine aroma. Without thinking I held the briefs to my face and inhaled deeply. I couldn't seem to control myself.

By the time I was finished cleaning up the house I was a basket case. I'd never been so turned-on before – which was confusing, because I had always thought of myself as straight, but all I could think about was what it would be like to be in bed with him. I went into the bathroom, pulled his briefs back out of the linen hamper, pulled my pants down, and then sat on the toilet and brought his briefs to my face. I breathed in, fantasizing that my face was actually in his musky crotch, then stroked my dick until I shot my load. As soon as my balls were emptied I felt as guilty as hell, and after cleaning myself up, dashed out of the house.

The next morning I let myself into his house. I was startled to hear a noise coming from the bedroom, so I crept up to the door and peeped in through the crack. He was naked and spread-eagle on his bed, doing some one handed reading and slowly working on his upright dick. He spat in his hand and then resumed his pumping action.

My heart rate increased, and my mouth dried, as I watched him pump his dick. I had never seen a hard-on before, other than my own, let alone seen another person jerking-off. His hand movement became faster and faster as he slipped it up and down the length of his spit lubed monster. Dropping the magazine he grabbed his nuts with his free hand and squeezed them tight as he beat his meat. His back arched, his long legs stiffened, and his toes curled downwards. Giving a loud wail, he gave one last downward stroke on his towering dick, and then spurted a tremendous amount of jism all over his body and the bed.

I quietly crept out of the house with my mind in turmoil; this had been the most sexually arousing experience of my life and I wasn't sure where it was leading me. After calming myself I once again let myself into the house, but this time making enough noise to ensure that he heard me. I busied myself about the kitchen, cleaning up the dishes from the night before; unsure of how I would react when I saw him. I was just putting the dishes away when, dressed in a short robe, he came into the room.

"Morning, Tony. You're up bright and early," his bubbly voice announced as he came through the door.

"Hi. Um ... sorry for the noise. I didn't know you were home. I thought you'd left ages ago," I stammered, hoping I sounded convincing.

"I decided to take the day off before starting to frame a new house tomorrow," he said.

He settled himself in a chair, leaned back, and began lightly scratching the blond mat covering his brawny chest. I could hardly keep my eyes off the erotic display, but busied myself making coffee. He got up and helped himself to some cereal. My eyes once again ogled him as he bent down into the fridge to retrieve the milk. I nearly dropped a mug when his short robe rose up, exposing his asscheeks and his hairy perineum. He plopped himself down onto the chair and began spooning cereal into his mouth. When he was finished his cereal he once again leaned back, scratched his chest, and then spread his masculine legs widely apart.

I poured him a mug of coffee then went about tidying up the kitchen. I could feel his seductive eyes following my every move, making me tremble with desire. My shaking hands rattled the dishes as I attempted to control this new and exciting feeling.

I jumped when he suddenly said, "For goodness sakes. Please sit down and have a cup of coffee. You're driving me crazy with all that racket."

Taking his advice I poured a mug of coffee and joined him at the table. I couldn't think of anything to say, too tongue-tied to utter a word. My cock was pulsating in my tight shorts and I hoped that I wouldn't be showing any telltale wet patches over the head.

He slurped his hot coffee, glancing at me over the brim of the mug. I just knew that he was trying to analyze my behavior, when even I didn't know why I was behaving in this strange manner. He pushed himself up from the chair, ambled over to the window to check the weather, then turned around and leaned on the counter sipping his coffee. His robe swung open as he moved, revealing his thick swinging appendage. I gulped my coffee down, nearly choking on the hot liquid. I could detect his distinctive male scent when he came over to the chair, clapped me on the back, and said, "Watch it. We don't want you to burn yourself."

When I'd recovered he suggested that I join him at the pool. "It's much too nice a day to spend indoors and I really would like the company," he added.

"Yeah, I'd like that, but I'll have to go home for a bathing-suit."

"Oh, don't bother going home; I'm sure I have one that'll fit you."

He went into the bedroom and rummaged through the drawers. "Here," he said, and threw a white bikini in my direction. "Try this on."

I went into the bathroom and slipped into the bikini. It fit me like a glove and did nothing to hide my aroused cock. I took a towel out of the cupboard and carried it in front of me hoping that by the time we got to the pool I would be back to normal.

He came out of his bedroom wearing a skimpy bathing-suit which consisted of a pouch up front, with a string waist band and a string between his asscheeks. A beach towel hung over his shoulder and a bottle of lotion was in his hand. As he plodded bare foot in front of me, my eyes caressed the mounds of his strong ass, watching the muscles move as he propelled himself forward on his high-arched feet. We entered the pool area which was protected by a high privacy fence and then, after spreading our towels on the lawn, we lay down next to one another in the warm sun.

After lying quietly for a short period he suddenly asked, "Would you mind putting some lotion on my back? I don't want to get burned."

I knelt next to his reposing body and began applying the lotion to his broad back, marveling at the smooth texture of his skin and his musculature. I slowly worked down to the waist band of his thong, not daring to touch his asscheeks. As if sensing my reluctance he said, "Make sure you do my butt properly. I don't want to get burned down there."

He placed his arms under his head and spread his legs apart giving me total access to his incredible cleft. I slowly applied the lotion to his pliable ass-mounds, gradually working my fingers into the hot crevice, admiring the way the sun glinted on the light sprinkling of blond hair that surrounded his pucker. The string between his muscular buttocks shifted as I massaged his flesh and I couldn't resist the temptation to run my fingers lightly over the small pink manhole exposed to my prying eyes. His asscheeks quivered as my finger slid over the tight orifice. I was so excited by the sight and by the feel of his hot body that my dick was leaking like a faulty faucet.

When I had finished applying the lotion to his hairy legs he rolled over onto his back and said, "You might as well put some on my front while you're at it."

My oily hands kneaded his hairy chest and shoulders, lingering over his hard pecs. He placed his hands behind his head, his well-developed biceps forming a frame around his handsome face, and then he closed his eyes and submitted to my erotic exploration of his body. I could detect an aroma arising from his arm pits as I bent toward his body. I thought about putting my nose right into his pits and taking a deep breath, but I was too chicken. Gradually I moved lower and lower until I was rubbing the exposed white flesh of his groin, edging closer and closer to the mound incased in the skimpy pouch, surprised to see that his cock was also leaking precum. His legs spread wide, so I moved between them.

He groaned loudly as my thumbs rubbed the hairy skin between his legs, inadvertently milking precum along his cock-tube, making it seep more and more into the tightly packed pouch. He bent his knees and spread his legs even further apart. His big balls were compressed so snugly that the pouch was unable to contain their fullness, forcing them out of the sides and into my view. My fingers continued their milking action stimulating the flow of blood into his big cock, engorging the shaft and head, until the pouch was pushed way out from his body.

"I think I'd like an all over tan, so I might as well get rid of this," he said, lifting his legs to his chest and at the same time pulling the thong from his body. While doing so, his asscheeks spread wide apart, giving me a perfect view of his tight pink hole.

He lowered his legs and rested his muscular thighs on mine. I was so excited I couldn't stop my hands from shaking. He wants you to play with his dick, went through my mind. I stared at it, wanting to touch it, but was too scared. What if I was misreading him? He'd kill me if I touched him. My hands moved towards him trembling in fear. I slowly grasped the shaft with my hand, pretending to apply suntan lotion, but in reality – masturbating him. I marveled at how smooth the long shaft was and yet how hard it felt under the skin. His precum trickled out as my hand moved up to the wide flaring head, and oozed down the sides over my hand, lubricating my gripping palm. A moan escaped his mouth when I smeared the precum over his knob. I looked up to see his blue eyes staring at me.

"Have you ever done this before?" he asked. I shook my head, not daring to speak. "Use your mouth on it," he said, spreading his legs further apart to give me greater access.

As my face fell towards his stiff dick I could once again smell his distinctive male aroma. I moved his cock towards my mouth and delicately licked the moist hole, running my tongue around the extensive head savoring my first taste of his semen. My lips opened wide and I sucked the big knob into my mouth, enjoying the feel and flavor of his stimulated sex organ.

"That's it, Tony – watch the teeth. Play with my nuts. Oh yeah, that's the way," he added as I complied with his request.

He allowed me to play with his nuts and his hard dick for a while then said, "Lie down I want to have a look at you."

I didn't want to. I wanted to keep sucking him. I'd been dreaming about doing it for a month, but when he pushed me away from him, I rolled onto my back. He tenderly rubbed my chest then brought his hand down to my bulging basket. He took hold of the bikini, pulled it down my legs, and tossed it to the side. I was now completely naked, lying like a sacrificial lamb ready for the slaughter. The feel of his hands on my body, lying naked in the sun, and the masculine aroma emanating from his body, was like a wet dream come true.

"Oh, man ..." he groaned, taking hold of my throbbing cock. "What a monster. I can't believe that such a small guy has such a big dick."

My face blushed scarlet as he slowly stroked my cock, watching as the skin slipped back and forth over the head. I gasped as he sunk his mouth down to the shaft, licking up and down the length. He moved the head of my dick to his mouth, opened wide and plunged down to the hilt, engulfing my entire shaft in one motion. I screamed in passion as I unloaded my juice into his widely opened throat.

"Oh fuck, I'm really sorry, Allan. I couldn't stop from shooting."

I thought he'd be mad at me for shooting in his mouth, and that he'd spit out my load, but he came off my still hard dick, and I could see his throat muscles working as he swallowed my load. When he was finished, he licked his lips like he had just tasted honey. "Ah, nice," he said, "nothing like the taste of young cum."

He rolled me over onto my stomach and ran his hands over my quivering ass. "What a great ass. I've always wondered what it would look like."

He spread my legs wide then slipped between them. Lying on his abdomen he brought his face to my ass and began to lick my sweaty cheeks, spreading them wide so he could gain access to my virgin orifice. He ran his tongue around my tightly clenched hole, forcing it open with his fingers to allow him entry. His tongue pushed between my tender tissues, making me grind my crotch into the towel.

He poured lotion onto my butt and his fingers, then pushed one into my hole, and rotated it around in my chute. He pushed another finger into me, then twisted them around and massaged my hard prostate gland. I whimpered softly as he stimulated my love gland, forcing semen through my still rigid cock. I pushed my ass onto his hand, wanting more than fingers in my hole. He pushed another finger into me and fucked my hole with his digits. I thought I would go crazy. My ass rotated around his fingers, pushing back on his hand. I had never been fucked, but I knew that's what I wanted. I needed to be dominated by him. I wanted his huge rammer up my ass.

Suddenly his fingers were withdrawn while at the same time he said, "Don't move I'll be right back."

I wondered where he was going. I watched him coming back towards me carrying a tube of lubricant and rolling a condom down his massive dick. I was excited. He was going to make my dream come true, but I was scared. Should I let him fuck me? Could I take his monster up my virgin chute? Would it hurt? But at the same time I didn't care if it hurt, because I wanted him inside me.

He once again lay down between my legs, using his tongue for a few moments, and then he lubricated my chute with three fingers. I was sure my hole must've been gaping wide from all the finger play, but I was still nervous. Rising to his knees, he slowly inserted his dick-head into my cherry hole. Once the head was in, he paused, waiting for my muscles to relax and accommodate his girth. As I began to loosen-up his cock pushed my tender tissues apart and probed my depths, not stopping until his pubic hairs were resting on my buttocks and his balls were lying on top of mine.

"Oh yeah," he murmured in my ear. "So tight, and hot ... just like I imagined."

He fucked me deep and slow in that position, letting me adjust to his huge size, and then he rotated my body around his staff, like I was impaled on a spit, and laid me on my back. His magnificent weapon once again began probing my innards. Arousing me in ways I had never imagined. He pushed my legs up until my knees were past my shoulders then began pounding my freshly opened channel.

He gasped when the head of my dick slipped into my own mouth. I didn't because I'd been sucking my own cock for at least a year. As he fucked me I stroked my shaft and sucked my knob in rhythm to the pounding I was getting. My semen flowed into my mouth each time his rammer thumped my prostate. He straightened his back and really ripped into my receptive hole, sinking down to the root then up to the crown. My tight ass muscles milked his hard shaft until he reached his peak and spurted load after load of hot jism while imbedded deep in my channel. As he let go, my own cock exploded, flooding my mouth with cum.

He gently pulled his cock out of my freshly fucked asshole, then collapsed onto my abdomen. His lips covered my mouth in a long passionate kiss and he sucked my cum into his own mouth.

"That was fantastic," he groaned into my ear. "I hope I didn't hurt you?"

"Fuck no," I answered shaking my head. "It was great."

"I've wanted to do that to you ever since we first met," he said. "I got hard every time you pressed your hard-on against my butt. I had to rush into the bathroom when I got home to jerk-off. Oh, by-the-way, I knew you were watching me earlier."

I could feel my face blushing as I twirled the hair on his chest. I changed the subject and then guiltily asked, "When will Rachael be back?"

"She's not coming back. I think she's found someone new."

"I'm sorry. You must be knotted?"

"Not really. Actually I'm happy about it. We haven't been getting on for a long time."

We lay like that for a while, and then he said, "Do you think you can start cleaning the place in the afternoon? I can't afford to take any more time off work. I don't know about you, but I'd like to do this again."

"Sure, that's okay, but what's wrong with now? Can you get it up again?"

Of course he could get it up again, and of course he was only too willing to oblige.

THE STRIPPER
COMES ON STAGE

Joshua was visiting the big city. He was anxious to check out a stripper bar he'd been told about, so on Friday night he headed in that direction. He was surprised when he walked into the dimly lit bar to see how busy it was. A long bar ran down one side of the room and at the one end of the room was a small stage where strippers performed. High tables and stools packed the rest of the room. Joshua chose a table in a dark corner.

A butch-looking waiter; dressed in ripped denim shorts, a black leather harness over his naked chest, and construction boots, took Joshua's order. When the waiter made his way through the crowded bar, the customers tweaked his protruding nipples, squeezed his ass, and through the holes in his shorts, grabbed his basket.

Joshua looked around the room. It's going to be an interesting night, he thought. I'm glad I came. It wasn't long before the MC announced that a stripper by the name of Adrian would appear next on stage. The music started and a handsome redhead, dressed in white briefs and western boots, strutted onto the stage. His smooth hairless torso, and well-developed arms and legs, appeared to glow in the spotlight as he did a bump and grind to the slow music.

When Adrian turned his back to the audience and showed the top of his butt cheeks, they cheered and shouted, "Take them off! Take them off!" He looked over his shoulder at the audience, winked, and then slowly uncovered his pale white backside. "All the way," they shouted. A cheer went up from the audience when his spectacular hard-on sprang out of his briefs, sticking straight out from his six-pack abdomen. He danced around the stage, swung his big dick at the onlookers, bent down low, and spread his asscheeks wide enough to show his tiny pink pucker. He moved to stage center and stroked his shaft, until Joshua was sure he was going to cum; but the music stopped, the stage lights dimmed, and he left the stage to loud applause.

When the cute waiter eventually arrived with Joshua's beer, he pressed himself up close between Joshua's widely spread thighs. The tables and stools were just the right height, so that the ass of the person standing was at groin level to the person seated. Joshua, under cover of the table, took the opportunity to give the waiter a feel. He ran his hand up the guy's furry leg, onto his bulging basket, and gave it a squeeze.

"You should get danger pay working in here," Joshua said.

"You got that right. By the time I get home I'm black and blue from all the groping."

"You mind?" Joshua asked.

"Not with you, handsome. You can grope me any time."

He spread his legs apart and pushed his butt against Joshua's thigh. Joshua's other hand moved to the waiter's rear-end and slipped through the gaping legs in his shorts onto his bare ass-cheek. When Joshua ran his fingers through the hairy valley, and probed the tight entrance to the waiter's chute, his middle finger slipped in right to the knuckle.

"Nice butt, boy ... I bet you'd like a big piece of meat in there, wouldn't you?"

The waiter pushed his rear-end against Joshua's hand. "Oh, man, that feels good," he said. "I bet you've got the equipment to keep me happy."

Joshua moved the waiter's hand to his erection. "You got that right. Feel what you've done to me."

"Shit. You're not kidding ... what a boner! I wish I had the night off, which reminds me, I better get back to work."

"Sure ... catch you later," Joshua said. He moved his finger to his nose and breathed in the erotic aroma left by the waiter's manhole.

The customers, obviously enjoying themselves, were drinking and cruising. The dancers, no doubt picked for their looks and endowments, rather than their dancing abilities, worked the floor, trying to entice customers into the backrooms, where they offered, for a fee, to put on private dances.

Adrian, wearing nothing but a jock and boots, approached Joshua's table and introduced himself. Joshua bought him a drink, and Adrian moved between Joshua's thighs. His eyes opened wide when he felt Joshua's erection pressed against his butt. They both laughed when he used the old line, "Is that a gun in your pants or are you just glad to see me?"

As they sipped their drinks, the dancers strutted around the stage exposing their wares to the audience. When Joshua's hand wandered under the table to Adrian's bulging jock, Adrian jumped, but he didn't move away. Joshua slowly moved the jock aside and freed the redhead's expanding dick. He stroked the hard shaft and pulled Adrian's rear-end against his hard-on. It was a strangely erotic feeling to know that the casual observer would think they were just sharing a drink while under the table it was a different story.

"Oh fuck," Adrian said with a groan. "We shouldn't be doing this out here. You're going to get me fired. You wanna come with me into the backroom?"

"No one's gonna see us. Besides, I like doing this out here. It really turns me on."

"If someone comes over, make sure you don't let them see what we're doing," Adrian said.

Adrian's hand moved below the table and slowly lowered Joshua's zipper. He had trouble freeing Joshua's hard rod, but eventually when it stuck straight out of Joshua's gaping fly, he gripped the exposed cock in his fist. "Oh yeah, that feels good. Stroke it," Joshua said. "I bet your beautiful mouth would feel even better."

"Well, that's one thing I won't be doing out here."

He let Adrian stroke his cock for a short time then he moved Adrian's butt over to his groin, and placed his hard shaft between the cheeks of the stripper's ass. He pulled Adrian onto his lap, spread the redhead's legs, applied a liberal amount of saliva to Adrian's smooth hole and penetrated his sphincter with his long middle finger. Adrian's hot breath sent tingles down Joshua's spine when he whispered in Joshua's ear, "This is a first for me ... I can't believe I'm letting you do this out here. I must be crazy."

The two of them were now oblivious to their surroundings. Joshua fucked the stripper's tight hole with his finger, opening him up for bigger things. He was getting into it, when the humpy waiter brought them both back to reality.

He dropped his tray on the table. "Would you two like another drink?" he said.

They didn't answer him. He stood his ground, waiting for an answer.

Joshua could see the light coming on in his eyes, "What are you up to, Adrian? Don't tell me you're getting it on right here at the table?" he said.

Without waiting for an answer, he moved in closer and dropped his hand between Adrian and Joshua. He felt Joshua's cock-head slide over the stripper's manhole. "Fuck. I don't blame you, Adrian. I wish I could get a piece of that monster."

Adrian gasped when the waiter's other hand stroked his hard dick. "Oh shit, David, please stop. You'll make me cum."

"Nice cock," David, the waiter, said. "I've wanted to do that for a long time."

"Please stop," Adrian said, grabbing David's hand. "You're not going to tell are you? It's his fault ... I couldn't stop him."

"Of course not ... why would I?" David answered. "Maybe you'll let me blow you sometime?"

"Sure, sure, anything you want," Adrian whimpered. "Oh, God, I can't help it ... he's got me so hot ... I want him to fuck me."

"Let me help," David said. Then he pulled a small tube of lubricant out of his pocket and smeared some on Joshua's shaft and up Adrian's chute. He held Joshua's dick at the right angle so that Adrian could back onto it.

"Oh fuck, Adrian, you sure know how to take it." David said when Adrian settled on Joshua's lap.

The waiter grasped Adrian's nuts in his hand, and pushed a finger into Adrian's chute alongside Joshua's dick. "Wow, what a hole, dude. I bet you like to get double-fucked." He poked around in Adrian's chute for a few moments, then he said, "Shit, I better get back to work before I get fired. Enjoy."

While the rest of the audience concentrated on another stripper on the stage, Joshua held Adrian's hips, and gently raised and lowered him on his stiff poker, probing deep in the stripper's moist channel. Joshua found it difficult to maintain his composure, but Adrian knew just how to move without attracting attention. His inner muscles gripped Joshua's shaft tightly as his rear-end slowly rose and fell.

"Fuck, you're good," Joshua said. "Maybe I should've taken you up on your offer and gone into the back room, then I could've really plowed you."

Joshua took Adrian's cock in his hand and began to masturbate him. Adrian quickly pushed his hand away and whispered, "No, dude. I can't cum. I've got more shows to do."

Joshua, turned on like he'd never been before, fired his load up Adrian's silky chute. He couldn't remember ever shooting that much jism before. He was still hard and probing Adrian's innards when the MC announced that the next dancer was Adrian. Adrian pulled away from Joshua. "What fucking timing."

Joshua was still zipping-up, when Adrian jumped onto the stage. The crowd cheered when they saw his boner protruding from the side of his jockstrap. He was hot now, and made every effort to impress. He ripped off his jockstrap, threw it in a corner, and danced around naked. His pecker – dripping semen, wildly swung back and forth. He moved onto his knees at the edge of the stage, and spread his thighs and asscheeks wide in the glaring spotlight. His pucker, still partly dilated, and an angry red color, was oozing Joshua's jism. There was an audible, and collective gasp, from the audience, when they saw the cum. There was no doubt about what he had just had up his ass.

Adrian, unaware of what was happening, continued with his performance. He pushed his massive endowment back between his legs, and slowly ran his hand up and down the full length of the shaft. His other hand moved to his smooth ass-cheek. When he slapped the tender skin his hand left a red imprint on the white surface. His hand moved into the valley between his cheeks and fingered his dilated hole. When he felt the wetness between his cheeks, his hand stopped abruptly. He rubbed the viscous fluid between his thumb and forefinger, as though trying to determine its origin. The audience cheered again when he brought his finger to his mouth, and tasted the substance. When Adrian realized what it was, his head jerked around in the direction of Joshua, his mouth open in shock.

The crowd went crazy. They screamed for Adrian to jerk-off. More and more cum oozed down his crack, and trickled down his perineum onto his balls. The over stimulated stripper appeared to be in shock. He was motionless, with his spotlighted backside sticking way up in the air. Before he realized was happening, an older man who sat within two feet of him, jumped up and glued his mouth to the stripper's hole. His hand reached through Adrian's legs and grabbed Adrian's cock. Adrian was lost. His over stimulated balls erupted as he struggled to get away from the old guy. Long volleys of cum spurted across the stage. Pandemonium ensued. The customers clapped and cheered. They gave him a standing ovation. "Encore, encore," they shouted.

A red-faced Adrian finally managed to dislodge the guy who clung to him like a limpet. He gave the guy a shove that sent him flying over his stool onto his back on the floor. Adrian moved slowly to his feet, a long thread of cum hung from the end of his still red, and swollen dick. Adrian was unable to find his jockstrap, so he was naked when he moved through the crush of the congratulatory audience toward the dressing room. They slapped his ass and tried to finger his still moist hole as he fought his way through them.

Joshua's rod had deflated somewhat after fucking Adrian, now it was once again pumped-up and hard. Needing to piss badly, he made his way to the restroom that was located downstairs at the end of a long dark corridor. When he passed one table, he noticed that one of the guys had Adrian's jockstrap pressed to his face.

When Joshua approached the restroom door, David, the humpy waiter, was exiting the room. He did an about face, grabbed hold of Joshua's belt, and pulled him into the end stall. Before Joshua knew what was happening, David, sitting on the toilet seat, had Joshua's shaft in his throat. His cock-sucking ability was superb. He opened his throat wide and bobbed his head up and down. He sank all the way down the shaft, to Joshua's short and curlies, and back up to give the head a good tongue bath. Joshua pushed his hips forward and relaxed, giving the waiter free access to his love-muscle. The waiter squeezed Joshua's balls in his hand, while his throat noisily milked the sinewy shaft. Joshua could feel his jism building up, making his knob swell to even greater proportions. He grabbed the waiter's head in his hands and plowed in and out of the receptive throat. He let out a loud bellow when his nuts spewed out their load deep into the gurgling waiter's gullet.

David jumped up, licking his lips. "Fuck, dude," he said. "That was great, but I gotta work. Maybe next time you'll fuck me?"

"Maybe," Joshua said. "It was fun." Then he pointed his dick at the toilet and emptied his bladder. Even though the waiter was in a hurry, he still found time to cup Joshua's nuts, and then milk the last drops of piss from Joshua's dick.

When David opened the door, there were a number of guys in the restroom, and Joshua had to push his way through them.

Feeling tired and satisfied, he headed home, knowing he'd be back for more of the action.

TREVOR GETS
A TONGUE BATH

On Saturday night, Joshua, dressed in a leather vest, leather pants, and black boots, entered the stripper bar and took a seat in a dark corner. It wasn't too long before David, the waiter, came over to his table. Tonight David was dressed in a black leather harness, black chaps, and black motorcycle boots. A dog collar, around his neck, and a leather strap around his right bicep muscle, completed his outfit. His bulging basket was encased in a black jockstrap and his rear-end was naked.

He sidled up to the table. "Hi, butch," he said. "How's it hanging? What'll it be?"

Joshua smiled at him. "Hi, David," he said, "nice threads. I guess we're both in the leather mode tonight. I am kind of thirsty so bring me a Bud, and make it snappy."

"Yes, sir," David said and hurried over to the service counter.

Joshua watched the stage show, and the audience. The management obviously went to great lengths to hire guys who were able to meet every customer's fantasy. David returned to the table and pushed himself between Joshua's widely spread thighs.

"Who told you to stand there?" Joshua asked. "Did you hear me inviting you?"

David backed away. "I'm sorry, sir. It won't happen again,"

"Don't do it again or you'll be asking for a whipping."

He looked down at the floor and mumbled, "Yes, sir."

"Okay, you can move closer," Joshua said.

David quickly moved back between Joshua's thighs. Naturally, Joshua had to take advantage of the situation. He ran his hand over the waiter's smooth buns, his fingers trailing through the moist cleft. "Oh, master," David said, with a moan, when Joshua's thumb pushed into his chute, and massaged his prostate. "That feels so good. Do you want to fuck me?"

"Maybe later if you're a good boy. Now get back to work"

"Yes, sir. Oh, by the way, poor Adrian is still trying to live last night down. He was in earlier and the customers were all giving him the gears, asking him to show them his asshole, and asking where the cum came from."

David fucked his dilated hole on Joshua's thumb for a few moments, and then said, "Oh shit. I could do this all night, but I need the job." He pulled himself free and made off for the bar.

When Joshua lifted the can of beer to his lips, he could detect the smell of David's manhole on his thumb. He made up his mind that he would be back to the bar sometime to pick up the hunky bottom. He looked like he could do with some discipline.

As Joshua sat drinking, one gorgeous dancer after the next appeared on stage. To cheers from the audience, they all completely stripped. At around eleven, the MC announced that Trevor was to appear on stage. The amount of applause clearly indicated that Trevor was one of the favorites, and when he appeared, Joshua could see why. He was a tall deeply tanned masculine brunet who wore his long hair in a ponytail. A small amount of dark hair covered his well-developed pecs and the centerline of his washboard abdomen. His skin-tight white underwear – that covered him from waist to mid-thigh, emphasized his muscular rear-end and the tube of meat which stretched from his groin to his hip. A pair of black western boots and black cowboy hat accentuated his height and strength. His routine was a fantastic demonstration of his athletic ability, and was more of a gymnastic floor exercise than a dance. He tumbled and rolled around the floor, did hand stands and the splits.

When he pulled off his underwear, there was a surge of applause. With his back to the audience, he bent over and placed his hands flat on the floor between his legs. His exposed, snow-white asscheeks highlighted the dark hair in his tight crevice. To demonstrate his strength and stamina, he slowly raised himself into a handstand. When he stood up with his hands on his hips, with his huge cock sticking straight out from his body, he resembled a statue of Priapus. Trevor was someone Joshua definitely wanted to see up close. He walked over to the stage and, making eye contact with him, slipped twenty bucks into one of his boots. There was tremendous applause when he completed his set and, carrying his underwear, left the stage.

When Trevor came over and introduced himself, Joshua signaled David over and ordered a drink for Trevor. He could see David's left eyebrow rise when he ordered the drink.

"Do you want a private dance in the backroom?" Trevor asked.

"To tell you the truth, tonight I'm in the mood for something more intimate and private."

"That sounds cool, but I don't go home with customers for free, I have to pay the rent this week, so I need the cash. Anyway I've already made arrangements with that guy over there in the corner."

Joshua looked in the direction indicated. A butch looking guy, who looked like he had just left a job at the construction site, sat huddled over his beer.

"You mean that blond in the blue denim?" Joshua asked.

"That's him. He doesn't look the type does he? It takes all types."

"Now that's a performance I'd like to see. I wouldn't even mind paying for the privilege. Do you ever give live fuck shows?"

Joshua could see that Trevor, the consummate exhibitionist, was thinking things over. "If I hide you in my bedroom closet, will you promise not to let the guy know that you're there?"

"I promise," Joshua said crossing his heart. "I'll give you a hundred bucks for the show."

The offer of a hundred bucks apparently convinced Trevor. "You're on. I get off at one. Why don't I take you home now ... you can wait there for us?"

"That sounds good," Joshua said.

"Listen I don't want that the guy to get any ideas, so I'll go and change and we can meet out front."

Joshua left the bar and waited on the sidewalk for Trevor.

"We'll have to hurry because I have another show to do before I'm finished for the night."

Trevor led him around the corner into an old apartment complex and up the stairs into a small one-bedroom suite on the second floor. The doors on the bedroom closet were within two feet of the foot of the bed and were louvered, so it would be easy to watch the action. Joshua placed a chair in the closet, took off his clothes, and waited for the stripper.

When Trevor finally arrived home, he took his time opening the door to the suite, making sure that Joshua had enough time to hide before he and the construction worker entered the bedroom. Trevor came over to the closet to hang up his jacket, his eyes popped open when he saw that Joshua was naked.

The two guys stripped quickly. Trevor lay back on the bed, saying, "You can put the fifty bucks on the bedside table. I like to get that out of the way before I start."

The butch blond took fifty dollars out of his wallet and laid it on the bedside table. As he slowly approached the bed his gaze swept up and down Trevor's body. Trevor was slowly stroked his huge dick when the blond sank onto the mattress. Trevor lay back, with his arms above his head and said, "I feel all hot and sweaty from my last dance. Why don't you clean me up with your tongue?"

Joshua could see by the blond's hesitancy he wasn't used to this type of request. If he doesn't do it, I'll do it Joshua was thinking, but he didn't have to because the blond slowly started giving Trevor a tongue bath. He licked Trevor's chest, paying special attention to the upright nipples.

Trevor pushed the blond's face into his hairy armpit. "Clean my pits. They must be all nice and sweaty by now. That's right, lick it, dude." When he was satisfied he moved the guy's head over to his other pit, and held him there.

The blond moved down Trevor's body licking Trevor's six-pack abdomen and hairy navel. He placed his hand on Trevor's dick, and was just about to put it in his mouth when Trevor said, "No ... not yet. My asshole needs some attention first."

The blond's face turned scarlet when he heard these words; however, he didn't hesitate when Trevor lifted his legs up to his chest. Trevor was obviously putting on a show for Joshua, because he stared at the closet door and winked when the blond started to tongue his sweaty crevice.

"That's it, dude. Eat that hole. Show Trevor how much you like his sweaty ass. Dig your tongue right in ... all the way in I said. Clean out my hole." He handed a tube of lube to the blond. "Put some lube on your finger and stick it in my ass, but don't get the wrong idea. I'm strictly a top. That's right, yeah. Move it around. Put another finger in ... yeah, that's it, finger fuck my ass."

Joshua began to fist his own cock when Trevor started stroking his long shaft. "Put another finger in me. There we go, that's it. Slip them right in. See if you can find my prostate, it needs some attention. Oh, yeah. That's it," Trevor said. Then he closed his eyes, opened his mouth wide, and let out a long groan.

Joshua wished it was his fingers up Trevor's muscular butt.

"Okay, that's enough. Do my balls now," Trevor suddenly demanded. The blond licked Trevor's sac then he took the sperm laden eggs into his mouth. "Stop being such a pussy. Chew on those nuts like you mean it," Trevor said.

Trevor licked his lips and stared at the closet as the blond salved his nuts. "Okay, that's enough," he said after a few minutes. "Get on your knees. I want to see your fuck-hole."

The blond straddled Trevor in a sixty-nine position. Trevor's thumbs opened the blond's manhole and he inserted one spit-lubed finger, and twirled it around. Another finger followed. As he fucked the tight hole with his two fingers. Joshua could see by the grimace on the blond's face, that the treatment he was getting was new to him. Trevor's other hand pushed the blond's head down to his crotch. Force feeding him dick, making the blond gag on the obstruction in his throat.

Trevor came to his knees. "I want your ass now. Get on your back."

"No way, man, I don't go that way," the blond said. "I just want to blow you."

"It's too late for that now, buddy. Your ass is mine."

Trevor quickly pulled a safe out of his bedside table and sheathed his enormous appendage. The construction worker's eyes were wide open, and Joshua could see a look of fear on his face when Trevor pushed him onto his back and lifted his long legs into the air. He slapped the blond's white asscheeks, poured some lube onto his fingers, and poked them into the blond's twitching hole. He lay on his side, held the blond's legs up with one arm and spread the blond's asscheeks apart so that Joshua could get a good look.

He stared at the closet as he slipped a finger into the blond's chute. He pulled it out and placed it in his mouth. "You taste all sweaty. Didn't you wash your hole today?"

"Sorry, sure I did, this morning. I've been working all day."

"Never mind ... I like the taste."

Trevor slipped two fingers through the stud's sphincter, twisted them around, and then he sprang to his knees and, in one quick lunge, embedded his dick-head in the blond's chute.

"Oh fuck!" the construction worker bellowed. "Take it easy ... you're killing me."

Joshua could see that even though the construction worker was protesting his rod was bone-hard. It was obvious that he wanted Trevor's steely pole up his chute.

Trevor slapped the blond's rear-end a few more times to distract him and slipped his piston all the way in. He spread his legs wide so that Joshua could see his shaft slipping into the blond's tight hole. Joshua had difficulty restraining his own gasp when he saw the formidable battering ram jammed in the butch construction worker's rear-end. It took all of his self-control not to rush out of the closet and join them.

"Oh fuck," the blond said again. "You're tearing me apart ... take it out."

Me thinks he doth protest too much, Joshua was thinking. The blond's pulsating root was bone-hard and, if anything, had grown since he had been pierced. Trevor grabbed the blond's ankles and held them tight. His shaft began to slide in and out of the breached hole. When he pulled back – until just the head of his dick was still in the blond's chute, at least eight inches of his thick tube glistened in the light. The blond's pain must've turned to pleasure because he grabbed his own legs, locked them behind his arms, and spread his perineum wide for the excited stripper. Trevor pounded the blond's ass, giving him his fifty dollars worth of meat.

"Oh yes," the blond screamed, "Fuck my ass. Gimme your juice."

He grabbed his stalk and fisted the slick shaft in time to the tremendous pistoning in his backside. "I'm coming, I'm coming," he said as his sperm shot over his head and landed on the headboard and pillows.

Trevor stopped moving. "Me too," he said. He pulled his still raging cock from the blond's rear-end, crawled up the bed, discarded the condom, and grabbed the guy's head. "Clean my dick," he commanded.

The blond tried to get away from Trevor, but before he could move, Trevor's dick was down his throat. Joshua could see the blond's eyes bulge with the effort of deep throating the stripper; however, it was obvious he was enjoying the rough treatment. He's going to remember his fuck session for a long time, Joshua was thinking.

"That's enough," Trevor finally said. He fell back on the bed and pulled his still hard rod from the blond's mouth.

They lay quietly for a short time. The blond obviously wanted to linger, but Trevor was anxious to get rid of him. He sat up and said, "Well, I hope that was worth the fifty bucks?"

The blond, his face a healthy pink, nodded, "It sure was. I can't believe what happened, but you can be sure I'll be back for more."

"If you've got the money, dude, I've got the dick."

The blond stood up and slipped into his clothes. When he was ready, Trevor showed him out of the suite. Joshua came out of the closet when Trevor returned. Trevor's rod was still hard, and so was Joshua's. The smell of cum and sex permeated the small room, making Joshua's pulse beat faster.

"Quick," Trevor gasped. "I haven't cum yet. I've been saving it for you."

Trevor fell onto the bed. Joshua, expecting a mutual masturbation, or at the most, a shared sixty-nine, lay down next to him.

"Oh fuck, man," Trevor begged. "No more fooling around. Put it in me. I want that big dick of yours inside me."

Joshua was overjoyed at this request. After watching the butch dancer putting the blond through his paces, it was the last thing he had expected. Trevor didn't waste any time. He handed Joshua a safe, tilted his pelvis, and spread his legs, doing the splits, to open himself completely.

"Quick," he repeated, "before I cum."

Trevor's hole, well lubricated by a mixture of sweat, lube, and saliva, opened up easily for Joshua's ramrod. He cried out when Joshua's rod sank all the way in with one push. Joshua, over stimulated by the erotic display he had witnessed, was also in a hurry. He rose up onto his hands and toes and jack-hammered his throbbing pole in and out of the sexy stripper's receptive hole. In no time what-so-ever, his balls were drawing up tight in his sac, ready to discharge their pent up juice.

Trevor hooked his legs behind his elbows and skewered his ass on Joshua's piston. "Give it to me ... all the way in, dude," he wailed.

Joshua was amazed when he saw Trevor move his head forward, and engulf the head of his own dick in his mouth. Trevor fell back on the bed, gasped for air, and whimpered as his nuts erupted. The juice, held back all night, spewed out of his dick-head in a steady stream.

The sight of Trevor coming was enough to take Joshua over the top. His own orgasm was just as earth shaking as Trevor's was.

"Fuck, dude," Trevor said. "That was really something. You sure know how to use that big weapon of yours."

"You're not too bad yourself. That was some workout you gave that guy. If I wasn't a top I wouldn't mind you throwing it into me like that."

After Joshua had washed up and dressed, he took out the hundred bucks and laid it on the bedside table. For a few hours work, if you can call it work, he was thinking, the pay is good. He leaned over and kissed Trevor on the cheek and went home. He dropped into bed and fell asleep almost immediately, dreaming about the cute waiter with the tight asshole.

THE COACH'S BOYS

I'd really pushed myself that evening. I'd been up and down the length of the college pool so many times, that I'd lost count of the number of laps I'd completed. My legs felt weak and wobbly and I was chilled to the bone when I finally decided to call it a day. I made straight for the sauna, lay down on a bench, and fell into an exhausted sleep. Sometime later, I awoke with a start, and had no idea how long I'd been sleeping. The gym was darkened and quiet when I left the sauna. It sounded as though everyone had left for the day. I had a quick shower, dried off, and then with my bathing suit in my hand, and a towel wrapped around my middle, I headed for the locker-room.

The light was on in the Coach's office at the far end of the corridor, so I thought I'd better let him know I was still on the premises. The office was empty. As I turned to leave, I heard voices coming from the treatment room which was adjacent to the office. The door into the treatment room was ajar, so I moved toward it. I stopped dead in my tracks when a whiny voice said, "Oh fuck, Coach, that feels so good."

I peeped through the crack between the door and the jamb. Peter, the college butterfly record holder, was lying on his back on the massage table. His ass was at the foot of the table and his legs were widely splayed with his feet resting next to his asscheeks. The Coach, naked, was on his knees at the foot of the table lapping Peter's asshole.

I was shocked. It wasn't the activity that shocked me – I've been in both those positions many times, it was the participants of the activity that shocked me. I'd been lusting after Peter from the moment I first saw him wearing a well-packed Speedo bathing suit. He's tall, muscular and buff, with smooth milky-white skin. Like all serious swimmers, he is shaved from head to foot. I'd always had the impression from his demeanor and from the company he kept, that he was as straight as they come. But here he was, lying on his back, spreading his cheeks for the Coach. I'd never seen him naked because he always stayed late for extra training. Now I knew just what the extra training entailed.

The Coach, an older guy, probably in his late forties, was the exact opposite of Peter. He has a swarthy complexion. His closely cropped hair and the pelt of hair on his chest are salt-and-pepper in color. On top of that, the Coach is straight, and married. This I knew because for months I'd been sucking off the Coach's son – nicknamed Baby Coach by the students, through the gloryhole in the toilet on the third floor of the science library.

"You're driving me crazy," Peter said. "Please ... please, stop."

Peter's asshole must've been real tasty though, because the Coach continued with his oral assault, using his thumbs to pry open Peter's anus. I would've given anything to exchange places with the Coach.

"Please, I'll cum if you don't stop," Peter said.

The Coach – his face wet with spit and ass-juice, reached for a package of safes on the floor, and then came to his feet. His huge uncut dick stuck straight out from his washboard abdomen. Ten inches, just like Baby Coach's dick, I thought. He opened a safe with his teeth, rolled it down his hard dick, and then lubed his dick and Peter's hole. He placed the head of his dick at the entrance to Peter's chute, and then with one lunge, planted it deep in the athlete's upturned ass.

"That feel good, boy?" the Coach asked.

"Oh, God, yeah," Peter moaned. "It feels great. Fuck me with that big dick."

The Coach hung onto Peter's ankle's as his shiny dick pumped in and out of the athlete's squirming asshole. "That's it, boy," he moaned as he slowly built up speed. "You really know how to take daddy's dick. Yeah, move that ass. Show me how much you like it."

His hips were pounding Peter's ass with such force that the massage table began to move, its legs screeching in protest on the concrete floor. "Oh fuck," he suddenly shouted, "Daddy's cuming in your ass, boy!"

I stood there in shocked silence, unconsciously stroking my throbbing dick as I witnessed this coupling of athletes. The Coach slowly pulled his still tumescent dick out of Peter's well plowed asshole. He pulled the safe off, milked the last drops of cum onto the floor, and then slapped the long shaft on Peter's rump.

All of a sudden the Coach stepped back from the table and came straight for the door. I must've made a noise for him to realize someone was out there. He grabbed me by my hard-on and dragged me into the room.

"Look what we have here," he said to Peter, "a peeping Tom."

I could see that Peter was shocked when he realized I had seen him getting shafted by the Coach. His face changed; however, when he saw my big hard-on in the Coach's fist.

"It looks like he enjoyed watching, Coach," he said as he pushed himself up from the table.

I was shaken-up being caught like that, but was ready for some of the man-to-man action that I had just witnessed. Peter's fleshy dick swung back and forth as he moved towards me and I could see precum dripping from the end of his big knob. He dragged me over to a wrestling mat, pushed me down onto my back, lay on top of me, then slipped his tongue into my gaping mouth. I sucked his tongue, squeezed his hot body, and ran my hand through his greasy ass-crack.

It didn't take long for the Coach to join us on the mat. He pushed his hand between our bodies and grabbed my cock. Peter turned around into a sixty-nine position, pulling me on top of him. He engulfed my pulsating dick in his hot mouth, and deep-throated me, keeping my rod buried deep in his gulping throat, until I wondered how he could breathe.

Peter's sizeable dick rubbed against my lips. My tongue came out and licked the bubbling hole in his cock, tasting his semen. I grabbed the shaft in my hand and sucked the head deep into my mouth. His long shaft followed the head down my throat until my nose rested on his big creamers. I gently rolled the weighty orbs in my hands as I came off his rampant dick, gasping for air. For me, it was a dream come true.

I could see his juicy asshole, so I pulled his legs up to his chest then started lapping at his recently violated end-zone, pushing my tongue deep into the crevice for a taste of his manly juices. His scrumptious ass stimulated my senses and drove me crazy with lust. I was right, he did taste good. No wonder the Coach didn't want to stop eating his ass.

The Coach rimmed my asshole, gently licked the tender tissues around my orifice, and then he plunged his tongue in and out of the narrow passage. While the Coach was busy at my asshole, Peter was sucking on my rod and playing with my balls. The Coach withdrew his tongue and began greasing my hole with his big fingers, sinking them deep into the hot cavity, until my channel was ready for his still raging dick. I tensed when I felt his monster touch my hole. I'd been fucked before, but I'd never taken such a big one. I was scared he'd split me, but I wanted to show Peter I could take it, so I relaxed as best I could. After pausing for a moment, I resumed blowing Peter. Meanwhile the Coach was pushing his big wrench against my tight muscular ring, trying to overcome the resistance. After taking a few deep breaths my sphincter began to relax and he was able to overcome my muscle spasm and slip his dick deep into my channel.

At first it felt as though a red-hot poker had been pushed into my body, but gradually the pain was replaced with exquisite pleasure. I tentatively started moving back and forwards, sinking my rod deep into Peter's throat on the forward thrust, then pushing my ass back onto the Coach's rigid dick. I nearly went crazy moving between the two of them, fucking myself senseless.

I could hear the Coach groaning as his shaft slipped in and out of my tight sheath. I moved my mouth back to Peter's cock and started urgently deep-throating him, wanting him to shoot his load deep in my throat.

I think I was the first to cum, but it was difficult to tell with all the action going on. The Coach's horse dick pumped his cum into my aching channel, while Peter spurted shot after shot deep into my throat. A gurgling sound emanated from Peter when my huge load squirted down his throat.

We lay exhausted on the mat for a while then, after a quick shower, headed for the sauna. It didn't take long for all three of us to work up a sweat in the heat, and it wasn't long before my dick was once again at full-staff.

"Would you look at that, Coach," Peter said pointing at my dick. "It looks as though he's ready for some more action."

The Coach reached over and grabbed my throbbing pole. "It sure does. How about you, boy?" he said, looking at Peter.

"You know me, Coach; I'm always ready for sex."

"Hang on, boys, I'm going for the protection," the Coach said, as he left the sauna.

I wanted a taste of the Coach's big boner, so as soon as he was back in the sauna I moved down onto the lower bench between his legs. I lost no time in sucking the hefty shaft into my mouth and had no trouble deep-throating him. Not after all the practice I'd had on Baby Coach. I wondered what he'd say if I told him I was doing his son.

"Yes, baby," he said. "That's the way daddy likes it. Suck that big dick. Make it nice and hard."

Whoa, I thought. What's this baby and daddy business? Maybe Baby Coach is doing him? Now wouldn't that be something?

Peter moved the Coach down onto his back then straddled the Coach's face, dropping his asshole over the Coach's mouth. I crawled onto the top bench, keeping the Coach's dick deep in my throat, while clinging to his low-hanging nuts, not missing a beat. The Coach had one of those huge cocks that are made for sucking. While it got nice and hard, it was always pliable enough to follow the curve of my throat.

I sucked on the Coach's dick for a long time, and then I moved my mouth down to his nuts. I licked his hairy sac then mouthed each of his nuts, rolling them around in my mouth, gently chewing on the sensitive spheres. The Coach pulled his legs up to his chest opening his perineum to my mouth. As Peter held the Coach's legs in place I began to lap at his asshole. I still could hardly believe that it was the Coach I was rimming.

I was suddenly brought back to my senses by a loud, "Fuck him. Fuck the bastard. Give him some of his own medicine."

I looked up at Peter to see if he was serious. "Go ahead," he said. "I've got him pinned."

I was anxious to fuck the Coach, so I quickly came to my knees, sheathed up, and then placed the head of my lubricated pole at the entrance to his channel. He was writhing around on the bench trying to get away from my dick-head and I could hear him mewling into Peter's manhole, but there wasn't much he could do to resist. Peter had him well and truly pinned down.

My dick slipped into his tight hole, not stopping until it was buried to the hilt. I nearly lost my load right then as I felt his hot smooth tissues massaging my rock-hard dick. I kept dead still as Peter's mouth covered mine, his tongue exploring my mouth.

"Fuck the bastard," he said, as he wiggled his rear-end on the Coach's face.

I lost no time in complying, resting on my hands and toes on the bench so that I could jack-hammer his tight hole.

"That's it," Peter said. "Fuck his ass. Let him see what it feels like to be on the receiving end for a change."

Before I knew it I was gasping for breath and my seed was being deposited up the Coach's chute.

Peter leaned over and whispered in my ear. "I want to fuck him too. Come around here and grab him before he can move."

I pulled my dick from the Coach's tight hole, got rid of the safe, then moved around to his head. Before he knew what was happening I had replaced Peter on his face and had his legs gripped tightly under my arms. The Coach's chute, now well lubed and relaxed after my fuck, opened easily to admit Peter's protected throbber. As he started fucking I could feel the Coach's tongue probing my recently fucked hole. Maybe he didn't want to be fucked in the beginning, but he was obviously enjoying himself now. I could see his big dong oozing semen onto his washboard abdomen so I bent over and sank it into my throat. He lifted me up, placed my dick-head in his mouth then pulled me into his throat, milking me with his throat muscles.

Peter was entering the home stretch. His buttocks were rising and falling like a battering-ram, his cock pounding the Coach's hole, massaging his tender prostate. Before I knew what was happening the Coach was shooting a massive load, nearly choking me with surprise. As I valiantly swallowed the Coach's cum, I could hear Peter bellowing as he too climaxed.

We were glad to see that the Coach had a big grin on his face when we finally released him and were ecstatic when the only thing he said was; "Well I guess we all know who the top boys are going to be this semester."

Next time I follow Baby Coach into the restroom I'm going to shove my cock through the hole and see what transpires. Nothing ventured, nothing gained.

GLORYHOLES GALORE

It was only a few months since eighteen year-old Nick had come out of the closet and lost his cherry. He was anxious to learn everything there was to know about the gay life, so when a friend told him about a place called *The Gloryhole*; he decided to give it a try. He was nervous when he entered the club on a Saturday night, unsure of what lay ahead. He was scared of the unexpected, but he was also excited, and hoped for some unusual sex.

The door of the club opened into a small vestibule that contained a small wicket on one side. When Nick stood in front of the wicket a burly guy behind the grille barked, "Where's your membership card? Don't you have one?"

Nick shook his head, "No I'm new."

"Let's see some ID. No chicken allowed."

Nick showed the guy his driver's license.

"Okay ... you're just old enough. That'll be twenty bucks ... fill out this form."

Nick filled out the form and handed it and twenty dollars to the guy. "Enjoy," the guy said, "nice to see some new meat. If you're still horny when you're ready to leave, come see me, I'll look after you."

The guy buzzed the inside door and Nick entered a dim noisy void. When his eyes adapted to the diminished light he was able to see that the room was packed with men. A long bar occupied one side of the room, and easy chairs and coffee tables were distributed around the circumference. Narrow corridors spread out like spokes from the main room. Nick was on his second beer, trying to pluck up enough courage to check out the corridors, when the tall guy standing next to him, dressed in a tight white wife-beater, blue jeans, and boots, spoke. "Ain't seen you round here before. You fresh meat?"

Nick could feel his face getting hot. He was glad it was dark in the room so the guy wouldn't notice. "Yeah," he said. "My first time."

"You're a cutie ... you having a good time?"

"Hope to. I've heard a lot about this place."

The guy stuck out his mitt. "Josh," he said.

Nick shook Josh's firm hand. "I'm Nick."

They guzzled their beers. The banging of doors drew Nick's attention. Guys were walking around, going in and out of the doors that opened onto the corridors. "This place sure is hopping tonight," Josh said. "Better check it out while they're still horny. Can't wait to get my big dicked sucked." He gripped the big tube of flesh angling down his left thigh, winked at Nick, placed his empty beer bottle on the counter, then walked down one of the corridors.

Nick watched Josh enter one of the doors. That guy is hot, Nick was thinking, maybe we'll be able to connect through a hole? I better get going before someone else grabs him. He walked down the corridor. The door adjacent to Josh's door was ajar, so Nick entered the cubicle and latched the door. There were huge gloryholes at crotch level on all three sides of the roomette. The smell of cum, piss, amyl, and sweat nearly overwhelmed Nick's senses. He grabbed a handle on the wall when he skidded on the slimy floor. He placed his beer on a small shelf, bent over and peered through the gloryhole on Josh's side. Josh's jeans and briefs were around his ankles, and a guy, in the cubicle on the far side, was sucking his cock. Damn, too late, Nick thought. Somebody got to him first.

The management had provided low stools for the cocksuckers to make themselves comfortable during their cocksucking, so Nick took a seat and watched the action in Josh's cubicle. His rod was stiff and throbbing, begging for attention, so he opened his fly and released it. He watched Josh's ass-muscles contracting and relaxing as he fucked the guy's mouth on the other side of the partition. When the guy, doing the sucking, passed his arm between Josh's legs, and pulled Josh firmly to his face, Josh spread his legs. The cocksucker pushed his finger into Josh's asshole and twirled it around.

Nick ran his hand up and down his own hard shaft. When Josh stepped back from the partition, a huge black dick poked through the gloryhole into Josh's cubicle. Josh bent over, sucked the proffered cock, and shoved his hairy perineum against the hole on Nick's side of the cubicle. Nick stared at the spectacular sight for a few moments then he gripped Josh's nuts in his hand and brought them to his mouth. As he chewed on the nuts he pulled Josh's throbbing pole back between his legs – as far as its stiff state would allow, and pumped his fist up and down the long shaft. He lapped at Josh's hole for a few moments, and then he sank a finger into Josh's chute.

A hand reached through the end wall and began to play with Nick's rod. The voice attached to the hand growled, "Yeah, baby, suck those big nuts. Finger that juicy hole."

Josh suddenly jerked his nuts out of Nick's mouth, swung around, and hit Nick in the face with his hard shaft. Nick opened his lips wide and sank down the long shaft until he had the whole thing buried in his throat.

The guy playing with Nick's rod once again spoke, "Suck that big fucker. Milk that shaft. Deep-throat him."

Nick backed off the long shaft to take a breath, then nibbled on Josh's pliant foreskin. He loved the taste of Josh's dick. He deep-throated Josh again, thinking, this is great, when another cock appeared through the gloryhole at the end of his cubicle. He continued blowing Josh while he fisted the other dick. Josh pulled his dick out of Nick's mouth and stepped back. A long thread of precum seeped out of the big hole in his cockhead and drooped to the floor. He crouched down and looked at Nick through the gloryhole. "Oh, it's you, cutie," he said. "Gimme that dick."

Nick quickly rose to his feet and poked his boner through the hole. Josh immediately engulfed it. He's an old pro, went through Nick's mind. I guess if you spend a lot of time in a place that specializes in blowjobs, it's only natural you'll develop your expertise in cocksucking. The guys who frequented the establishment are evidently into cocksucking, and they're proud of their skill. I'll have to come back for more practice.

Josh pulled his mouth off Nick's dick and said, "Join me in the end cubicle. We'll have a good time in there."

Nick nodded and they both stood and pulled up their jeans. When he came out of his cubicle Josh was waiting for him. He took Nick's hand and led him down the corridor into the far corner. They entered a cubicle that wasn't much bigger than the previous one Nick had been in; however, it was big enough to accommodate a leather armchair and the mandatory stool. The gloryholes in the cubicle were even bigger than the holes in the last one. Josh quickly undid Nick's jeans, pushed them and his briefs down his legs, and then pushed Nick into the armchair. When Josh removed Nick's boots, jeans, and briefs, Nick was naked from the waist down, and sprawled in the armchair.

Josh quickly removed his own boots and jeans, and made himself comfortable on the stool in front of Nick. He buried his face in Nick's crotch and chewed on Nick's nuts. He rolled them around in his mouth for a few minutes, and then he licked up and down Nick's rigid shaft. His thumbs pried the hole open in Nick's dick-head, so that he could lick up the oozing semen, then he held Nick's cock at the base, and sank down the shaft, not stopping until his lips encircled the root. He kept Nick's tool buried in his throat for a long time, swallowing around the throbbing shaft. Eventually he backed-off and took a big breath. While Nick lay back in the chair getting his pecker sucked, anonymous arms appeared through the gloryholes, some of them stroking Nick's chest and others stroking Josh.

After feasting on Nick's cock, Josh pushed Nick's legs up to his chest and licked his hole. He sat back and said, "Nice an' tasty, boy. You ever get fucked?"

Nick nodded. "Yeah, I did, once."

"You're pretty much still virgin then."

Josh dived back between Nick's legs and rimmed him like he was starved for butt. He reached over to a shelf and retrieved a tube of lube, then he smeared lube on his finger and pushed it into Nick's chute. Nick spread his legs and hung them over the arms of the chair. Josh pushed a second finger into Nick, then a third followed by a forth. Nick's rear-end rotated on the fingers up his chute. When Josh's fingers found his prostate he groaned loudly. He wanted to tell Josh to fuck him, but he was too shy.

After playing with Nick's dilated hole for a few minutes more, Josh stood up on the seat of the armchair, bent his knees, and shoved his pole down Nick's throat. Nick's legs were pinned to his chest in a spread-eagle position, leaving his crotch and butt fully exposed to the guys on the other side of the partitions. Nick's throat muscles were working overtime on Josh's big reamer when he felt something wet and hot envelope his cock. He pushed Josh to the side to see what was going on. A scrawny, butch looking number had apparently found the door unlatched and was now sucking-off Nick. Both Nick and Josh stared in astonishment at the intruder; however, given the fact that he was young and hung, they went back to their previous preoccupation.

As Nick continued to suck on Josh's cock, the number on the floor moved his mouth to Nick's exposed asshole. His hot tongue wormed its way through Nick's dilated sphincter into his unprotected chute. Nick wiggled his ass. God, he thought, it feels fantastic. What'll I do if he starts fucking me? Josh'll think I'm a slut if I let him. While Josh continued to hammer away at his mouth, two fingers bored into Nick's channel, and massaged his prostate. Josh pulled his tool from Nick's mouth, squatted down over Nick's thighs, and pushed the guy away from Nick's butt. The number on the floor moved his mouth to Josh's asshole.

Josh reached over to the shelf for a safe and lube, passed them to the butch number on the floor, and said, "Put it on his dick."

Aw, fuck, Nick thought. That's not the way I wanted it. He's supposed to fuck me. After the guy had sheathed Nick's erection and applied a liberal amount of lube, Josh moved his feet and placed one on either side of Nick. Nick lowered his aching legs. The butch number, still on the floor between Nick's splayed thighs, took hold of Nick's dick and held it at the entrance to Josh's hole. Nick gasped when he felt Josh's tight pucker open up and engulf his dick-head. After sliding all the way down Nick's shaft, in one long plunge, Josh's backside rose and fell as he fucked himself on Nick's rigid rod. Nick being athletic and supple, was able to bend his head forward and cover Josh's dick-head with his mouth. The two stimulated guys, sweating from all the exertion, soon reached a tremendous climax. Nick's implanted cock was the first to erupt, spilling his wad into Josh's grasping channel. Nick nearly choked when Josh's spurting cock blasted in his throat. He tried to get away, but Josh held him tightly, and forced him to swallow every drop.

The guy on the floor pounced on Nick's rod when Josh rose and released it. He quickly removed the condom, deep-throated Nick, and beat his own meat. Josh, his tool still stiff, stepped behind the guy and pulled him up so that he was bending over and still sucking Nick. He reached for another safe, rolled it down his boner, applied lube to the guy's hole and, as quick as a wink, shoved his dick up the guy's ass. Josh, seemingly, as horny as ever, pounded the guy's rear-end. The guy getting the tremendous fucking screeched around Nick's shaft when he shot his load. Josh pulled his rod out of the guy's hole, removed the safe, and quickly jerked-off, his cum shooting out all over the bending guy's backside. If Nick hadn't seen it with his own eyes, he would never have believed that anyone could shoot so much cum, twice in a row.

The three guys now completely exhausted quickly dressed and left the cubicle. On his way home Nick thought about Josh. He'd enjoyed the session, but he was disappointed Josh hadn't fucked him with his huge cock. I should've been more assertive and told him to fuck me, flashed through Nick's mind. Oh, well, maybe next time I'll get lucky. He climbed into bed knowing he'd be a regular at *The Gloryhole.*

THE HORNY CREWMAN GETS PLUGGED

I was brought up sailing around the Great Lakes on the family yacht. One day, while looking through a sailing magazine, I noticed that someone was seeking an experienced hand to crew for him on a month long cruise around Georgian Bay. The money was good, so I decided to apply. When I went down to the yacht club to talk with Brian, who was the yacht's owner, he informed me that a friend of his was also going on the trip. Brian was an experienced sailor, but because his friend, Doug, was a novice, they had decided that an extra pair of hands was required to manage the forty-two foot cutter. The trip would not be too strenuous since there would be no overnight sailing and we would anchor every afternoon in a different location. Brian was impressed with my experience so I was signed up for the trip.

The day before the sail, I took my gear down to the dock and spent that night on board. The next morning Brian and Doug arrived in a pickup truck with all the necessary supplies. Brian, a ruggedly handsome guy, with dark wavy hair and surprisingly deep blue eyes, was dressed in a brief pair of white shorts and deck shoes without socks. His long legs were well-formed and were quite hairy. His bare chest was covered in dark hair. His well-developed biceps and pecs spoke of a guy who worked out daily. The earring in his left earlobe, and the tattoo of an anchor on his left upper arm, gave him a nautical look.

Red-headed, hazel-eyed, Doug, was Brian's polar opposite. He was shorter and although he had a great body, he didn't have Brian's muscular definition. He was dressed in long white baggy cargo pants, and the long sleeves of his oversized white shirt hid his arms. You could tell by the Tilley hat he wore that he was one of those pale skinned guys who had to protect themselves from the sun. Doug also seemed quite shy compared to Brian's gregarious personality.

I'm proud of my own body which is compact and well-developed. When I'm not sailing I'm kept busy with my college gymnastic team, my specialty being the floor exercises. I'm what you call a dirty-blond, but because my tan has been built up over a long period of

97

time, I don't have any trouble with the sun. I like to wear short shorts without a shirt, and I don't were briefs or socks – that way I don't have to worry about the laundry. I always wear a baseball cap when I'm sailing, and tie my hair back in a ponytail.

We spent a few hours packing away the supplies and then, after checking out all the onboard equipment, we took off on the first leg of the trip. The weather was great, with a steady breeze blowing from the right quarter – which meant we didn't have to do much tacking or gibing. The sky was clear and the sun hot so, for protection, we put up a Bimini awning over the cockpit. Brian and I plotted the course and took turns steering; while Doug lazed around in the cockpit. Once we had settled into a routine Brian spent some time teaching Doug the fundamentals of sailing and navigation. Before long he was pitching in, helping with the sails and taking his turn at the wheel.

We found a quiet cove the first evening; then after setting two anchors, we changed into our bathing suits and jumped into the cool water. Refreshed, we settled down in the cockpit for a light snack and drinks. It was pretty obvious that Brian and Doug were close friends by the way they kept ribbing each other. Brian's small white bikini didn't hide his hefty equipment very well, and once the fabric was wet, the ridge of his cockhead was quite evident. Doug thought this was a great joke and kept laughing and poking at the mound – bringing it to my attention. I could see that Brian was really getting horny, trying to control his obviously hardening dick, which began tenting out his bikini.

They were clearly gay, which at first bothered me – I wasn't sure if I'd made the right decision to accompany them, wondering if they'd take advantage of me, but gradually I began to relax and enjoy their companionship.

After a few more drinks we decided to call it a day. They had the bigger forward V-berth, while I had a smaller cabin below the cockpit in the stern. I read for a while then realized I needed to empty my bladder. Rather than use the head I went up on deck to piss over the side; enjoying the feeling of walking around naked. I was just shaking the last drops off my dick when I heard a low moan coming from the forward hatch. Not being able to resist the temptation, I crept forward and peered into the partially opened hatch, which was situated directly above the V-berth. The propane lamp was quite bright, so I had a good view of Brian's and Doug's lower bodies.

Even though I'd accepted the fact that they were gay, I still wasn't prepared for what I saw. They were naked and were lying side-by-side fisting each others dicks. I was too shocked to move. I don't know why I was shocked. I mean at some level I knew gays did this, but I had never really put much thought into it. It just wasn't something I'd dwelled on.

I was mesmerized by the sight of their cocks. Brian's was long, thick and uncut, with a plum shaped head. Doug's, although not as long or thick, was still a hefty piece. What confused me even more was the fact that my own rod had firmed up and that I had unconsciously started stroking it as I watched them in action.

I stood dead-still as Brian swiveled around and then in one move, swallowed Doug's dick, right down to his red pubes. I almost gasped out loud when I witnessed this feat. Although still confused, I couldn't help wondering what it would be like to have my cock down Brian's obviously talented throat.

"Oh yeah, baby," Doug moaned. "All the way down."

Brian appeared only too pleased to comply. He planted Doug's rod deep in his throat, then held it there as he rolled Doug's nuts around in his hand. I could tell by the noises that Doug was making that he had his mouth full and wished that I could see him working on Brian's big rod. They continued sucking for a while and then Brian lifted his mouth off Doug's pecker and said, "I'm gonna cum."

He lay back with his eyes closed – but carried on fisting Doug, then uttered a long drawn out wail as his cum sprayed over his chest and face, big globs hanging from his cheeks. Doug's pecker exploded, as he too let out a cry of ecstasy, his jism joining Brian's. I though it wise to beat a hasty retreat at that point.

My heart was pounding in my chest and my dick was bone hard as I quickly moved down the companionway back to my cabin, hoping they hadn't heard me up there. Of course as soon as I lay down, one hand went to my throbbing pole, stroking the shaft while the other hand squeezed my aching nuts. My hand slid up and down my long slick shaft until I too shot a load all over my chest and stomach. What interested me most, about the whole episode, was the fact that I had been so turned on by the sight of two gays getting it on. You're straight, aren't you? Kept circling through my brain. It took a long time before I fell into a deep sleep.

The next morning I got up bright and early – went through my daily exercise routine, then had a long swim in the cool fresh water. Brian and Doug had a swim and then, after a quick breakfast, we raised the anchors and started the second leg of our trip. After a good day's sail, we again anchored in a quiet cove and were soon in our berths. Once I was sure they were in their berth I crept up on the deck anxious to see them at it again. Sure enough the hatch was fully open and I could hear groans coming from the cabin. This time I could see Doug sucking Brian's big dick, sliding the plum shaped head between his lips. He was having difficulty getting much of the shaft into his mouth and throat because of the size. I couldn't help wondering what it would feel like to suck on such a big dick.

Doug lifted his head and said, "Please, baby ... I want you to fuck me."

He turned around, lay on his stomach, and then Brian moved between his legs. Brian ran his hand over the redhead's milky-white ass-mounds and then he pried the cheeks apart, exposing Doug's tiny pink pucker. My mind was in a whirl. Was he actually going to fuck Doug with his massive dick?

I was even more shocked when Brian lowered his mouth to Doug's rear-end. He started licking Doug's butt and then moved in on the main target; which he attacked with gusto. "That's what I need," Doug sighed. "Eat my ass, baby."

After rimming Doug for a long while, Brian reached over to a locker and pulled out a safe and some lube. He sat back on his haunches, rolled the condom down his shaft, and then he lubed his cock and Doug's manhole. I watched as he fingered the tight orifice, with one finger, then with two. "Fuck me, baby," Doug groaned. "Give it to me."

Brian lay on Doug's back and slid his dick into the waiting hole. "Feels good, doesn't it?" he said, as his hips began to rise and fall.

Their voices were now silenced and I could hear slurping. Since I couldn't see their faces, I could only surmise that they were kissing. Brian's rear-end started moving faster and I could hear him grunting with the exertion. "Oh yes, baby," he suddenly cried. "I'm coming."

I had been stroking my own dick throughout this performance, and was practically ready to shoot, so I thought I had better head back to my cabin. Once I was on my bunk I began playing with my nuts and dick. I was strangely turned-on by the fact that Doug had wanted Brian to fuck him in the ass and that he had obviously enjoyed being shafted. Without even thinking about it, my fingers started probing my virgin hole. I brought my fingers to my mouth for some saliva to lube my hole and was turned on by the taste of my chute and the smell of my man-scent.

My bunk was under the cockpit, so there wasn't much headroom. When I bent my legs up to my chest, to open up my chute, my feet were planted on the roof. Because of my flexibility my pecker was mere inches from my face. I slipped my spit lubed finger into my tight orifice and twirled it around, stimulating myself as never before. After only a few more strokes on my pole, my load shot out spraying over my face and neck. My mouth, wide-open in ecstasy, was the main recipient of my load. Without even thinking I swallowed my creamy load, tasting cum for the first time.

On route to our next port of call the following morning, Brian asked me how I had slept. I told him I had slept well. He said that he thought he'd heard me on deck during the night. We came to the conclusion that he must have heard a bird or something else, since it hadn't been me. I realized that I would have to be more careful in future.

We docked in a small fishing port that evening to get some fresh supplies. Doug pulled out his cellphone and made a number of calls. The last call didn't sound good. Someone was in hospital. After he'd hung up, he told us his mother had taken ill and that he would have to take the bus home. After packing a small overnight bag he called a cab and left for the bus terminal.

I could see that Brian was upset at this sudden change in plans. He had been planning this trip for a year, he told me, and now suddenly all the excitement was over. That night I crept back on deck, but the forward cabin was dark and quiet. The next morning it seemed senseless to go back home, so Brian and I decided we would spend a few more days cruising Georgian Bay. After a good sail we arrived early at a small secluded cove and were able to tie up to the shore.

By the amount he was drinking, I could see that Brian was still upset. "Fuck, what a time for his mother to get sick," he complained, "right at the beginning of our trip."

After a while he suddenly said, "Shit am I ever horny today. It must be the sun and the booze."

As the afternoon wore on I could see that he was getting hornier by the minute, rubbing his mound more frequently, pushing at the hardening cock as though wishing it away. Of course I too was getting turned-on watching his performance. He leaned back against the gunwale. When his legs spread widely apart, his big nuts bulged out of the legs of his bikini. He shook his head when he was unable to push them back inside his bikini. "What the fuck!" he said, "might as well let them hang out."

From where I sat, directly across from him, I could detect a masculine aroma emanating from his body. He kept looking at me, then down at his bulging pouch, as though trying to send me a message. I knew what he wanted, but there was no way I was going there! Suddenly he said, "Maybe if we take a swim it'll cool me down. You game?"

"Sounds good," I said.

Without further discussion, he stood up and dropped his bikini. My breath caught in my throat as his half-hard cock came into view, swinging around as he moved. I stared at his muscular ass as he bent over to remove the bathing suit. His cheeks were very white and I could see a thin coating of dark hair in the muscular crevice. It was one thing to see him in the semi-dark cabin, but quite another thing to see him fully exposed in the light of day. He was a magnificent specimen, from head to foot. He climbed up onto the gunwale then dived into the clear blue water. I lost no time in joining him, anxious to get in before he saw my hardening dick.

We swam around for a while, and then I followed close behind as he climbed up the stern ladder. What a view I had. I could see his tiny asshole when his cheeks spread wide, and had a good view of his big balls swinging in their hairy pouch. His dick had shrunk a little, but was still something to behold. We soaped ourselves and I undid my ponytail and shampooed my hair.

"Want some?" I asked, offering him my bottle of shampoo.

"Yeah," he said, "that'd be great." He sat down on the deck and said, "You wanna do it for me?"

I thought, why not? So I stood behind him, poured shampoo onto his head, and massaged his scalp. As I moved, my dick hardened up and rubbed across his smooth back. I quickly moved away from him. "All done," I said, and then dived into the lake. He stood up and followed me into the cool water.

After our swim, we went forward and spread our towels on the deck, drying our naked bodies in the hot afternoon sun. As we chatted, I noticed he was looking into the partially opened forward hatch, and I wondered what was going through his mind.

We had another drink, then he said, "I think I'll go below and take a nap. Call me when you feel horn ... ah ... hungry."

I could hear him moving about down below, and then it became very quiet. I lay still for a short time, trying to put my mind on other things, but all I could think about was his magnificent body. I rolled over onto my stomach so that I could peep into the hatch. My heart practically stopped when I saw him. His lower body was fully exposed in a bright shaft of sunlight and I could plainly see his hand stroking his dick. The head was shiny and leaking precum, while the long fat shaft was as stiff as a rod. My own cock; which was pressed between my body and the hard deck, hardened up fast as I watched him playing with himself. My hips rose and fell as I pumped my throbbing shaft on the warm deck, watching as his hand glided up and down his slick shaft.

I inadvertently let out a low groan as my pleasure increased. We both stopped moving on hearing this sudden noise. I held my breath hoping he wouldn't realize that it had been me. Very slowly his hand once again began to move up and down the slick shaft. I breathed a sigh of relief and started humping the deck once more. My relief was short lived; however, because he suddenly spoke out loud, "You might as well come down here. You'll have a much better view."

I was horrified. He'd caught me spying on him. I lay still hoping the whole thing would go away, but it was not to be. He knelt on the bunk, opened the hatch wide and beckoned me in. I rose slowly from the deck, then slipped through the hatch onto his bunk. As I dropped to the bunk, I could see him staring at my stiff rod. He resumed his reclining position and then; ignoring me completely, went back to working on his still uncontrollable dick. I was entranced. Never before had I witnessed such blatant exhibitionism. He was horny and didn't care who knew it or what he did to relieve himself.

I lay on my side with my head up close to his crotch, marveling at the sight of his throbbing manhood. His legs spread slightly as I watched, giving me a view of his huge balls and his hairy perineum. As he continued to stroke himself, my own hand moved imperceptibly toward his torso, settling eventually on his rigid abdomen. His muscles jumped slightly, as my hand came to rest, the only indication that he was aware that I had touched him. His eyes were closed, his lips were slightly parted, and it appeared as though he was in a trance.

I couldn't believe how turned on I was. I wanted him. I wanted to see what it felt like to suck cock. My body moved closer to his as I raised myself on my elbow, moving my mouth over the head of his shiny dick. I opened my lips and gently mouthed the head of his dick as he stroked the shaft. My mouth sunk lower on the smooth head, sucking his semen from the wide-open piss hole, as he continued to jerk on the slick shaft. His hand moved lower on the shaft giving me more of the rod to suck into my mouth. Eventually he removed his hand completely, lying back and giving himself to me. My hand replaced his as I sucked his enormous cock, trying to get the whole thing down my restricting throat.

"Suck that big dick," he groaned. "Deep-throat me."

I spread his legs and moved between them. Lying on my abdomen as I once again brought my mouth to his lust-engorged tool. I licked the solid shaft then moved to his big balls, rubbing the sac over my lips then sucking the big creamers into my mouth. His groaning became louder as my sucking became more assertive, while his legs spread wider to give me greater access to his sexual organs. I could smell his maleness emanating from his crotch as I persisted with my sucking. He raised his legs to his chest, uncovering his whole perineum.

My mouth moved to the pink pucker that I had seen on the ladder, remembering how I had enjoyed the taste of my own hole. My tongue hesitantly rimmed the clean virgin hole, licking the dark hairs surrounding the orifice. He placed his hand on my head and pushed my mouth hard against his manhole.

"Oh yeah, baby," he groaned. "Eat my ass."

Even though I had never rimmed anyone before, I was hungry for his asshole and pigged out on the virgin tract of male flesh. His ass twitched and his hips rolled as I rimmed him, driving him crazy with lust. He lowered his legs then pulled my head back to his saliva-coated dick, pressing the head to my parted lips.

"Suck my dick. Go on ... suck it," he groaned.

My mouth opened wide as he fed me his dick. He pushed on the back of my head, forcing my mouth down his thick shaft, until the throbbing monster was in my throat. He slowly fucked my mouth sinking more and more of the slimy shaft down my throat, until I was able to swallow about half of the length before gagging.

His hand came off of my head and I heard him speak. "I know you were up there watching the other night, so you know what I want, don't you, Chris?"

My mouth slowly came off his huge dick, as I looked into his eyes. There was nothing menacing about him. He was only making a statement. I was scared of his big cock, but Doug liked it, so I thought, why not give it a try? "I've never done this before, Brian. If you promise you'll take it easy I'll let you try."

He looked long and hard at me, then as though ruminating rather than questioning said, "Are you really a virgin? Of course I'll take it easy. If I hurt you, let me know and I'll stop."

He pulled me up onto his body and then gently licked my lips. My mouth opened to admit his tongue and we French kissed for a while. I rolled onto my stomach offering him my ass. His hand stroked my smooth mounds, parting the cheeks, then he gently played with my exposed hole. "You've got a fantastic ass," he murmured. "I've wanted to fuck you ever since you came aboard."

He continued playing with my hole, attempting unsuccessfully to insert his finger into the tight orifice. He spat in his hand then brought the saliva to my hole; spreading the lubricant around and then bit-by-bit sinking his finger into my tight channel. My ass moved around attempting to engulf his big finger, while my throbbing dick fucked the bunk.

He reached over to the locker and retrieved a tube of lubricant and a safe. After applying a liberal amount of lube to my orifice and his finger, he continued working on my hole, gradually loosening up the tight sphincter, until I could feel him deep in my chute. His chest pinned down one of my asscheeks, while he spread the other with his free hand, and probed deep into my hot cavity. He slowly inserted a second finger then a third, twirling them around and around, setting my virgin ass on fire. He was taking his time loosening me up, knowing the size of his dick, and feeling the tightness of my chute.

I held my breath as he came to his knees, scared and yet at the same time determined to satisfy his needs. He quickly sheathed his rammer then went back to fucking my tight hole with his fingers.

He placed the big head of his dick against my dilated hole then, slowly withdrew his fingers, replacing them with his knob.

"Fuck me," I said when I felt his knob at my entranceway. "Give it to me. Stick that big dick up my ass."

I was so worked up that I hardly knew when the head of his big dick breached my virgin hole and penetrated my clinging channel. His hands spread my asscheeks wide as his massive shaft, inch by inch, sunk into my innards, massaging tissues that had until then been dormant. The feeling was incredible. His shaft spread the tissues apart stretching them to their maximum, giving them their first taste of male sex.

My ass began to move on its own, milking his probing pole. He spread my legs with his knees, and then sank his cock in my ass, all the way to his balls, screwing the tender flesh of my virgin ass. His big cock-head probed my very core time and time again; sinking all the way in before coming back to the surface, making me cry out loudly as it rubbed against my prostate. He was over stimulated and could wait no longer. "Oh yes," he said. "I'm gonna cum."

His cock pounded my ass driving me to the edge of climaxing. My ass rose to meet his inbound shaft, the sheath of my channel spreading for him. He pulverized my ass with his rammer, jack-hammering my tender prostate, triggering the most tremendous orgasm I had ever had. My balls spewed out their load all over his bunk, as his own cock exploded up my tight chute. He lay on my back breathing heavily until I had to ask him to move.

For the next few days we continued sailing before heading back to our home port. By the time we arrived home my ass was well and truly run-in. All I could think of was, lucky Doug.

LIVE SEX IN THE THEATER

Troy was walking along Main Street when he noticed Leo, a butch looking tennis instructor that he'd been lusting after, turn into a gay movie theater. He couldn't believe it. He'd always thought that Leo was straight. Maybe he doesn't know what kind place it is? Troy thought. Maybe I should follow him and see what happens?

Troy was familiar with the gay porn theater because he'd been there on numerous occasions. When he entered the lobby, Leo had just purchased a ticket and was heading downstairs to the restroom. Troy quickly purchased a ticket and followed him downstairs. The restroom, which was empty, had a number of urinals down one side and three cubicles down the other. The middle cubicle door was closed. Troy went into one of the empty cubicles, closed the door, pushed his jeans down to his boot tops, and emptied his bladder. He made sure to stand well back from the toilet so that Leo could see his cock through the large gloryhole.

By the time his bladder was empty his dick had hardened up considerably. Troy took his time, milking out the last drops of piss, making sure that his erected shaft was close to the gloryhole. He was surprised when Leo's dick, without any forewarning, slid through the gloryhole. So much for thinking he was straight, flashed through Troy's mind. Since he was the one usually getting the blowjob, Troy hesitated. Leo doesn't know me, he thought, so who's going to know I'm sucking cock in a restroom?

He ran his hand up and down Leo's substantial endowment for a short time, and then a disembodied voice said, "Suck my dick."

Troy sat on the toilet seat and, without any further preliminaries, began to blow Leo. He ran his tongue around the smooth head and sank the eight inch shaft down his throat. His inhibitions forgotten, he bent himself to the task. He was just getting into the swing of things when Leo withdrew his dick, and wiggled his finger through the hole.

Troy stood up and shoved his cock through. It felt good when a hand grabbed his shaft and a wet tongue licked his knob. Leo pulled Troy's balls through the hole and chewed on them. With his abdomen flat against the partition, his cock and balls were completely available to Leo. Although Troy had been blown through

107

the same gloryhole many times before, the cocksucker had always been a stranger.

Leo concentrated on his nuts. He gripped the skin between Troy's nuts in his fist and compressed them in their sac. Oh yeah, Troy was thinking, squeeze my nuts. He groaned loudly when Leo chewed on the sensitive orbs, and stroked his shaft. Still holding securely onto the sensitive nuts, Leo moved his mouth to Troy's knob. He circled the head with his tongue and then deep-throated him.

Troy couldn't move, so he relaxed and let the hot mouth blow him. He's a natural cocksucker, Troy was thinking, and can probably deep-throat a horse. Troy was amazed at Leo's ability, and gave himself up to the once in a lifetime blowjob. He hung onto the top of the partition, and clenched his asscheeks. Unable to restrain himself, Troy cried out loudly when he climaxed and flooded Leo's throat with his seed.

Trembling after his earth shaking orgasm, Troy slowly withdrew his organ and pulled up his pants. He was doing up the fly when he heard Leo leave the restroom. Troy followed him out of the restroom, up the stairs into the balcony, and when Leo settled down in the second row from the back, Troy moved quickly into the seat directly behind him.

Leo slouched back in the seat, his asscheeks pushed to the edge of the cushion, with his legs draped along the arms of the seat in front. He concentrated on the action on the screen for a short time, then he opened his fly and took out his tool. Troy had a good view of the long shaft that he'd just been sucking. Leo stroked up and down with one hand, and played with his balls with the other.

Troy was still turned on by the hunk. He was thinking about joining Leo, he wanted another taste of Leo's massive dick, but before he could move, there were two guys moving toward Leo, like vultures zeroing in on a decaying carcass. One guy moved into the row in front of Leo, one seat over. The second guy moved into the same row, with one seat separating the two of them.

Leo ignored the two guys and continued to stroke his dick as if he was the only one in the porn theater. The guy in the same row as Leo moved over into the seat next to Leo, and placed his hand on Leo's thigh. When Leo removed his hand from his cock, it stood straight up from his open fly. He lay back, as though he was trade, as if to say, 'It's all yours. Go ahead.' The guy next to him immediately took over the hand action, stroking up and down the tall cock.

When the guy leaned over and sucked Leo, Leo ignored him, and watched the movie. Troy, from his seat behind them, could hear the slurping sound of the guy's mouth working its magic on Leo's manhood. The guy in front of them swiveled around in his seat to get a better look. He leaned over the back of his seat and rubbed Leo's thigh for a short time, and then he climbed over his seat back and joined the sexually engaged couple.

The guy just joining the couple started stripping Leo. First, he pulled Leo's T-shirt up, locking the front behind Leo's neck and, after undoing Leo's belt; he had Leo raise his hips, then he lifted Leo's legs into the air, and removed the pants completely. Leo, now naked, sprawled out in the seat with his muscular legs spread wide apart, his gaze fixed on the screen, leaving all the work to the two guys. Troy popped the buttons open on his jeans so that he could work on his rod – which was once again hard and ready for action. The action in the row before him was far superior to the action on the screen, so that's what he concentrated on.

One of the guys knelt between Leo's legs, and sucked on Leo's nuts. The other guy persevered with Leo's dick, over, and over again, he deep-throated the long hard piece of meat. Leo continued to ignore the action around him. The seats all around the trio, including the one next to Troy, were beginning to fill up. Troy felt a hot hand rest on his thigh, so he glanced at the guy who had taken the seat next to him. It was a young guy who hardly looked old enough to be in the place; however, Troy knew that the porn theater didn't admit minors so he relaxed and allowed the guy to feel him.

Troy leaned back in his seat, spread his legs to give the guy access to his crotch, and watched the guys in front of him. He felt wet lips encircle his knob. The guy mouthed the knob and slid down the shaft toward his churning nuts. Troy's hand moved down the cocksucker's back, gliding over the skin-tight T-shirt toward the waistband of his satin shorts. Troy pushed the shorts down and bared the upturned backside for all to see. His hand fondled the exposed muscular asscheeks, moved into the moist crevice, and then his finger gently rimmed the crater and probed the quivering hole.

The guy's hole needed some lubricant so Troy moved his finger to the cocksucker's mouth for some saliva. His finger, now wetted down, returned to the waiting manhole and drove right in. Troy could hear the guy groan around his shaft when his finger invaded the tight sphincter.

The trio in front moved into high gear. Leo's legs were pinned to his chest and both guys were on their knees taking turns to rim him and to suck his nuts. After a few minutes Leo pushed them out of the way and dropped his legs. One of the guys shucked his jeans, straddled Leo, placed his feet on the adjacent seats and, over Leo's head, looked into Troy's eyes. When his asshole swallowed the long shaft between the tennis instructors's splayed legs, his mouth opened in a gasp, and then he bounced up and down on the pole.

Troy was so turned on by the spectacle before him that he too wanted a piece of ass. He pulled the guy up from his cock, and bellowed, "Get your ass up here." His command was louder than he intended it to be, drawing the attention of other patrons. The young guy was quick to obey. He immediately removed his shorts so that he could mount Troy's rod. The muscular young stud turned his back to Troy, spread his cheeks with his hands, and lowered his manhole to the waiting stalk.

When Troy's dick-head penetrated his slit he moaned and said, "Fuck me with that big cock, dude."

The two guys being fucked were mouth-to-mouth. They tongued each other's oral cavity while the two studs below them plowed their asses.

The men, who frequented this porn theater, were often active participants in the sexual acts which took place in the seats. Being voyeuristic by nature, they enjoyed a good live sex show. The audience surrounding the copulating guys all had their cocks out, jerking-off and shooting cum all over the place. Troy had his hands around the young guy's waist. He bounced him up and down on his rod, and pounded the receptive channel. Leo was lost somewhere below the mass of bodies.

Troy whispered in the guy's ear, "I'm coming, dude." Then he lost his load.

The guy above Troy leant back against his chest, and impaled himself on Troy's throbbing boner. He grabbed his own dick, and masturbated wildly. Troy could feel the guy's chute clamp tightly around his organ when his load erupted in long streams over the seat back, covering Leo and his trick.

"Asshole!" Leo bellowed.

There was a collective gasp from the audience when they witnessed the tremendous climax; many of them lost their own loads in the process. The trick lay back against Troy's chest, and rested his head on Troy's shoulder. Troy could feel the guy's heart racing as he milked the last drops of jism from him.

The stench of cum, and sweat, permeated the air; however, Troy was far from satiated. He'd already cum twice, but he knew he could carry on all day if he wanted. He tucked his dick in his pants and then climbed over the seat back into Leo's row. He removed his jeans, pushed the guy off Leo's dick, straddled Leo, and then pushed his rear-end into Leo's face. Leo immediately attacked Troy's hole. Delving his tongue into Troy's tight hole and squeezing his nuts. He pushed two fingers into Troy's hole and wiggled then around. When Troy's dick reached for the sky, the stud that'd been getting fucked by Leo immediately pounced on it, sucking Troy down to the pubes.

Troy stood between Leo's legs then bent them up to his chest. A guy on either side of Leo held his legs in place, exposing his spit-covered upturned asshole for all to see. Troy dropped to his knees and clamped his mouth on Leo's hairy hole. Leo groaned when Troy slipped two fingers into his hot chute. This so-called straight guy wants to be fucked, Troy thought as he shoved a third finger into the butch tennis instructor's manhole. Troy placed his dickhead against Leo's hole then shoved his dick into Leo's silky smooth chute. Leo let out a yell when Troy hit bottom. "Asshole!" he shouted, "That was virgin territory."

Not anymore, Troy thought as he grabbed Leo's ankles and hammered his chute. It didn't take long for Troy to shoot his third load of the day deep into Leo's gripping channel. When he withdrew his dick, he placed a foot on both sides of Leo, lent forward, clamping Leo's legs in place, then fed Leo his dripping dick. Leo tried to get away, but Troy held his head still until he opened his mouth and sucked Troy's dick down to his pubes. Troy felt someone behind him. He swiveled his head and noted that someone else had moved in and was fucking Leo. Leo groaned, but sucked harder. Troy let him suck him for a few moments, then he pulled his dick free, tucked it into his jeans, stepped over all the bodies, and left the theater.

THE COWBOY
GETS RIDDEN

I have always been interested in horses, and attended a local riding school to perfect my riding skills. One day the instructor informed me that a friend of his who owned a dude ranch was looking for some summer help. I naturally took advantage of this opportunity and immediately applied for the position. The owner hired me, and told me I could start work at the beginning of the season.

When I arrived at the ranch the owner informed me that I would be sharing a room in the bunkhouse with his son. The ranch house was under renovation and therefore space was at a premium. His eighteen year-old son, Aaron, was the same age as me, and was tall and blond with a deep tan. He would be responsible for my training.

The first week was hard work, so I was pretty bushed every night, falling into a deep sleep as soon as I hit the pillow. Aaron informed me that Thursdays would be our day off each week, so that we could rest-up before the arrival of the week-end guests. When the first Thursday rolled around he suggested that we pack a lunch and ride up into the hills where we could relax next to a small lake. I jumped at the chance of spending the day with him out in the hills away from the hustle and bustle of the ranch.

It was mid-morning by the time we arrived at the picnic spot. It was a great place with grass and trees surrounding the deep blue spring-fed lake. After tying up the horses to a tree, we unpacked our saddle bags, spread a blanket on the grass, opened a couple of cans of beer, then relaxed in the shade of a big willow tree. It felt great lying around shooting the breeze after the hectic pace at the ranch.

After our first couple of beers Aaron suggested we take a swim to cool down. We were soon stripped out of our clothes, helping to remove each other's boots. I couldn't help admiring Aaron's nicely tanned body, noting the contrast of his smooth white tail and long cock. We jumped into the cool water, shivering at the sudden change in temperature. After a short romp around in the deep lake we quickly jumped out of the water. Since we had not brought towels we moved the blanket into the sun and lay down in the warming rays.

Aaron reached over to his saddle bag and pulled out a joint. After lighting the joint and taking a deep drag, he passed it over to me. We passed the joint back and forth till we were both feeling nice and mellow. It felt cozy and intimate lying in the nude in the hot sun with Aaron's warm body next to me. I must have dozed off for a few minutes, but was awakened by a noise from Aaron. I raised myself to my elbow and looked at his sleeping form. He was flat on his back with his legs spread apart, but what really caught my attention was his dick. It had grown into a rock-hard piece of meat since I had last seen it, and was now lying on his abdomen moving slightly with each heart beat.

I was captivated by this sight. I had never before seen a hard cock besides my own. My own cock started to rise while I stared at Aaron's smooth dick. It was a hefty piece of equipment topped by a plum shaped head, and was oozing semen onto his hard abdomen. The shaft was an ivory white with a small amount of dark-blond pubic hair at its base. I'm not sure how long I stared at his dick, but I just couldn't take my eyes off him. As I looked at him I was slowly stroking my own cock.

His hand moved slowly to his groin. He lazily scratched his nuts for a while, then he began to milk the shaft of his throbbing pole, squeezing more precum out onto his rigid abdomen. I glanced at his face and I saw that he was wide awake and fully aware of what was taking place. I was very confused not knowing how to react, but he seemed to be in full control of the situation.

"I don't know about you," he said, "but I always get hard lying around in the nude, especially when I'm with a hunky stud like you."

I was in a trance when Aaron placed his hand over my hand then moved it to his hard dick. I couldn't resist, knowing that I wanted this as much as him, so I allowed him to take the lead. He held my hand around his stiff shaft, then moved it up and down, demonstrating the action he desired. When he was satisfied that I understood, he placed his hands behind his head and watched as I stroked his manhood in the hot sun.

"That's it," he whispered. "Milk that big dick."

After I'd been stroking him for a short time he turned around on the blanket into a sixty-nine position. I gasped as he took hold of my dick and sunk it into his mouth, slurping on the sensitive crown for a few moments, and then sinking down the stiff shaft. I lay there hanging tightly onto his dick enjoying the feeling of him giving me my first blow-job. Naturally I'd heard of this before but had never experienced the intense joy of having my dick deep down a milking throat. Seeing that I was in a trance he once again demonstrated what action he required by placing a hand behind my head and pulling it into his masculine smelling crotch.

"Go on, suck it," he said. "I know you want to."

I wasn't sure about any of this. I was scared and confused, I mean I liked girls, but as soon as my lips touched his dick my tongue tentatively lapped at his oozing cock-hole. He groaned loudly around my dick when my tongue circled his pink cock-head. He lifted his head to watch me then, after saying, "Oh, man ... does that ever feel good," went back to my stiff shaft. I sucked the head of his dick and pushed it down my throat. I hadn't done it before, but I knew what to do. After we'd sucked for a while he rolled onto his back and pulled me over him. My mouth opened wider and I dived back onto his dick. I placed my hands on his warm thighs and forced his dick into my tight throat, swallowing hard as the large head stimulated my gag reflex. I continued bobbing my head until I was able to take more and more of the smooth stalk into my tight throat, not satisfied until my lips came in contact with his silky pubic hair.

As we continued our sucking, I slowly became aware of an added presence. My heart nearly stopped with fright when I opened my eyes and saw a scuffed pair of cowboy boots standing next to us. I immediately tried to break away from Aaron, but he continued to hang onto my ass and deep-throat me. I raised my eyes from the boots, taking in the long chap covered legs, pausing briefly to admire the bulging crotch at the junction of the chaps, then continuing up past the narrow waist, across the muscular chest, arriving eventually at the handsome smiling face of the ranch foreman.

"Howdy, boys," he said. "How you all doin'?" He poked Aaron's rear-end with the toe of his boot. "I see it didn't take you long to get into the new guy's pants. At least you could've invited me along to share his meat."

Aaron said, "I didn't invite you 'cause I knew it wouldn't take you long to follow us up here. Why don't you take your clothes off and join us? I'm sure Brent won't mind."

As you can imagine I was shocked at this sudden change in events, but didn't say anything as the foreman dropped his knapsack on the blanket and stripped. Aaron resumed his cock-sucking, hardly missing a beat. What the hell I thought, and went back to his solid chunk of meat, once again slipping the head into my mouth and sliding down the smooth shaft. It hasn't taken you long to become a practiced cocksucker, I thought as I rolled his nuts in my hand.

When he was naked the foreman kneeled on the blanket and lifted Aaron's ass onto his muscular thighs. Our foreheads were together when his tongue moved back and forth over Aaron's small puckered asshole, rimming the edge then probing the tight hole. His tongue moved to Aaron's balls wetting them down, then slowly one at a time he drew them into his mouth, rolling them around, nibbling on the pliable sac, causing Aaron to increase his deep-throating of my pulsating dick.

After chewing on Aaron's balls for a short time, the foreman held Aaron's dick at the base then watched as I attempted to deep-throat him. "Oh yeah, I can't wait to feel those pretty lips on my dick," he said. "Suck his big cock. Take it all."

The foreman moved his mouth over to share Aaron's shaft with me. We both tongued the shaft then reaching the head at the same time, he placed his hand behind my head, pulled my mouth to his, and French kissed me. It felt weird to feel his rough day-old beard on my face. Our mouths dueled over Aaron's dick, and I watched in admiration as he sucked Aaron's cock deep into his throat. These two have been doing this for a long time, flashed through my mind.

We shared Aaron's dick, taking turns to demonstrate our cock-sucking expertise, deep-throating the bloated shaft until Aaron shouted, "Stop, or I'll cum." The foreman pulled Aaron and me over so that I was on my back and Aaron was on his knees. He reached into his knapsack and pulled out some lube and a handful of safes. After rolling a safe down his huge dick, and covering it and Aaron's hole with lube, the foreman placed the bulbous head at the entrance to Aaron's chute. I continued with my sucking as I watched his dick slip into Aaron's body. I would not have thought it possible, but with my ring-side seat nothing was left to doubt. His steely rod sliced into the gripping tissues of Aaron's ass until it was buried to the hilt, at the same time forcing Aaron's cock deep into my throat. I placed my hands on Aaron's ass and circled the deeply imbedded stalk, testing the pulsing girth with my fingers.

Meanwhile Aaron had moved from my shaft to the virgin territory between my asscheeks. Pulling my legs up and clutching my ass to his face, he began to tongue my hole just as the foreman's bloated cock started to pound in and out of his tight hole. I was engrossed with the action before my eyes. The big cock slipped out of the clenching hole until I could just discern the ridge of the crown, exposing at least eight inches of oversized dick, then plunging forward again through the pouting lips, until both sets of swinging balls knocked together above my wide-open eyes.

Aaron sat up and impaled himself on the foreman's stiff shaft. "I want my cock in your ass," he said to me.

I wasn't sure if I was ready for that new experience, but by then was so turned-on that I wanted to feel his cock between my virgin cheeks. I rolled a safe down Aaron's slimy shaft and covered it with lube. Next I fingered my hole, making sure I was well lubed. It felt strange shoving a couple of fingers up my chute, especially in front of two guys, but it also felt good. I wanted to see what a cock felt like up my ass. I was scared, but Aaron was enjoying it, so why wouldn't I?

I slipped between their legs and turned onto my stomach placing my asshole against Aaron's stiff dick. He began a slow fuck between my asscheeks, rubbing my anus with his lubed rammer. Gradually his movement changed until the knob of his dick was pushing at the very entrance to my virgin hole. His rimming and my fingering had loosened me up considerably allowing the knob of his big dick to breach my tight pucker. I gasped in pain as the head slowly entered my spasming hole. Gradually the pain abated, being replaced by a feeling of pure ecstasy as my hole opened up and his rod slipped all the way home.

Aaron lowered himself to my back and began pummeling my ass, sliding the full length of his stiff dick in and out of my slippery hole, massaging my prostate for the first time. My ass tingled with desire, hungry for this new found pleasure. I pushed up hard against his thrusting dick, spreading my tight cheeks wide. I could feel when the foreman resumed his fucking action by the increase in Aaron's pressure on my ass. Each time the foreman hit home Aaron would bounce on my ass thrusting his own cock deep into my bowels, jack-hammering my tender prostate. His cock felt like an extension of the foreman's cock, and I could feel him twisting about on top of me trying to get more cock up his ass, while at the same time attempting to thrust his own cock as deep as he could into my newly breached hole.

I knew it would only be a matter of time before I exploded. My ass was on fire while my cock pressed between my body and the blanket, was draining a continuous stream of precum. Aaron's thrusts became faster, making me feel as though I had a bucking bronco on my back. I could hear both him and the foreman grunting with exertion as they fucked themselves senseless into the writhing assholes surrounding their dicks.

Aaron began a long drawn out wail as his throbbing dick began to spurt load after load of molten cum up my destroyed asshole. I could hear the foreman climax as he too lost his load up Aaron's ass, pumping the cum out of Aaron's prostate into my receptive hole. My own dick splattered the blanket with a thick coating of jism as the two of them pounded ass.

We lay like that for a while, too exhausted to move, and then Aaron whispered in my ear, "Was that good?"

I nodded shyly, milking his dick with my ass muscles to let him know just how good it had been.

"Now that you've been tamed by this young stud," the foremen said to me, "it'll be easier for me to show you how it feels to get ridden by a real man."

After a quick swim we headed back to the ranch. I could feel saliva and lube oozing out of my tender asshole as we galloped down the winding trail. That summer turned out to be my best ever. The three of us often rode up into the hills to fuck, and the foreman was right, it wasn't long before his hefty shaft felt right at home in my rear-end.

THE HITCHHIKER
GETS THUMBED

I was sitting by the side of the loneliest road in the world, trying to hitch a ride to Reno. An uneasy feeling came over me when the sun, in a burst of orange, sank behind a mountain range. The thought of being stuck overnight in such a desolate place was terrifying. I'd heard how rattlers liked the warmth of the human body, so there was no way I was going to roll out my sleeping bag in those surroundings. I could hear the growl of the eighteen-wheeler approaching long before I could see its lights. I heard the trucker downshifting as he neared, and breathed a sigh of relief as he finally stopped next to me.

"What the hell are you doing out here in the middle of nowhere?" the driver asked as I climbed into the cab.

"I was scared I wouldn't be picked up."

"You been waiting long?"

"My last ride dropped me here nearly four hours ago."

"I guess it's a good thing I came along then."

"Yeah, thanks for stopping."

He seemed happy to have my company, and talked non-stop as we headed down the highway. I was glad my underpants were tight because the warmth of the cab and the vibrations from the motor caused my cock to raise its head and strain against my jeans.

After a couple of hours, I saw the lights of a motel in the distance. "I'm going to stop there for the night," the trucker said. "I've done the maximum hours allowed. What are you going to do?"

"Can I sleep in the cab?"

"Sorry, it's against company policy, I could lose my job."

"I'll just sit outside then. Can I ride with you in the morning?"

"Sure you can ride with me, but there's no need for you to sit out here. You can share my room. It won't cost you anything. The company pays for it."

I felt a little awkward, since I didn't know him well, but I gratefully accepted his offer. When we entered the room I saw there was only one double bed. He hadn't given me any hints about his sexual orientation, so you'll have to be careful, I thought as I dropped my bag on a chair. Yeah, I've fooled around with other guys – nothing major, just mutual hand jobs, but I've never actually slept with another guy. This would be a new experience, and I was excited.

We dropped our bags and headed for the coffee shop for a quick meal, which he paid for. On our way back to the room, he purchased a cold six-pack of Bud at the office. We decided to take showers before hitting the sack. He went into the bathroom first, eventually coming out with a towel wrapped around his hips. In his state of undress I could see he was bigger than I had thought, at least six two and 180 pounds. His closely cropped dark hair was still damp. The gold band on his left ring finger sparkled as he ran his fingers through the pelt of hair on his chest. Oh fuck, he's straight – you'll have to be careful, crossed my mind. His huge, tattooed biceps, probably a result of steering big rigs, flexed as he moved his arms.

I luxuriated under the warm shower water. It had been a few days since I had showered, so I spent a long time washing away the sweat and grime. My cock started to expand again. I wanted to jerk-off – it had been a while, but I was scared he might come in and catch me.

"What's taking you so long in there?" he called out. "You ain't jerking-off, are you?"

Shit, he must be a mind reader, I thought as I quickly rinsed the soap off, dried myself, and slipped into a pair of bikini briefs. When I came out of the bathroom, he was sitting on the bed in the Lotus position, sipping on a cold Bud, watching a news channel. He was still only wearing a towel around his middle.

"Feel better?" he asked.

"I was beginning to stink."

"You didn't smell bad at all. Just a little raunchy, but then, so did I. Have a beer, they're nice and cold."

I opened a beer, joined him on the bed, and leaned up against the headboard. I wasn't much of a drinker so, by the time we were on our third beer, I could feel the alcohol kicking in. It was a nice feeling to be relaxing with a sociable guy after my week on the road.

"I wonder if there's anything decent to watch." he said, picking up the remote control and surfing the TV channels. One channel indicated if you wanted a pay-for-view triple X adult show, all you had to do was call the office and they would bill your room.

"That looks interesting," he said. "I think I'll check it out."

He picked up the phone and called the office. Within a few seconds, an adult show, in progress, appeared on the screen. I'd never seen any porn movies before so was entranced at the images on the screen. As we watched, a well-endowed young man rammed his dick in and out of a petite blond's gaping pussy. The sight of his hairy perineum and his big balls swinging back and forth, as he plowed her, hardened my dick. I was embarrassed because I had no way of hiding my woody in my small bikini briefs. I was just deciding to slip into some shorts when I noticed his dick throbbing under the towel, slowly lifting the loose folds from his muscular stomach. He didn't seem self-conscious, so I relaxed.

I kept glancing at his throbbing dick, which seemed to grow more and more as the show progressed. His towel became undone and slowly parted, revealing first his hip, gradually slipping further and further apart, until I could see the head of his uncut dick peeking out the side. I had difficulty concentrating on the TV. I wondered what he'd say if I told him the sight of his dick turned me on more than the movie?

Mesmerized, I watched his hand move to his lap to rub his shaft through the towel. His cock became fully hard, causing the head to slip out of its prepuce. As he stared at the TV, he moved his thumb over his cock-head. Precum oozed from the hole in his dick and pooled on his thigh. The towel slipped further back and exposed the full-length of his huge dick.

He patted his shaft, like he was trying to calm it down, then he raised the stalk from his thigh into an upright position. My own cock had appeared above the waistband of my bikinis and I was startled to realize I had also been playing with the knob while observing him at play. Hoping he wouldn't notice, I slowly pushed my briefs down my thighs until my balls and cock were fully exposed. My hand moved up and down my shaft, matching his moves. My other hand gently rolled my nuts around in their sensitive pouch.

As I watched him watching the TV, he spread his legs apart, completely exposing his dick and nuts. My breathing increased as I watched him stroke himself, all pretenses of watching the movie now gone.

Suddenly he spoke, "Fuck. Did you ever see anything like that before? Would you look at her deep throating him. I sure could do with some of that." He looked over at me and watched as my hand caressed my hard dick, the TV forgotten for the moment. "That's some pecker you've got there, boy. It looks like you're just as turned on as me."

I felt my face flush as he looked at me. I'd never been in such a situation before so was at a loss as to how to react. As though sensing my embarrassment, he said, "Don't let it bother you. We're just two horny guys enjoying ourselves in private."

Relaxing a little, I continued to manipulate my dick, proud of the way it stood up high between my thighs. I was even prouder when I noted the way he kept glancing at me. I pulled my undies off and threw them onto a chair so I could spread my legs. He bent his legs up and rested the one closest to me on my thigh. The erotic sensation of his hairy leg resting on my thigh caused my excitement to go up another notch. His hand rubbed his thigh, and then, as if by accident, his hand slipped onto my leg, his hot palm covering my inner thigh. His other hand continued to stroke his dick. The hand on my thigh inched toward my crotch.

I gasped aloud when his hand contacted my swinging pouch. I moved my hand and placed it on his hairy thigh. He leant back against the headboard and spread his legs. My hand slipped down his thigh and touched his nuts. His leg crossed over mine, opening up his groin to my hand, putting his dick within grasping distance. Our hot bodies pressed tightly together. He took his hand off his dick and rubbed his leg. His cock swung free and rested on my hand. My hand, seeming to have a will of its own, turned over, gripped his shaft, then slid up and down the long expanse of man-meat.

His hot breath sent tingles down my spine when he placed his arm around my shoulders and whispered in my ear, "Have you ever done this before?"

I could feel my face once again blush, as I shook my head in response. I shivered in ecstasy when he gently nibbled on my earlobe. Slowly he moved his mouth to mine. I was lost, completely captivated by the horny trucker. My mind was in turmoil. This was so much more than a mutual jerk-off with a buddy. But I knew I wanted him to possess me. I'd wanted this for a long time. I was more than anxious for this man-to-man sex. My mouth opened to admit his probing tongue. I marveled at the strange feeling of a man kissing me. He ran his hand over my smooth chest, lightly pinching my nipples, then he moved his hand down to my groin and milked my shaft. He placed his hand between my legs, gently fondled my nuts, rolling them around as though testing their weight.

We kissed like two lovers who have been parted for too long. He leaned back against the headboard and his hand pushed my head towards his crotch

"Suck me," he whispered.

I had to pretend that I didn't want to. "Uh-uh, I'm no fag."

"Neither am I, but I'll suck you too. Just to see what it feels like. There's no harm in that, is there?"

His dick, only inches from my mouth, hypnotized me. His hairy chest felt erotic against my cheek as my head slowly, but surely, descended to the throbbing rod in my hand. I was confused. I was mixed-up. Should I suck him, or should I back away?

Even though he had just showered, I could detect a distinct male aroma arising from his manhood. My lips touched the smooth knob. I had wanted to suck him ever since he'd come out of the bathroom, and yet I was still scared. His hand moved down my back to my ass-cheeks. My mouth engulfed his dick. The wide head lodged in the back of my throat. He groaned out loudly as I forced the head further into my throat. His hand moved between my moist ass-cheeks and his finger tickled my virgin hole.

He lifted his hand to his mouth, coated his big middle finger with saliva and moved it to my tight sphincter. His lubricated finger gradually penetrated my asshole making me squirm with pleasure. As he lazily fucked my tight hole with his finger, his dick slipped down my throat, his semen greasing the passageway. I swallowed deeply as he lay imbedded in me. The peristaltic movement of my swallowing made him cry out. I took his nuts in my hand and massaged them as I gave my first blowjob.

"Oh, yeah, that's the way," he said. "You're a natural."

His hand came to my mouth for more saliva. I play with my asshole when I masturbate, so I recognized the smell and taste of my own hole on his fingers. My sphincter relaxed as two of his fingers pushed inside and massaged my tender tissues. His fingers slipped out of my hole. His thumb replaced them and probed deeply. I could tell when he contacted my prostate.

I pushed my rear-end back as he fucked me with his thumb. I wanted more of him inside. I released his dick. "That feels good," I said.

He lay back and made me straddle him in a sixty-nine position, with my asshole directly over his mouth. His tongue probed my virgin hole, driving me crazy with lust. His hands held my rear-end tightly to his face as he tongued my chute. He pushed me forward onto the bed, climbed between my widely spread legs and once again brought his mouth to my manhole. He groaned as he spread my cheeks wide and dipped his tongue into my gaping channel. My ass twitched in desire as he fucked my hole with his tongue.

A voice on the TV was crying, 'Fuck me! Fuck me!' and before I could think I had joined in the chorus crying, "Please. Fuck me with your big cock."

I watched over my shoulder as he pulled a tube of lube out of his bag. He lubed his dick and my hole, then he placed the big head at the entrance to my chute, and slowly pushed it home. He was balls deep before I realized it. I tentatively milked the large trunk up my ass, testing my inner muscles. He groaned loudly in my ear as he felt me grip his boner.

"Oh fuck," he murmured. "What a tight hole."

He sank his shaft nuts deep in me and then withdrew it completely. He slapped my cheeks with his dick, and pounded it back in to me, as though he wanted to ream out my channel. My asshole was taking the first pounding of its life, and I was in heaven. When my hips lifted spontaneously to meet his downward thrusts, our bodies slammed together. He seemed out of control, fucking my ass like a wild man, pummeling my prostate with each thrust, and I loved it.

His movements became faster and faster, and I could feel his knob probe deeply into my innards as he opened up new territory. He bellowed out loudly when his man-juice spewed out of his pounding rod, depositing load after load up my newly opened chute. I was still on fire. My cock was hard and begging for release. I couldn't stop my ass from twitching around his throbbing manhood. He slowly withdrew his dick from my gripping hole, groaning as the head broke free.

He rolled me onto my back. We both stared at my cock, watching it sway back and forth like a metronome. He lifted my buttocks to his chest and rimmed my ass, soothing the tender tissues. His mouth moved up to my balls, licking and chewing, as he went. He pushed two fingers into my dilated chute and massaged my prostate, then he swooped down and engulfed my dick. Right down to my short and curlies. I squealed out loudly and thrashed my legs around in the air as his velvet throat brought on an immediate orgasm and I shot a week's worth of sperm into his throat. He sucked me dry then gently released my dick, licking the last remnants of cum from the sensitive head as it cleared his mouth.

"Your cum tastes really nice," he whispered. "I hope there's more where that came from?"

I nodded.

"I can see we're going to get on just fine. Maybe we'll spend another day here before moving on. What do you think?"

"That sounds great."

He turned off the TV and we climbed into bed and fell asleep in each other's arms. I guess things must have been just fine with him, because I stayed with him for a week, before I headed back home a new man.

JARED GOES SUNBATHING

Jared had a couple of days off work, so he decided to drive to the beach for a day in the sun. It was going on ten when he parked his Corvette on the side of the road. The stretch of beach where he liked to sunbathe was usually deserted, so he was surprised to find a red Mustang convertible parked in his usual spot. He changed into a bikini, then grabbed his bag and started off across the dunes.

In the distance he could see a tall redhead disappearing over a dune. Always on the lookout for a new trick, Jared waited for a short period, and then he walked in that direction. He dropped to his knees when he reached the area and crawled up to the top of the dune. The redhead had removed his clothes and was spread out on a blanket with his bare ass exposed.

Jared watched for a few minutes, and then came to his feet. He could feel his dick swelling in his tight bikini as he approached the prostrate redhead. He stopped when he reached the hunk's feet, his eyes taking in his stunning physique. His glance lingered on the white asscheeks, and the shiny red hair visible in the tight crack.

Jared gave a little cough to attract the redhead's attention. "Nice day isn't it?" he said.

The redhead jumped and his head whipped around in Jared's direction, his eyes wide open in shock.

"Sorry, didn't mean to startle you," Jared said. "Had no idea there was anyone here until I came over the dune."

The redhead gave Jared the once over, his glance lingering on the protuberance in Jared's brief bathing suit. "It's okay," he finally said. "I didn't know there was anyone else around. Why don't you join me? There's lots of room on the blanket."

Jared sat down next to the redhead. "I'm Jared," he said.

"I'm Allan," the redhead said, sticking out his hand to shake.

Jared stretched out on his back in the hot sun. "This feels really great," he said. "It's nice to get out in the sun. I've been cooped up in the office for days."

"Yeah. It's great, isn't it?" Allan said.

"Do you come here often?" Jared asked.

"I spend a lot of time at the beach, but today I wanted to get some rays on my backside, so I decided to try this deserted area."

"It is kind of isolated. I come here whenever I can."

"Why don't you take off your bathing suit? It feels really great," Allan said.

Jared removed his bathing suit and lay back on the blanket. "Yeah, that does feel great. I love the hot sun shining on my dick. Unfortunately it usually gives me a boner."

"Same thing happens to me," Allan said. He rolled onto his side, propped himself on his elbow, and ran his hand over Jared's chest. He stared into Jared's eyes, and twirled Jared's chest hair between his fingers. "I'm glad you joined me. I thought I'd be having a quiet day all by myself, and now it seems to be getting exciting."

It's getting better all the time, Jared thought. I'm glad I decided to check him out.

Allan lowered his mouth to Jared's mouth and chewed on his lips. Jared placed his hand behind Allan's head, held him in place, and opened his mouth to Allan's invading tongue. They kissed for long moments, and then Allan moved his mouth to Jared's chest and chewed on Jared's sensitive nipples. Jared raised his head and watched as Allan's hand moved over his abdomen down to his stiff dick.

"That's some piece of meat you've got down there," Allan said as he took Jared's dick in his hand. "I bet you know how to use it too?"

"You got that right," Jared said. "It's had plenty of practice."

"I bet it has," Allan said as he ran his warm hand up and down the length of Jared's dick.

"I hope no one's around," Jared said. "I'd hate to be caught."

"No one's gonna see us out here. I'll check and make sure we're alone." Allan stood up and looked around. "No one's around. It's all clear." He dropped back down to the blanket, this time with his head above Jared's crotch and his dick next to Jared's head.

"I love uncut dicks," Allan said. "They're a real turn-on." Then he chewed on Jared's foreskin, and lapped up his precum.

"Oh, yeah," Jared groaned. "That feels great. Suck it."

Jared licked Allan's dickhead, and then went right down on him. He could feel his own dick being engulfed by Allan's tight throat. They hung onto each other's ass-cheeks, and deep-throated each other, for a long time, as only two experienced cocksuckers can do.

Jared held Allan's shaft deep in his throat, fingered the wet spot between Allan's ass-cheeks, and then slipped his finger in to the knuckle. Allan made mewling sounds around the shaft embedded in his throat when Jared inserted a second finger. He ground his rear-end against the invading digits, opening himself completely. Jared moved his fingers in and out of the gripping hole, then he dug deep until he could massage the hard knob of Allan's prostate.

Allan handed Jared a condom. "You're driving me crazy," he said. "I want your cock up my ass."

Jared was feeling ambivalent. His mind was in a whirl. He was supposed to be going steady, but here he was, again, getting ready to fuck a stranger. Maybe just this one time, he thought. Besides, he rationalized, Brad will never know.

Allan must've seen the doubt in Jared's face. "What's wrong? Don't you want to fuck me? Please, give it to me ... I really need it."

Jared couldn't resist the appeal. He quickly checked to make sure that they were still alone. While he rolled the condom down his shaft, Allan lubed his chute. Jared positioned himself between Allan's long hairy legs and pushed them to his chest. Allan quickly grabbed Jared's dick and guided it to his receptive manhole. With a jerk of his hips Jared buried his shaft right to the hilt.

Allan gasped when Jared penetrated his orifice. His hands grabbed Jared's hips to stop him from moving. "Oh, man ... you're so big. I've never had such a big piece. Stop for a minute."

Jared rested on his elbows. When Allan relaxed, he rammed his joint in and out of the receptive chute, banging into the upturned ass-cheeks with such force that Allan's body shook with the shock waves.

Allan, an experienced bottom, spread his legs as wide as he could and hooked his knees behind his elbows. "Give it to me," he said.

The hot sun on his naked ass, and the risk of being caught by a park ranger, stimulated Jared. He was just getting into a steady rhythm when he was shocked to see a pair of hairy muscular legs standing next to Allan's head. He looked up into the hazel eyes of a rugged bear of a man. He gasped. "What the – "

"Howdy, boys," the hairy bear drawled. You all interested in some company?"

129

Before Allan or Jared could answer, the stranger dropped his shorts and knelt next to Allan's head. His huge blood engorged dick and nuts, bloated by the tourniquet effect of the leather cock-strap, looked menacing. "Don't let me stop you," he said. "I've been watching you for a while, and couldn't resist the temptation."

Allan's response was quick. He grabbed the stranger's huge knobbed appendage and pulled it into his mouth.

"There we go," the bear cooed. "Show Daddy how much you like his dick. Nice and slow ... all the way down. That's a good boy. You sure know how to suck Daddy's dick."

Jared, who hadn't moved since the stranger's arrival, slowly recommenced fucking Allan. He was just getting back into the swing of things when the stranger once again spoke. "Why don't you let me have a go at that juicy boy hole? I bet you've got it nicely primed for Daddy."

Allan didn't seem to object so Jared shrugged and said, "Sure, why not."

Jared lifted himself up and moved out of the way. He helped the bear safe-up, thinking, fuck, I wouldn't let him any where near my asshole with that big whopper, he'd split me in two! The bear dropped to his knees and, in a nanosecond, was buried balls deep in Allan's chute.

"Yeah," Allan said rotating his ass around the jawbreaker, "fuck my ass with that big monster. That's it. I can feel it way up inside me."

"That's a good boy," the bear growled. "You sure know how to take Daddy's cock. Just as well or Daddy would've had to spank you." He turned to Jared. "Gimme that dick, boy. Daddy wants to suck you."

Jared was quick to comply. He ripped off the safe and squatted over Allan's face. He could feel Allan's tongue on his hole when the bear swallowed him in one lunge.

Allan took hold of his own organ, rubbed the semen around the head, ran his fist down the long shaft, and slapped his hard-on against the bear's hard abdomen. His other hand pulled at his nuts, as though he was trying to squeeze his sperm from them.

The stranger pummeled Allan's chute, driving his dick in and out as though it were a piston. Suddenly he came to his knees and said, "Oh yeah, Daddy's there." He pulled out of Allan, ripped off the condom and, with only two strokes, shot his massive load over Allan's abdomen.

"Stand up, boy," the bear ordered Jared. "I want you to cum in Daddy's mouth."

Jared jumped to his feet and plunged his dick back into the bear's mouth.

"Oh yeah ..." Allan panted, "... getting close. Cum with me, dude."

"I'm coming," Jared said, and flooded the bear's throat with his load.

Allan climaxed next.

They had hardly caught their breath when the bear jumped up and pulled his shorts on. "Thank you kindly, boys," he said. "Daddy really needed to get his rocks off."

They laughed as they watched him disappear over the dune. "He's sure in a hurry," Allan said. "Do you think he has a bus to catch?"

They lay side by side, gradually recovering from their marathon fuck. "That was great, man. I can't remember ever having such a good reaming. Do you think we could get together again?" Allan said.

"Yeah, it was great, wasn't it? It would be nice to see you again, but that's not possible. I'm ... uh ... kind of going steady," Jared replied.

Allan laughed. "I understand," He leaned over and kissed Jared on the cheek. "I've been there. A quick roll in the hay is fine, but anything more than that would be cheating. Your partner is a lucky guy."

"No, you're wrong," Jared replied. "I'm the lucky one."

He slipped into his bathing suit, winked at the redhead, and then headed home.

ORGY AT THE LEATHER BAR

Cliff wanted to try the leather scene. He'd heard all kinds of weird stories about what went on in leather bars, and was determined to experience the scene first hand. He'd dressed in tight faded blue jeans and, to show off his pumped delts and biceps, a white tank-top. His black western boots, he thought, added just the right touch. He was sure he'd pass muster if he put on a butch act. The last thing he wanted was to appear Nellie. They would laugh him out of the place.

It was going on ten when Cliff entered the bar. It was dark inside, and Cliff had to pause at the entrance until his eyes adapted to the change in lighting. With the exception of the barman, the place seemed deserted. However; he could hear the sound of pool-balls clicking in the background. The dark-haired, butch-looking barman, dressed in leather pants and cycle boots, gave him the eye as he approached the counter. His upper torso was naked. A wide leather band circled his left bicep, and a hoop earring pierced his left nipple.

"Well what have we here," he said to Cliff. "Are you sure you're in the right place, boy? You know what kind of bar this is?"

"Sure ... I know it's a leather bar."

"Good. Nice to see some new meat in the place. What'll it be?"

"A Bud, please."

After he had paid for his beer, Cliff wandered around to check out the place. He moved through an archway into the pool-table area, and leant against the wall. There were four guys in the room. He could feel his face flush when the four guys all turned and looked in his direction.

Two guys were leaning against the wall watching two other guys playing pool. One of the guys leaning against the wall was ruggedly handsome and was about six feet tall. He had dark closely cropped hair, and a small strip of beard covering the cleft of his chin. Shiny black leather pants clung to his muscular legs. His well-developed upper body was completely naked. A barbed wire tattoo encircled his left bicep and a hoop earring pierced his left earlobe.

The other guy leaning against the wall was a long-haired brunette. He was shorter, and stockier, than the first guy, and was clad in old blue jeans, with rips across the knees, and a white T-shirt. He was clean-shaven. Cliff slowly made his way around the pool table and settled on a stool close to the two guys. As he rested his butt, the two gave him the eye. He smiled at them and nodded.

"Hi," the tall one said. "Haven't seen you before. You visiting?"

"No. Just thought I'd drop in for a drink. How 'bout you? You visiting?"

"We're regulars. I'm Eric," he said, offering his hand, "and this's Randy, and before you ask, yeah, he's always randy."

Randy grinned. He too offered his hand. "Hi, handsome. What's your name?"

"Cliff."

"Hi, Cliff. You play pool?"

"Nah, not really. I've tried a few times but it's not my thing. I prefer to watch."

"And tonight it's worth watching, ain't it?" Eric said. He nodded in the direction of the table.

One of the players was dressed in a miniscule pair of ragged denim shorts, a leather harness, and a pair of construction boots. He lay across a corner of the table, getting ready to shoot. With his legs spread the way they were, the onlookers had a good view of his bulging jock through the gaping legs of his shorts.

Randy stepped over to the guy spread on the corner of the table, ran his hand inside the guy's shorts, and gripped his nuts. The guy miscued. There was loud crack and the white ball flew off the table onto the floor.

"Dude," he said, "look what you made me do. I coulda sunk that one."

Randy laughed. "Who're you kidding? The only thing I've ever seen you sink is a big cock down your throat, and a gallon of recycled beer."

Everyone laughed. Randy continued to fondle the guy's nuts. Cliff noticed that even though the guy had complained about missing his shot he remained in position and seemed to be enjoying the manhandling by Randy. When Randy sank to his knees and pressed his face into the guy's rear-end, Cliff's rod hardened-up.

"Well, I guess that's the end of this game," the guy's partner said. He dumped his cue and came around the table.

"That's Lenny," Eric indicated with a nod of his head towards the guy spread on the table, "and this big fucker's Mitch," he added when the other guy joined them. "This is Cliff."

Cliff took a good look at Mitch. He was a bear of a guy. Probably six-three, Cliff estimated, and built like a linebacker. He was dressed in leather pants and a leather vest. His shaved head contrasted sharply with his exposed hairy chest and goatee. Mitch's biceps bulged when he pulled Cliff up from the stool, took him in a bear hug, and ran his hand over Cliff's butt.

"Nice bod, dude," he said. "Where you been hiding?"

Mitch's other hand cupped Cliff's hard dick. The big bruiser's technique wasn't what Cliff was used to, but his cock seemed to relish the attention it was getting. Mitch gripped Cliff's shaft through the denim. "Get a load of this," he said. "Nice piece, boy."

Eric's hand joined Mitch's at Cliff's groin, and the two guys played with Cliff's meat. They held him between their bodies, Eric in front and Mitch behind. Cliff opened his mouth to Eric, enjoying the taste of Eric's tongue, the erotic smell of warm leather, and the sensational feeling of the two studs enveloping him with their masculine aroma.

They were all startled when a loud voice bellowed, "What the fuck's going on in here?"

Cliff turned his head towards the voice. The barman stood at the entrance to the poolroom glaring at them. "You want to get us closed down again?"

"Don't be such a pussy, Billy. I've seen you getting it on in here before," Mitch retorted.

"Sure you have ... but that was after closing."

"Well yeah, you're right," Mitch said. "The place was closed, but all we're doing is kissing."

Billy pointed at the pool table. "You call that kissing?"

Cliff looked in the direction of the table. Lenny was still spread-eagle. He was now; however, butt naked with Randy's face pressed between his asscheeks.

"Yeah, well, maybe ... I guess we are getting carried away," Mitch conceded. "Why don't you lock the door and join us?"

"Are you crazy? You want me to get fired?"

"Just do it, Billy," Mitch said. "If Steve gives you any grief, tell him that I made you do it."

Billy looked confused, as though undecided. "Oh, what the fuck. Why not? Just remember, Mitch, if I get in trouble it's your fault."

Someone undid Cliff's belt and lowered his jeans to his boot-tops. He ran his hands down Eric's naked back onto Eric's leather encased mounds of ass-flesh, and held on. Mitch's strong hands spread his butt cheeks apart, then he slowly worked on Cliff's asshole, opening it up with his thumbs, and penetrating it with his tongue.

"Oh yeah, boy, you taste real good. You need to get a look at this sweet ass," Mitch said to Eric.

"Let's get him on the table so we can get a good look," Eric suggested.

Mitch stood up and waved his dick. "I need some action on this first," he said. "Get your lazy butt over here, boy," he commanded.

Cliff wasn't sure who Mitch was addressing although it was obvious that the others did. Lenny jumped up from the table and dropped onto his knees in front of Mitch with his head bowed in submission. Mitch held Lenny's head with one hand, and slapped his face with his blood-engorged cock. The cock-head was a dark purple color. Probably from the tight silver cock-ring, Cliff thought.

"You wan' it?" Mitch asked Lenny.

Lenny strained toward the rod held a few inches from his mouth. "Please, sir ... I want your cock," he said, with a whine.

Mitch slammed his cock into Lenny's mouth, all the way down his throat in one lunge. Lenny gobbled on the rigid shaft as it slid in and out of his mouth.

"What are you waiting for?" Eric bellowed at Randy.

Randy dropped to his knees in front of Eric and wolfed down his hefty dick. As the two bottoms pleasured their masters, Cliff watched in awe. His gaze moved in the direction of the naked barman, who now leant against the pool table, using two hands to slowly stroke his extra long shaft. Cliff moved in front of the barman and sank to his knees. He took the hard-on in his hand. "Nice dick, Billy," he said.

"Suck it, dude," Billy directed. "That's it, chew on my skin. Oh, yes ... that's the way. I knew you'd be a good cocksucker the minute

I saw you mince through the door. Chew on my nuts. Oh, yes, dude ... get them all wet and juicy."

Cliff was just getting into his stride when he heard Eric suddenly blurt out, "Okay, that's enough. I want to taste the new boy's ass."

Eric and Mitch pulled Cliff to his feet, and tugged his T-shirt over his head. They placed him on his back on the pool table next to the other three guys, removed Cliff's boots and jeans, and pushed his legs up to his chest.

Eric's tongue zeroed in on Cliff's manhole. "You weren't kidding," he said. "Nice and yummy."

Mitch, who had stripped, climbed onto the table and pulled Cliff's mouth to his dick. "Suck my cock, boy," he ordered. "Show me what a good cocksucker you are. That's right all the way down. You've done this before. You know how to take a big cock." He forced Cliff's mouth all the way down his shaft, ignoring Cliff's attempts to free himself.

Cliff felt a hot mouth on his dick. He shoved Mitch out of the way and looked down. Billy, the barman, was giving him head. The sensations, which coursed, through his aroused body, threatened to overwhelm him, but he tightened up when he felt something hard press against his sphincter. He looked down. Eric was smearing a big gob of lube on his hole. He relaxed. Two of Eric's fingers slipped into his chute and poked around. He pushed back on the fingers, and groaned when two more fingers slipped inside. Eric withdrew his fingers and rubbed the head of his latex covered dick against Cliff's anus. Cliff relaxed and let him in.

Cliff couldn't restrain himself when he felt Eric's dickhead massage his prostate, "That's it, give it to me, hard and fast," he said. "That's the way I like it."

Eric grabbed hold of Cliff's ankles and pistoned in and out of his receptive chute. "There we go," he said. "Is that what you want, boy ... all the way in?"

Cliff couldn't respond because Mitch had forced his bloated shaft down his throat again. Lenny and Randy joined them. Cliff was turned on by all the action; he wasn't sure who was doing what. All he knew was that there seemed to be hands and mouths everywhere as Eric's dick pounded his rear-end into oblivion, giving him the fuck he needed.

Billy, the barman, pulled Eric out of the way and, reaching unheard of depths, pounded his latex covered dick into Cliff's well lubed chute.

Mitch said, "Stop hogging him. I want a piece of that ass too."

Billy ignored Mitch, and plowed Cliff for a good five minutes. When Billy finally withdrew, Cliff felt the sudden void. "He's all yours. I've got him all juiced up for you," he said.

Mitch crawled between Cliff's legs. Cliff looked down. Mitch, on his knees, held his unprotected dick at Cliff's dilated asshole. "Here we go, boy, just what you need, a prime piece of meat."

"Not without a safe," Cliff shouted, when he realized Mitch intended to fuck him bareback.

"Yeah, boy, that's the way I like it. When you get a feel of this big smooth hog up your ass you'll never want it any other way – "

"Are you crazy," Cliff burst out when he felt the head beginning to enter his body. "I said no!"

Mitch was undeterred by Cliff's protests and continued to push forward. Cliff suddenly kicked Mitch in the chest, sending him flying off the pool table. "You asshole!" he shouted. "What's your problem? I said no!"

Cliff was standing on the floor when Mitch came to his feet. He lunged for Cliff. "Nobody fucks with me. You goddamn pansy. I'll get you for that."

Cliff was too quick for him. He let out a loud yell, spun around on one leg and, then with the sole of his foot, kicked Mitch on the chin. Mitch landed on his butt on the floor.

Mitch once again came to his feet, but much slower this time.

"Stop this shit, Mitch," Eric yelled. "Get a grip on yourself. How can you even think of fucking bareback? You must be crazy."

Mitch seemed determined to have his way. He once again started to move towards Cliff. Billy jumped between them. "That's enough," he bellowed. "Leave him alone, Mitch. I always knew you were a bully, but I never knew you were also stupid. Now get dressed. I'm gonna open the doors."

Cliff quickly dressed and followed Billy out into the main bar area. Billy unlocked the door for Cliff. "I'm sorry about that," he said. "That asshole won't be allowed back in here after I speak with the boss."

"Thanks, Billy. I appreciate your help, but I could've flattened him if I wanted."

"I think you probably could've. That was some move. What was it?"

Cliff laughed. "I'm a Tae Kwon Do black belt."

"That right? Well, I'd hate to mess with you."

Cliff said, "Well, I'd like you to mess with me. I'm sorry about what happened I liked you plowing me with your big dick. I wouldn't mind a second round."

"That so? Come back at closing time and we'll see what we can do about it."

THE BUILDER GETS HIS PIPES CLEARED

Chad was hot and thirsty, so he dropped into his local pub. The only vacant stool was between a woman, and a butch guy dressed in a ragged T-shirt and paint-stained blue jeans. Chad squeezed into the open spot and ordered a Bud. He was trying to think of a way to start up a conversation with the guy, when the hunk gave him an opening. The hunk rotated his head, like he was exercising his neck, and gave a low groan. Clearly, he was in pain.

Chad glanced at him. "You had a rough day?"

The hunk, still attempting to exercise his neck, said, "You better believe it. It's been a real bitch. I'm a builder. I've been on the go all day trying to satisfy the customers. It's nice to finally relax and enjoy a beer. Name's Justin," he said, offering his hand.

"I'm Chad," Chad said as he shook the hunks calloused hand.

Now that they were talking, Chad was able to get a good look at the handsome dude. His left nipple peeked through a rip in his T-shirt and both of his boney knees showed through tears in his jeans. A pair of scuffed construction boots completed his attire. His muscular biceps, tanned forearms, flat abdomen, and well-defined pecs, all indicated that he was a man who was used to hard work. The earring in his left earlobe, and the black baseball cap were, to Chad, a real turn on.

They were chatting for some time, gulping down the cold beer, when coverage of a hockey game began on the television. "Oh good, the game's starting. I've been looking forward to this all day," Justin said. "Are you into hockey?"

"Sure," Chad said. "I try to watch whenever I can."

"Let's move over to a table," Justin suggested. "We'll be able to see much better from there."

"Sounds like an idea."

They picked up their beers and crossed the barroom floor to a nest of tables in front of the television.

"I used to play in the minors, so I know some of the players on the team," Justin said. "It makes it a lot more exciting for me."

They sat down at the table. The television screen went blank.

141

"What the fuck!" Justin shouted.

The barman quickly came over to the television, but he was unable to revive the ancient set.

"Shit. It's about time you got a new set. You make enough bread," Justin said.

"Sorry 'bout that," the barman said. "I'll talk to the boss 'bout it."

Maybe I can get him to invite me to his place, Chad thought. "It wouldn't be too bad if I could watch at home," he said, "but my set's also on the blink."

"Listen," Justin said. "Why don't you come over to my place? I live just around the corner, and I've got a fifty-two inch plasma set."

"Great," Chad said. But, it worked, was going through his mind.

He followed Justin out of the bar around the corner into a large three-story house located on a quiet street. The house was old, but well maintained. The dirty dishes in the kitchen sink, and the newspapers and empty beer cans scattered around the living-room, all spelled bachelor. Justin led the way down to the basement, where he had a nicely set up recreation room that included a wet-bar. Justin grabbed a couple of Buds from the refrigerator and they settled down on a settee in front of the television. Chad was enjoying himself sitting around shooting the breeze with Justin. He liked cruising men who were obviously straight. He watched Justin out of the corner of his eye.

Justin was caught up with the action on the screen, and must've been real thirsty, because he drank one beer after the next, downing at least two to every one of Chad's. Justin frequently used the toilet next to the bar, leaving the door open so he wouldn't miss any of the game. The sound of Justin's piss hitting the water turned Chad on, and he could feel his shaft slowly expanding in his tight briefs. The last time Justin came back from the toilet he had a small wet patch covering the head of his dick, which further aroused Chad.

By the time the game was over Justin was flying. He staggered when he went to get another beer. When he came back to the settee, he flopped down and spilt beer into his lap. He jumped back up with a disgusted look on his face. "Oh, shit ... that's fucking cold."

Oh good, Chad thought, just what I needed. An excuse to get him stripped. "You better get those wet jeans off," he said. "I'll get you a towel."

When Chad came back from the bathroom carrying the towel, Justin was hopping around on one foot, trying to get his other foot out of the tight jeans. He fell back on the settee, his legs hopelessly entangled in the jeans.

Chad knelt before him. "Here. Let me give you a hand," he said. Chad's hands ran up and down Justin's hairy legs as he struggled with the tight jeans. Justin's hefty equipment was clearly visible through his wet bikini briefs. Get a grip on yourself, Chad thought. The guy's straight. If you make any stupid moves you'll jeopardize everything. After his jeans were off, Justin retrieved his beer and continued to guzzle the liquid, seemingly unconcerned that his cock was practically on display.

Justin turned to look at Chad. He tilted his head back and grimaced with pain. "Shit, my fucking neck is killing me."

"I've been told that I'm pretty good with my hands. Why don't you sit down here on the floor and I'll give your neck a rub?" Chad suggested.

Justin rubbed his neck. "I'll try anything to get rid of this pain."

He settled on the floor between Chad's knees, and leant back against the settee. Chad's hands trembled with excitement when he placed them on Justin's neck. He'd wanted to touch Justin ever since they'd met in the bar, and now at last, his hands were on him. As Chad's fingers massaged the tense muscles in Justin's neck, Justin groaned and moved his shoulders. "Let's get this out of the way," Chad said tugging at Justin's T-shirt.

Justin lifted his arms, allowing Chad to remove the T-shirt. Justin was now practically naked on the floor between Chad's thighs. Chad pulled Justin back against his crotch. "Here," he said lifting Justin's arms onto his thighs. "I'll be able to massage your delts better in this position. The scent emanating from the builders armpits, and his warm back and arms, gave Chad an immediate hard-on.

Chad rubbed the strong neck for a long time, then said, "Why don't you lie down on the floor, so I can do your back muscles?"

Justin stretched out the floor in front of Chad and made himself comfortable. "It's hard kneeling in these tight jeans. You mind if I take them off?" Chad asked.

143

"No, go for it."

"You have any lotion I can use?" Chad asked.

"Yeah, there's some in the bathroom."

Chad collected the lotion then removed his jeans. He straddled Justin's backside, poured lotion on Chad's back, then recommenced the massage. His hands worked the slabs of muscle on the tanned back before him and then, bit-by-bit; he worked his way down Justin's back. He concentrated on the stud's lumbar-sacral joints for a long time, slowly nudging Justin's briefs down, until the mounds of Justin's butt-cheeks appeared above the waist band. When Justin didn't object, Chad slowly lowered the briefs until he could see a smattering of auburn hair peeking out from between the studs cheeks. A tattoo of a phoenix, looking like it was taking flight from the luscious crevice of Justin's butt, covered the area. Justin lay completely relaxed as Chad continued to work at his muscles. He seemed in a trance when Chad pulled his briefs down his legs and off his feet. He moved between Justin's legs and massaged Justin's asscheeks digging his thumbs into the muscular mounds. He lifted Justin's hips and pushed a cushion under them.

Justin groaned loudly when Chad's thumbs slipped into the crevice of his rear-end. Chad stared at Justin's spectacular ass. His hands moved the mounds apart to reveal the hairy valley between them. He could tell that Justin was hard by the way he fucked the pillow below his hips. Chad moved forward slowly, scared to spook the guy spread before him, but determined to taste the virgin manhole. He held the cheeks apart with his strong hands, and took a deep breath. Wonderful, he though as the raunchy aroma arising from the hunk's crevice assailed his senses. His tongue gently licked the moist hair surrounding the tiny pucker.

"Oh shit," Justin said. He lifted his head, and groaned with pain when he looked at Chad over his shoulder. "What the fuck you doing, buddy?"

Chad ignored the question. He held Justin's ass tightly in his hands, so the stud couldn't move, and licked the quivering asshole.

"That's fucking weird, buddy. You gay, or what?"

Chad lifted his head and stared at Justin. "Haven't you had your ass eaten before? Don't you like me doing it to you?"

"Yes ... I mean no ... Fuck; I don't know what I mean. It's just ... I mean ... you know ... it's what fags do, and I'm not queer, and you don't look like a homo."

"I know you're not queer. I'm just trying to make you feel good."

With a groan, Justin's head fell back to the rug. But his asscheeks remained spread apart before Chad's mouth. The tangy taste of Justin's butch ass turned Chad on, so he decided to give Justin a rim-job he'd never forget. His mouth, and tongue, worked Justin's hairy crevice from end to end. By the time his tongue was fucking Justin's tiny hole, the stud was squirming around on the floor, whimpering in pleasure.

"Fuck, buddy. I gotta admit, that really feels good. I guess ... oh fuck ... I don't know, maybe I am queer."

As Chad worked at the asshole spread before him, he eased his own briefs off, and fingered Justin's rear-end. He pushed his finger in and out of the tight hole, trying to relax the tightly gripping sphincter. Chad lay on Justin's back and began to run his ramrod back and forth between the muscular mounds of ass-flesh.

"Oh fuck ... I don't know about this," Justin said. "You're really getting carried away, buddy."

Chad went back to rimming the tight sphincter. He quietly pulled a safe out of his pants pocket, and rolled it down his shaft. He squirted lotion between Justin's cheeks then moved onto Justin's back and slid his rod between the muscular mounds of flesh. He placed the head of his knob at the entrance to Justin's chute and gently but determinedly pushed it home.

When Chad's weapon breached his virgin hole, Justin bellowed, "Take it easy, buddy." He wiggled his ass, and squirmed around, as though trying to get away. The movement of his rear-end; however; only facilitated with his deflowering.

Chad's cock slowly forced its way through the tight elastic ring, his dick, slowly, but surely, entering Justin's hot channel. Justin gasped when Chad's shaft finally reamed his virgin hole and probed his innermost core. "Oh fuck," he said. "You're killing me."

"Relax ... take a deep breath," Chad said. "The pain'll go away."

Chad lay still, but when he felt Justin flex his ass, he realized that Justin was ready for the fuck of his life. Chad spread Justin's thighs apart with his knees, making sure the stud's hole was unobstructed, and with a grinding movement of his pelvis, he fucked the newly opened hole. His hard shaft slipped in and out of Justin's tight chute stretching the hole to its limits as his hips moved faster and faster. He was out of control and howled loudly when his cum flooded the ravished stud's bowels.

Justin fucked the pillow below his hips, and his ass continued to milk Chad's shaft. When Chad slowly withdrew his still hard ramrod from Justin's freshly breached hole the tight lining of Justin's chute clung to his shaft, as though trying to keep him in. As soon as his knob was free, Chad rolled Justin over onto his back. Justin's lust-engorged cock, oozing a copious amount of precum, throbbed against his abdomen. Chad could tell that Justin was on the brink of coming, so he dived down onto the tool, and swallowed it, balls-deep, in one gulp.

Justin's hands grabbed Chad's head to hold him down on his organ as it spewed forth its jism. "Oh fuck, buddy," he said. "You're taking my load."

Justin fell back on the rug when he had cum. He appeared totally exhausted from the heavy session. Chad could feel Justin's rapidly beating heart against his ribs when he rolled him over and took him in a tight embrace. They lay in silence. Chad placed the pillow under Justin's head, and covered him with a throw rug from the settee. Justin never said a word, when Chad gave him a kiss on the cheek, then dressed. "Take care, Justin," he said. "Is it okay if I come back sometime?"

Justin opened his eyes and looked at Chad. "Sure, I'd like that."

THE SAILOR PLOWS HIS BUDDY

I had been in the navy for a short time and was just finishing boot-camp. All the new recruits in my group had been worked hard during basic training, and were now finally getting some needed R and R. I had become quite close to another new recruit by the name of Dale, who was a tall, well-built, energetic blond. We had met on the first day we arrived at the barracks, and since we were both from small towns in Utah, and were both pretty naïve, we hit it off right away.

Dale and I headed into the closest town anxious to begin our time off. That evening, after checking into a small cheap hotel, we hit the bars. Dale was throwing back his drinks one after the other; while I was being more careful, coasting most of the time. It became clear to me that he wasn't going to last very long at the rate he was going, so I suggested we head back to the hotel and take a break. At first he was reluctant but I finally managed to drag him back to the hotel. He seemed to be getting more drunk by the minute, with me having to support him through the lobby and into the elevator. I was glad when we got to our room because he was beginning to wear me out.

I dragged him over to his bed and sat him down. I was kneeling on the floor removing his shoes when he passed-out and fell back onto the bed. I stood up and looked at him for a while, miffed at him, wondering what to do. Since I didn't want his clothes to get all wrinkled I thought it best to get him out of them. It was quite a struggle, but eventually I had him lying on the bed in his white briefs. I was pretty hot and bothered by then, so I stripped off my clothes as well.

I couldn't help admiring his smooth body, the kind that only blonds have. His skin was flawless, and except for a luxurious growth of blond hair over his pecs and abdomen, he seemed to be as smooth as a baby's bum. My mind was in a whirl. I had been brought up in a very strict religious environment and was taught to repress my sexual urgings, but the sight of his body had me in a dither.

This was the first time in my life I'd ever really had a good look at another body, male or female, so I was really intrigued. A voice inside of me kept telling me that this was wrong, but a stronger influence seemed to be goading me on. Fate had placed my unconscious buddy at my disposal and I knew that I wanted to check him out. The circumstances would probably never arise again, so this might be my one and only chance.

My heart was beating fast as I ran my hand over his chest, feeling the solid musculature and fuzzy hair over his pecs. Next his rigid washboard abdomen caught my attention so I moved my hand further down and ran my fingers through his pubic hair. It was just about then that I realized I was getting hard. This seemed strange to me since I had never been attracted to men before. I stopped for a while contemplating my next move, knowing all along that what I really wanted was to see him completely stripped. I gripped the sides of his briefs and gently pulled them down his long smooth legs, taking them off completely.

Dale was now lying fully exposed, naked as the day he was born, with his smooth pink cock nestling on the balls between his legs. I ran my hands over his muscular thighs, getting closer and closer to the main attraction. As my hands moved nearer to his manhood I could see it starting to stir. It was slowly expanding and rising from its nest, and by the time my hands had reached his crotch his big dick was fully hard. It had grown from an inconsequential thing to a huge piece of male meat. The shaft was smooth, thick, and long, and was topped by a large head which lay over his navel. I was fascinated by the change. I had often had glimpses of his soft dick in the showers, but never guessed that it would grow so big.

My mind was in a whirl. Here was this aroused man completely in my power, and I wasn't sure yet what to do about it. I knew that for some strange reason I was sexually attracted to him but wasn't sure as to why. I wanted to feel his big rod so I tentatively began to slide my fingers up the ivory shaft. My own cock was definitely responding to this action, and had become hard, peeking out the top of my briefs. My hands spread his legs apart, giving me room to climb between them. I started masturbating his bulky dick, watching as the precum began to ooze out of the big hole in his dickhead.

I wanted to feel his big balls so I splayed his legs wide, and then lifted his buttocks onto my thighs. In this position his whole crotch was widely displayed before my eyes. I could see the hairy area between his legs, from his balls right down to his asshole. I took his big nuts in my hands and gently squeezed them, feeling the texture of his sac, realizing for the first time in my life that I had total control over a male body. I wasn't sure at first, but gradually became convinced that I could smell his sex organs. I lowered my head for a closer smell and was intoxicated by the aroma. I rested my head between his thighs and closed my eyes. He had a clean masculine smell which made my mouth water.

Although I'd never been in such a position before, I wasn't totally ignorant. I mean I was in the navy and the rest of our crew certainly talked about having their dicks sucked, some even hinted that they'd heard the best cocksuckers were men. I was scared and nervous but I wanted to try sucking a cock. First, I licked his shaft, running my tongue all the way from his balls to his cock-head, not yet ready to go all the way. But then I thought, why not, no one will ever know I sucked him. I opened my mouth, put my lips around the head of his dick, and sucked. It felt great, so I let more of him into my mouth. I knew right away that I'd always wanted to suck cock; I had been too scared to admit it to myself. My mind was spinning as I sucked his big dick.

I came up for air and checked his face to make sure he was still out for the count. His gentle snoring convinced me that all was well. I climbed off the bed and removed my briefs, then standing at the bed-side I stroked my hard cock, wondering what to do next. I rubbed my throbbing dick over his pouty lips, watching as my precum dripped into his partly opened mouth. I was scared he'd choke on the fluid so I bent over and licked his lips, then planted my lips on his and ran my tongue into his mouth. I stood up and pushed my cockhead into his mouth. When he groaned in his sleep I jumped back in horror. I was starting to loose control of myself. He would kill me if he woke up and caught me doing that to him. This thought did not seem to deter me in the least so I went back to my molestation of his perfect body.

I got back onto the bed and resumed my former position. This time my hard dick stood up between his legs, rubbing the hairy skin between his legs. I pushed his legs up against his chest until I had a clear view of his tiny asshole. The small button was begging for attention, but I wasn't ready for that yet. I went back to his dick, sucking the shaft into my mouth, practicing deep-throating him, getting more and more proficient with each try, eventually able to take most of the monster into my throat. I sat up and milked his big cock with my hand, watching the precum bubble out of the well in his cock-head.

Deciding that I wanted to see his backside, I jumped up and rolled him onto his abdomen. This side was just as gorgeous as the front. The curve of his white rear-end drove me wild. I once again climbed between his legs, spread his butch ass with my hands, and gazed at his little pink orifice. I suddenly realized that what I wanted most was to fuck his ass. I sat there for a short while trying to remember if we had any oil to lubricate his asshole, when it dawned on me that spit would do just fine.

Bending forward I hesitantly ran my tongue over the tight aperture, tasting his manhole. My hands forced his cheeks wide as my mouth covered his exquisite hole, my tongue delving into the smooth chute. His elastic sphincter dilated as I rimmed his ass, lubricating the channel in readiness for my thick-veined dick. I made sure that I left plenty of saliva at the entrance to his manhole before I straddled his back. Then positioning my dick, I very gently slipped it through the restricting muscle. I was amazed at how easy it was. The hole just seemed to open and I was in.

I lay flat on his back and pumped my cock in and out of his asshole, realizing that it wouldn't take me very long to shoot a load up his silky hole. My hips began to rise and fall as I pumped his tail, sinking my rod all the way into his juicy channel, then taking it all the way out, relishing the feeling of his rose bud opening and closing around my cock-head. My pistoning increased as I jack-hammered the gob's rear-end, until with one last plunge, I flooded his innards. I couldn't ever remember shooting with such intensity.

Sitting back between his legs I watched as my thick cock came sliding out of his well fucked hole. The sight of my big dick-head popping out of his tight chute, followed by a stream of cum, was a sight to behold. I placed my thumbs at the entrance to his chute, holding his anus open so I could take a better look at his ravished love channel. The sight was too much. I bent my head down, and fixing my lips to his hole, began felching him. I went wild on his moist crevice, sucking and chewing at the tender tissues surrounding his channel, practically suffocating between his ass-mounds.

My cock was still rock-hard so I got back on top of him and rammed it back into his hole, sinking it to the hilt in one lunge, then I recommenced fucking his hot and oozing channel. His inner muscles seemed to be gripping my rod even harder than before, milking my shaft like a tight sleeve. Within minutes I deposited another big load of cum deep within his chute.

This time I rolled off his back well and truly drained. As I lay there recovering, he turned his head in my direction and said, "I hope you enjoyed fucking my ass? Now how about some relief for me?"

He rolled over onto his back as he said this, shaking his rock-hard cock at me. Of course I realized then that his passing-out had all been a big act, and I had fallen for it. I leaned over and started sucking on his heavy equipment, trying to give him as much satisfaction as he'd given me. My tongue circled his big dick-head then my mouth engulfed his throbbing cock, sliding down the shaft until it was buried to the short and curlies.

He climbed off the bed and turned me onto my back with my head hanging over the edge of the bed, pushed his long hard dick back into my mouth, and fucked my wide open throat. I thought I would suffocate from the bombardment, but managed to keep my throat muscles wide open for his onslaught.

He pulled his long slimy shaft out of my mouth saying, "I want your ass, turn around."

I wasn't sure if I was ready to be fucked, but he had let me screw him twice, so I decided to give it a try. He twisted me around and raised my legs to my chest. I stared at his huge dick, doubting I'd ever be able to take him. He spat in his hand and applied the saliva to my virgin hole. I was scared but excited, wanting to feel him deep in my body, wanting to see what it felt like.

"Take it easy," I said as he placed the big knob against my pucker. "I've never done this before."

The pain seemed unbearable when he breached my hole for the first time, making me cry out in anguish. Sensing my discomfort he rested with just the head of his plunger planted in my hole.

"Relax, Alex," he said. "Breathe deeply and push down. The pain'll go away."

He was right of course. As soon as I began to relax the pain disappeared and my sphincter opened up allowing him to slide all the way in. The feeling was incredible with his big dick-head seeming to find new ways of stimulating me each time he moved. He grabbed my ankles then began to pile-drive in and out of my fully dilated hole, massaging my tender prostate with each lunge.

My cock was rock-hard; it had never really softened up at all, so I quickly grabbed the shaft and started to jerk-off. I had never felt such pleasure before. My solitary jerk-off sessions had been good, but this was heaven.

"Oh fuck," Dale said. "I'm coming." Then he erupted deep in my milking chute.

I wasn't far behind. "Ah yeah. I'm coming too," I cried as my cock exploded, spurting my seed all over my chest and face, forced out of my prostate by his big dick-head.

Dale collapsed on my abdomen in exhaustion, his rod still implanted deep in my chute. He looked into my eyes and said, "I've wanted to fuck you ever since I saw you in the shower that first day we met. I knew you were an uptight virgin. I hope I wasn't too hard on you?"

I shook my head, "No, I really enjoyed it. I hope we'll be doing it again?"

"You better believe it. My ass is still tingling from the pounding it took but it'll be ready any time you ask."

"Good. Now let's get cleaned up so we can get something to eat."

"Not yet, Alex," he replied, moving his still hard rod in my chute. "I'm still horny."

I groaned in delight as he once again started moving his shaft in and out of my now widely dilated channel. He pulled my head up from the bed, planted his lips on mine, then sunk his tongue into my mouth. As he slowly fucked my abused and aching rear-end, he held me in a bear-hug and kissed me deeply. I was happy and contented in his embrace and hoped that we would be repeating those sessions whenever we could.

FLIP-FLOPPING JOCKS

It was around midnight. We had taken a breather from the college football team's party in the beach house and were sitting on the dock with our feet in the cool lake water.

"Did you hear that?" Mark asked. "It sounds like someone's in the boathouse." He put his finger to his lips and signaled me to follow him as he crept toward the boathouse near the dock.

I joined him on the roof of a shed next to the boathouse. As we peered through the broken boathouse window Mark's hot body pressed against me. Inside, just a few feet below us, two of our football teammates were drinking beer. Empty beer cans were strewn over the floor. One of the dock lights was shining through the big French doors, so they were clearly visible to us.

"It's Rick and Todd," Mark whispered. As we watched, Rick began to rub his crotch. "Fuck," I heard him say, "am I ever horny. I'm glad you came to the party or I'd be going home with swollen nuts."

"Yeah, me too," Todd said. "Who needs pussy when I've got you?"

Mark looked at me, his eyes wide. We should've backed away but instead we ducked a little lower and kept looking. Rick and Todd started to make out. I could see Mark was just as shocked as I was – finding out these two butch jocks were queer was a real surprise. And these two were hot guys. Like Mark and myself, they were both around six foot and well-built, smooth-bodied and cute. Not only was I turned-on by what I was seeing, but I knew I was more excited by the feel of Mark's body behind me. I wondered how he would react if I leaned back against him.

Rick and Todd opened each other's jeans, freeing their hard dicks. My own dick was hard and I could feel Mark's hard-on pressed against my butt.

Todd sank to his knees and began giving Rick a blowjob. We could see Rick's big dick sliding in and out of Todd's mouth as he deep-throated it. Then I heard the sound of a zipper and realized that Mark was opening his fly. I glanced down. He was pulling out his hard cock. I watched in a trance as he began to slide his fist up and down the shaft, not seeming to care that I could see him

153

I'd seen Mark pulling his dick before, a month earlier in the gym shower after hours. He didn't know I had seen him from outside the shower room. Water had cascaded over his pumped up pecs and six-pack abs. His pelvis was tilted forward, thrusting out his cock. His left hand stroked his dick. It was the image that I conjured up during my jerk-off sessions. And now his hard dick was right next to me. My own cock was aching to be free, so I took it out and stroked the stiff shaft.

Mark whispered in my ear – the touch of his face and his hot breath causing me to shiver. "Have you ever ... ah ... done anything like that, Kelly?"

I shook my head but looked into his dark eyes, wondering what he'd say if he knew that I had dreamed about doing it to him. "No," I finally answered. "What about you?"

He shook his head, and then we turned back to the window. They had switched places. Rick was now getting his cock sucked by Todd. Mark groaned, and I couldn't stop myself from looking at his spit-lubed dick sticking straight out from his body, shining like ivory in the moonlight. His hand was moving up and down the shaft in time to the sucking taking place in the boathouse.

Mark whispered, "Why don't we try that?"

I was shocked and scared. Did he really mean it, or was he testing me? I shook my head, "Um ... I don't think so, dude. I'm not gay."

"I know. Neither am I, but I'd still like to try it. Just to see how it feels. I mean ... what harm could there be in that? Fuck ... I mean if those two can do it, then no one's ever going to call us fags."

Before I could answer his hand moved down to grab my cock and he started pumping it. It felt great to have my dick stroked by big butch football-stud Mark, and I figured if he could do it to me, then why couldn't I do it to him. I placed my hand around his hot thick dick, and loved the new erotic sensations coursing through my body. We continued to stroke each other as we stole more glimpses of the blowjob action in the beach house.

I was enjoying the sensation of Mark's hand on my cock when he surprised me again. "Shit, I'm so fucking horny," he said. "I want to see what that feels like." Suddenly all my fantasies became reality. He dropped to his knees, and then taking my uncut dick in his hand, he unsheathed the head and began to lick the sensitive crown. I gasped in pleasure as his hot mouth enveloped my manhood, allowing my dick to slip between his silky lips. The feeling was incredible. His mouth slid up and down my shaft, giving me my first blowjob. Maybe Mark never did it before, but let me tell you he was a natural. He was able to open up his throat wide and swallow my shaft to the hilt.

Next, Mark released my cock and then sucked my nuts, gently chewing on the pliable sac. He worked my nuts for a while then he stood up and said, "How was that, did you like it? Did it feel good?"

I felt my face flush red as I nodded, "Oh yeah, it sure did."

"It felt great sucking your cock too. Why don't you give it a try?"

Since he did it first I didn't need much coaxing. I went down to my knees in front of Mark and stared at his cock. I could smell his male scent, and knew how much I wanted to suck his dick. I gently held onto the shaft, then started licking the bloated head, tasting the precum oozing from the tube in his dick. He groaned above my head as he sank his shaft into my mouth. I tried very hard to duplicate what he'd done to me, sucking his cock as deep as possible into my mouth. I held my mouth steady for him to fuck, while I ran my hands up and down his muscular hairy legs.

I was really getting into it when he pulled his dick from my mouth, then bent over and whispered, "Dude, you've got to see this. These guys are into everything."

I came to my feet to observe the action. Carefully peeking in the window. I couldn't believe my eyes. Todd was bending over a crate, and Rick was eating his butt. I watched enthralled as Rick spread the asscheeks before him and licked Todd's butch ass. Mark undid the top button of my jeans and pulled them and my briefs down my legs. When he knelt down behind me I realized he wanted to taste my virgin asshole. His hot hands spread my cheeks wide as he tentatively ran his tongue through my buttcrack, moving down and zeroing in on my tight pucker. He wanted to really spread me wide, so he lifted my foot and slid my jeans and briefs all the way off. Then he pushed my legs apart and once again dived right back between my cheeks, rimming my tight hole, then reaching between my legs to stroke my throbbing dick.

I was embarrassed at first, but then I relaxed and enjoyed the fantastic feeling of his tongue on my hole.

Meanwhile, the guys once again switched roles – Todd was tonguing Rick's butt – and I knew that I too wanted a taste of Mark's hot ass. I pushed away from him and then pulled him to his

155

feet. Before you could count to five, I had his jeans off and was admiring his jock-ass. I spread his big butch asscheeks apart, entranced by the sight and smell of him. His pendulous balls swung between his legs as he moved. A thin layer of dark curly hair covered his firm meaty ass. I often saw his athletic butt in his football outfit and in the shower, but had never dreamed of getting this close to it.

My tongue began to lick along his muscular butt, then down between his cheeks, until I gradually moved toward the center. I could feel his tight pink hole directly against my tongue. A strong masculine odor assailed my senses. I grabbed his cheeks, spreading them apart as I licked his hole and pushed my tongue into the tight ring. He was bent over at the waist and I could tell that he was enjoying the rim-job by the way he pushed back against me.

I pulled his hard dick back between his legs, ran my tongue down the shaft, then worked my way back up to his quivering hole.

Then Mark pulled me to my feet again to see what was happening with our friends. Todd was bent over, and Rick was slowly sinking his rod into his hot asshole. Standing behind Mark as we peeked at the fuck session, I ran my hand over his ass, letting my finger stroke his slicked hole. Mark's legs spread slightly as though offering himself to me. My finger began to probe his spit-lubed slot as we watched Rick pound his buddy's asshole. I slipped a second finger into Mark, and then probed him deeply while my hard cock rubbed against his moist asscheeks. After fingering his hole for a short while I moved behind him, placed my rod between his butch cheeks, and slid it back and forth over the bulls-eye.

Mark reached back and placed my knob at the entrance to his chute. He grabbed my hips and pulled me into him. "Fuck me, Kelly. Give it to me. I've dreamed about this since the day I saw you watching me in the shower."

He groaned loudly, as I entered him. I grabbed his hips and pounded his silky-smooth chute. His big muscular ass was made for fucking. He was able to squeeze his tight sheath around my rod, massaging my shaft as it moved in and out slowly for long beautiful minutes.

"Oh no," I groaned as I watched Todd and Rick switch positions. I knew that would mean that Mark would want to switch as well. But at the same time I did want to feel his huge cock in my hole – though I was scared to death because of its size. Sure enough,

Mark straightened up, taking my throbbing dick from his asshole. Then he was on his knees, lubricating my tight hole with his velvety tongue. I spread my cheeks wide, baring my virgin hole. He attacked my ass with a vengeance, chewing at the tender entrance, tonguing my tight assring, driving me crazy with lust.

Mark inserted a finger into my chute, twirling it around, opening me up. Two more fingers slipped in, stimulating me in ways I thought not possible. I kept my eyes glued to the guys in the boathouse when Mark rose up and rubbed his cockhead around my rim. I panted with lust as he started his offensive, his big rammer poised at the door of my virgin hole, ready to violate my chute.

It was painful as the head of his dick gradually stretched my hole. "Take it easy. It's hurting," I said. He stopped and allowed me to adjust. He rubbed my butt and whispered in my ear, "Relax, Kelly," he groaned in my ear. "Push back on me."

I did what he said. He gasped in surprise as my muscle suddenly relaxed allowing him to plant his huge slab of meat deeply into my pulsating body. I flexed my asshole around his rod, feeling a man up my hole for the first time.

"Oh fuck, Kelly," he groaned in my ear. "That feels so good – I knew it would." Mark's rod slowly began to piston in and out of me, gradually building up steam, until it felt like a jack-hammer up my newly opened channel. He placed a hand on my neck and turned my face to his. Before I could react his lips were locked on mine and his tongue was probing my mouth. Without thinking, I returned his kiss, more excited than I had ever been.

I could feel his long dick probing my insides, forging its way up my tight sheath, touching places that had never been touched before. My ass gripped his hard pounding dick as he slammed it into me. I could tell that he was close to coming by the way he picked up speed, and by the gasping in my ear. He suddenly blasted off in my ass, filling me with his hot jism. He pulled me upright and continued to pound my hole as he jerked me off. In seconds that brought on my own orgasm. I couldn't help groaning out loud as we both finished coming.

You can imagine the look of surprise on Todd and Rick's faces when they looked up and saw us fucking at the window – even as they were still going at it. It didn't take them long to climax after that. Of course we got together afterwards to compare notes. The four of us have been close friends ever since that fateful night.

THE VOYEUR JOINS IN

I was brought up in the country close to a national park. Most of my teenage years were spent in the outdoors, either hiking into the park or fishing in one of the nearby streams. There weren't any other kids my age to hang around with, so basically I was a loner. One day I came across a young straight couple making out in the backwoods. They were very energetic in their lovemaking and I watched for hours as they fucked and sucked in the sun. Since this was my first exposure to anything sexual, I learned a great deal watching the two of them perform.

After this episode I became a real voyeur and used to purposely sneak around trying to catch couples having sex. This happened a lot more frequently than you would expect. Hardly a weekend would go by without me witnessing at least one overt sexual act.

My most enlightening experience took place in the middle of summer. I hiked way out into the hills, carrying some food, water, and a small pup-tent. This was not unusual since I often camped out on my own in the park. It was about midday by the time I arrived at my destination. I pitched my tent in my usual spot, and then stripped down into my bathing suit, intending to take a dip in the cool stream before settling down to lunch. I was making my way through the bush to the nearby stream when I heard voices, so I quietly crept in the direction hoping that they would be putting on a show for me.

A small sandy beach about ten feet wide, surrounded by bushes, ran along the side of the stream. As I came up to the beach I stood quietly in the bushes to begin my voyeuristic activity. There was a man wallowing around in the stream, and as I watched he lifted himself out of the water and came towards the bank. He was well-built and had a mass of auburn hair which hung to his shoulders. His hairy, muscular chest, contrasted with the smooth paleness of his exposed skin. I stared at his fantastic body as he came out of the stream, watching his thick cock and low hanging nuts swinging as he moved. While I had seen lots of sexual activity I hadn't seen anyone parading around in the nude, so this was a new experience.

He approached a nude blond who was lying face down on a big blanket. I couldn't see the blond's face because of the long curly hair. The well-built guy dropped to his knees on the blanket and began rubbing the blond's pale white ass. He moved the blond's legs apart then, after settling himself between them, started eating the blond's ass, spreading the cheeks wide so that he could get his tongue right into the cleft. I had never seen anyone eat ass before so this too was a new experience. My cock immediately hardened at this sight and my mouth watered watching him eat ass. He pulled the buttocks up, getting the blond onto their knees and then continued with his anal assault, running his tongue through the deep valley.

Two unexpected things happened simultaneously. A deep and obviously male voice cried out, "Oh yeah, Barry, eat my ass. Stick your tongue in my hole." The person being rimmed lifted his head and I was amazed to see that it was a handsome young man. You can imagine my shock. I was absolutely unprepared for this abrupt revelation, for suddenly the whole sphere of gay sex was revealed before my eyes. I had never really thought about whether I was gay or straight, but I immediately knew that I was more turned on watching the two men, than I had ever been watching a straight couple. I watched fascinated as the blond placed his hand behind Barry's head and held it tightly to his ass. My cock seemed to be harder than ever as I slipped my bathing-suit down to my knees. My hand moved to my rod and began a slow jerk as I witnessed the gay sex act.

Barry turned the blond over onto his back then took the well-endowed blond's cock in his hand and stroked the shaft. My hand continued to stroke my shaft as Barry pulled the blond's buttocks up to his hairy chest and spread the mounds of ass-flesh. His tongue once again commenced exploring the blond's asshole, this time giving me a much better view. I stared dumbfounded as his tongue circled the tiny orifice, his saliva making the blond hairs surrounding the hole glisten in the sunlight.

He licked the blond's big balls and at the same time milked the blond's big dick. My own rod was throbbing wildly, leaking like a faucet, as I clandestinely spied on them. Barry pulled the blond's dick up to his mouth and started sucking on the big head. I had seen women sucking men before, but I never seen anything like the expertise demonstrated by this big butch man. He pigged out on the blond's dick, sucking the knob like crazy, then sinking his lips all the way down the shaft, right to the hilt. It was amazing how he managed to engulf the dick without apparently feeling the least bit of discomfort.

The blond grabbed Barry's head and pulled it tightly to his crotch. "Suck it ... take it all. Oh yeah, that's it, all the way down," he moaned as his dick disappeared in Barry's mouth.

As I watched Barry deep-throat his buddy I suddenly came to the realization that I too would like to experience the thrill of having my cock sucked by that expert.

Barry pulled his mouth off the spit lubed dick saying, "Get on top of me, Dale, I want you to suck me."

Barry then lay on his back and pulled Dale over him into a sixty-nine position. Barry's widely spread legs were pointing towards me, giving me my first full view of his throbbing dick which was thick, long and uncut. The wide head was still partially covered by his foreskin and was oozing a large quantity of precum. Dale placed his cock-head at Barry's mouth, sunk the shaft balls deep into the able throat, then he lay down on top of Barry and reached for Barry's throbbing pole.

Dale's hand gently pulled the skin back, exposing the chunky vermilion shaded head of Barry's dick. I watched in awe as he slipped the skin back and forth over the sensitive head and licked the clear fluid seeping out. His lips opened wide to envelope the head and I could plainly hear the sucking noises created by his mouth. His lips gradually took in more of the long shaft, but it was clear he didn't have the expertise of his buddy.

Dale bent Barry's legs up and hooked them behind his arms, exposing the butch stud's manhole. His hands played with Barry's big nuts, squeezing them in their pouch, as his mouth continued to suck Barry's thick-bodied dick. They continued this mutual sucking for some time – the slurping noises driving me crazy with lust, then Barry pushed Dale onto his back and once again crawled between his widely spread legs.

"I want my cock in your ass, baby," Barry said as he fished a safe and lube out of a bag. He rolled the safe down his dick, squirted lube into his hand, and then lubed his dick and Dale's asshole.

Even though I had never witnessed this activity before, I knew instinctively what was going to happen and once again wished that it was me on my back. I watched in awe as Barry's huge cock slipped into Dale's hole. Dale wiggled his ass to accommodate

Barry's invading manhood and then placed his legs around Barry's waist pulling the dick into his hole.

"Oh yeah," he whimpered. "That feels so good. Give it to me, all the way in. Fuck my ass."

My head was whirling, stimulated by Dale's raunchy commands; while my own hole contracted in empathy, as though it was longing to feel that big rod buried between my cheeks. As I watched, I wet my finger with saliva then started fingering my virgin asshole, unconsciously spreading my legs in the process, forgetting that my bathing suit was around my ankles. I don't know who got the biggest surprise, me or them, when I lost my balance and fell through the bushes onto my back, landing right on the blanket next to the fucking pair.

"What the fuck!" Barry bellowed as he moved back onto his haunches, his big wet shiny cock waving around like a flag-pole.

Dale, who was still on his back with his legs up on his chest, stared at me in shock. "Where the fuck did you come from?" he asked.

I couldn't think of anything to say. I'd never been caught spying before, so I just lay there, petrified, wondering how I was going to get out of my predicament. Of course it didn't take them long to assess the situation. My still hard dick and the fact that my bathing suit was wrapped around my ankles made it quite apparent.

"Well what do you know, another cocksucker," Barry finally managed to get out, "and what a cock. Glad you could join us, dude."

Barry reached over and began stroking my throbbing dick, holding the distended pole up high, testing its circumference and length. Without further fuss he sank his hot talented mouth down the shaft engulfing my pecker in his throat. I groaned in delight as my wish came true, and his throat muscles milked my shaft. I had never felt anything so wonderful. My best hand-job had never felt so good.

Dale, now over his initial shock, moved onto his knees then held his pole to my mouth, rubbing the moist end over my lips. "You scared the shit out of me you asshole. Now suck my dick."

I tentatively licked the proffered dick, exhilarated beyond my wildest dreams. My lips opened wide and slipped around the smooth head of his dick. My hips moved up and down, pumping my cock into Barry's silky throat as I attempted, for the first time, to accommodate a big cock in my throat. I now knew what it felt like to be sucked and to suck at the same time.

Dale pulled his cock from my mouth then, after straddling my head, lifted his balls onto my lips and commanded, "Suck my nuts."

I was only too pleased to comply. I sucked them into my mouth, chewing on the firm spheres, making him cry out with passion. "That's it, dude ... that's it. Suck those creamers."

Barry pulled my bathing-suit off then moved between my legs. He pushed them to my chest and then and rimmed my virgin asshole. I pictured in my mind how it had looked when he had rimmed Dale and was further stimulated. Dale's nuts were exchanged for his manhole. I stared at his hole in wonder, not yet sure about eating ass. It looked so small and tight and yet I had seen it spread wide to admit Barry's massive shaft.

"Eat my ass!" he commanded as he rubbed his hole over my protruding tongue.

My tongue tasted the juicy hole, which contained a mixture of his juices and Barry's saliva, then my hands spread his firm mounds of ass-flesh allowing my tongue to enter his chute. He rotated his ass over my face and pushed his dilated hole onto my mouth, while Barry continued with his assault on my virgin hole.

I could feel something solid entering my chute and knew that Barry was fingering my tight orifice. I spread my legs as wide as possible, wanting to assist with my deflowering. His finger dug deep in my channel, massaging my prostate in the process, causing my ass to tremble and wiggle. A second finger joined the first as he continued to dilate my hole, stretching my aching sphincter for the first time.

I just knew that I was about to be fucked when I felt Barry's brawny thighs pressed against the backs of my legs, and I couldn't wait. I wanted him inside of me. I concentrated on the asshole above my mouth trying to relax my tight hole for the coming intrusion. Dale grabbed my ankles and held my legs tightly against his chest as Barry placed his big sheathed dick-head at the entrance to my chute.

"Fuck him," Dale said. "Show the voyeur what your big dick feels like."

I panted deeply as I felt the dick stretching my tight hole. Determined to let him in I pushed back onto his rigid dick forcing the big head into my tightly clinging chute. I cried out around Dale's ass as I felt Barry breach the portal of my ass, taking my cherry. He stopped for a moment, letting me adjust to his wide girth and then his slimy dick slid through the parted flesh and didn't stop until it was buried balls deep.

Dale turned around to face me, once again slipping his dick into my mouth. He lifted my head and began to fuck my mouth with short fast strokes. "Suck my dick, take it all. Show me what a good little cocksucker you are."

Barry began to jack-hammer my now unobstructed channel. I could feel his big rod sliding in and out of the tender tissues probing my depths, seeking release. Dale rolled a safe down my rigid pole, then moved his ass back so that he could plant my dick into his well lubed chute. He moved back and forth on my chest, fucking my mouth with his dick, while at the same time skewering his ass on my dick.

The feelings were unbelievable. I was getting three erogenous zones stimulated at the same time, the cumulated affect taking me quickly over the edge. My cock detonated up Dale's ass spewing my load deep in his bowels, while Barry's ramming pole spurted his jism deep into my newly aroused chute.

Dale wasn't far behind. His muscular ass milked me dry while his thrusts became faster and faster into my aching mouth. "I'm coming, I'm coming," he cried, with an ear splitting wail, as he pulled his dick from my mouth and sprayed his cum over my face.

After our sensational session it took quite a while for us to return to normal. They couldn't stop laughing when I told them what had happened and were also astounded to hear that this had been my first sexual experience. I was pleased to learn that they were spending a few more days up in the hills and quickly agreed when they asked me to join them at their camp site.

By the time I went home I was a no longer the naïve young guy who had set out for a lonely weekend.

THE BIG–DICKED COP

It's after 1 a.m. and I'm leaning against a lamppost. I've got my skintight cruising jeans on. I don't wear underpants when I'm cruising, so the slab of meat snaking down my left thigh is on display. The seam in the backside of my chinos is ripped wide open, so to cover my crack, I've got my shirt pulled out of my jeans.

My shirt's unbuttoned, and I'm playing with my nipples. I'm horny, extremely horny. I hope I'm picked up soon.

A cruiser pulls up next to me.

"Hey, you," the cop yells.

I lean on the cruiser and poke my head in the window. "Yeah," I say.

"What're you doing hanging around here?"

"I'm waiting for a friend."

"You think I believe that crap?" he says.

He climbs out of the cruiser and comes around to me. He looks like a linebacker in a cop's uniform. His dark hair, sprinkled with grey, puts him in his fifties. He's my kind of man.

"Put your hands on the hood and spread your legs," he says.

That's a first for me, on the sidewalk, that is, but I comply with his command.

He runs his hands over my legs. My cock starts filling out when his warm hand rests on it. I become fully hard when his other hand slips into the rip over my butt and his fingers slide over bare skin. He prods my hairy crack, like he's looking for contraband. I gasp when his finger explores my quivering hole. He twists his big digit around and probes deeply. Fuck, it feels good. I bend over so he can really finger me. He pulls his finger out of my hole, spits on it, then shoves it back up my chute. It feels so good; I can't help wiggling my ass.

I come to my senses, remembering I'm on the sidewalk. I pretend to be shocked. "Wow," I say, "what're you doing?"

"What the fuck does it look like?"

"Don't tell me this is how you frisk everyone? It could get you in a lot of trouble."

He opens the cruiser door. "Get your ass in there and stop sassing me."

165

"You arresting me?"

"You want I should cuff you and call for back-up?"

"What're you charging me with?"

"I haven't decided yet, but I could add resisting arrest to the charge. Maybe a night in the slammer with the other scum will smarten you up. I'm sure that ring through your nipple will turn them on. You won't even have to take your pants off. They'll be able to fuck you right through that rip. By the time you get released you'll have cum dripping out of your asshole. Now get in."

I climb into the cruiser.

After sitting looking at me for a few seconds he says, "You smell like a brewery. Maybe a night in the drunk-tank will straighten you out."

I remain silent.

"Yeah, that's what I'll do," he ponders aloud. "Maybe next time you'll be a little more cooperative when questioned by the police."

"Look, I'm sorry – "

"Too fucking late. I'm taking you in for questioning. Maybe you'll be a little more civil with me at Central."

"I'm really sorry, officer," I say, in a contrite voice. "Is there any way we can resolve this without you taking me in?"

"What. Now you're trying to bribe me?"

"No, that's not what I meant."

I watch as he sniffs and licks the finger that was buried in my asshole. "What exactly did you mean, then?" he asks.

"Just ... um ... I've heard that sometimes things can be worked out."

He turns around and looks at me, examining me from head to foot, like I'm a side of beef hanging in cold storage. I can see he wants me.

"Whadda you mean?" he says.

"I wanna suck your dick, sir."

"Do I look like a fag to you?" he asks.

"No, I can see you're straight, officer, but you'll enjoy it. I'll do all the work."

Tires squeal on the pavement when he takes off.

"Where're we going?" I ask.

"I'm taking you to a private place where we can close the deal."

He calls in to let them know that he's taking a break. I guess when you've got three stripes on your sleeve you don't have to ask permission. He turns off the highway and drives down a narrow lane which ends in front of a small cabin in the woods. He gets out of the cruiser, comes around, and lets me out. Silently he unlocks the door of the cabin and holds it open for me.

He flips on the lights, locks the door, closes the drapes, and then flops down in an old armchair. His tattooed biceps bulge below the cuffs of his short-sleeve shirt. His intimidating dark eyes stare right through me. He rubs his hand over the mound in his pants. "Okay, get your ass over here and put those pretty lips around my big dick."

I hold back, pretending I don't want him.

"What ... you change your mind?" he says. "Stop stalling, I don't have all night, you know."

I'm more turned-on than I've been in ages. I kneel between his widely spread legs and excitedly rub his crotch.

"Oh for fuck sake, would you get with it," he says, "You're acting like a young virgin. We both know that you're dying to get your mouth on my dick."

He's right. He can read me like a book.

He stands up, strips off his shoes, pants, and briefs, and then he resumes his position in the armchair. His dick is enormous. It's still soft but it's already thick and long. The big bulbous head rests on a spectacular set of nuts.

He lies back in the armchair, pulls my face into his moist crotch, and says, "Now stop messing around and blow me."

I lift his cock to my lips and run my tongue around the tasty knob. I slurp his precum into my mouth and run my tongue up and down the length of his shaft.

His dick expands into gargantuan proportions. I've got an eight-inch dick, but he's bigger, much bigger. When I hold his rod in my fist, at least an inch separates my fingers from my thumb. It's so long that three fists could hold the shaft at the same time.

When I look up at him, he's taking off his shirt. He'd be at home at a convention of bears. He runs his hands through his luxuriant growth of salt-and-pepper chest hair and tweaks his nipples.

"You like that big dick, boy?"

"Oh fuck, yes."

I put the head into my mouth and suck, taking it in as far as I can. He places his hands behind my head and fucks my mouth, force-feeding me his rigid length of flesh, pushing until I gag. I consider myself an expert cocksucker, but I know I can't deep-throat him. I use my hand on his shaft, jacking him off as I suck his big knob. I try valiantly to get more of him into me, but it's no use.

"That's the way," he says. "I knew you'd be a good cocksucker the minute I first laid eyes on you."

I suck his stiff boner in lust-engorged ecstasy. I come off his knob and gasp for air. I can smell his manly aroma when he bends his legs and places them over the arms of the chair to give me full access to his sexual organs. I bend down and lick his nuts. His groan of delight tells me I'm on the right track. I slurp on his nuts trying to get both of them into my mouth, but can only get one in at a time.

"Oh yeah. Chew on my balls. That's what I like."

His asscheeks slip to the edge of the seat. He pushes my mouth down to his asshole, and then he spreads his cheeks so my tongue can probe his moist fissure. The sight of his pink hole, surrounded by a pelt of dark hair, stimulates me beyond words. I grab his massive thighs, push my tongue into his asshole, suck his juice into my mouth, and nibble on his sensitive tissues.

I push a finger into his tight soggy channel and finger-fuck his butch ass. He rotates his ass as though he wants me deeper, so I push another finger in. When my palm's flat against his muscular cheeks, I probe for his prostate. When I hit home he groans, "Oh yes, that feels great."

My confined rod needs attention, so I loosen my chinos and push them down to my knees. My released dick springs out like a jack-in-the-box. I spit in my hand, and jerk on my rod, while I work on him.

His pliable hole confirms that he likes getting his chute reamed, and tonight that's what he's gonna to get.

I always keep a supply of condoms and a tube of lube in my pocket when I'm out cruising – you never know when you're going to get lucky – so I pull a safe out and roll it down my throbbing boner. I push him further back in the armchair until he's flat on his back, with his knees resting on his chest, and his heels on the arms of the chair. His manhole is completely available for my use. His eyes are closed, and his mouth is wide-open, like he's in a trance. I chew on his asshole, and then I lube three fingers and twirl then around in his chute. He doesn't complain, so I fuck his hole with four fingers. I know that with more lube, and more pressure, my hand would glide right in, but I'm in a hurry to fuck him, so I come to my knees, pull my fingers out of his gooey channel, and replace them with the head of my cock.

ted me to."d eases into his wide-open hole, quickly followed by my shaft. The smooth hot lining, of his channel, fits me like a glove. When I hit bottom, his eyes pop open, and a look of surprise suffuses his face. I'm buried balls deep in him before he realizes what has happened.

He places his hand down to check his hole. "Oh shit, boy ... your cock's up my asshole."

No kidding.

I grab his ankles and pile-drive my rod into his squirming hole before he can unseat me. He must be enjoying the sensation, because he hooks his knees behind his elbows, grabs my butt with his hands, and pulls me hard into his sensational ass. His muscular butt is made for fucking. I sink my dick right to the hilt, and then back out until just the head is encased. He grabs my head and pulls my mouth to his. His tongue slips into me. I stop fucking so that we can exchange saliva, and then I resume reaming his rear-end. I slow down. I'm enjoying him too much to cum, but he won't let me prolong the fuck. He grabs my asscheeks, pulls me hard against him, and grinds his butt against me. I can't hold back. I'm creaming inside him.

I collapse on top of him. His tight muscular chute milks my shaft until it expels me. He drops his legs, jumps up, pushes me onto the floor, pulls my chinos and boots off, and then rips the cum laden safe from my still hard dick.

"Okay, boy," he says, when I'm naked, "now it's my turn."

He pushes my legs up to my chest and glues his mouth to my hole. He chews, licks, and tongue fucks me. I seldom get fucked – I prefer being on top – but he's got me so worked up that, for a change, I want to be dominated.

He smiles when I reach for a safe and roll it down his shaft.

"Fuck me," I say. "I want that big dick in me."

He lubes his fingers, then he slips one finger up my chute and works it around. Another finger soon joins the first, and then a third follows. I'm wide open and ready for his huge rammer. When he places his dick-head at the entrance to my chute, I stop breathing. I know it'll be a tight fit, but I want him inside me. With one steady push, he buries his mighty organ to the hilt. The sensation astounds me. I feel like I've been split in two, and he's touching areas that have never felt a cock before.

He rests on top of me, gently probing until he feels me relax, then he starts pounding. Time, and time again, he pulls his dick completely out of me and then, like a heat-seeking missile, rams it back in. His big dick-head has my prostate in an uproar. He keeps at it for what seems like hours, but I don't mind, I wish it could go on all night. He's hyperventilating when he shoots his load up my tight chute.

I throw him off me and roll him onto his stomach.

"Ah," he says when he sees my hard-on, "the stamina of youth."

I lower my mouth to his wet hole and taste his man-juice as it oozes from his recently breached fuck hole. I kneel between his widely spread legs, sheath up, and plunge my dick into him. His backside rises to meet my downward thrust. I spread his thighs wide apart with my knees and fuck him like a dog. I pull his mouth to mine and kiss him deeply as I ram his butch cop ass. I can feel the hard muscles of his hole clinging to my dick as it plows in and out of him.

"Oh fuck," I groan, as my cock erupts deep in his inner core. "I'm coming."

I lie exhausted on his back.

"I wish you could do it again," he says.

"When you get home I'll be ready for more, Derek."

He rolls over and smiles. "Fuck, for a minute I thought you were going to fist me."

"Next time I will," I say.

"Great ... I'm looking forward to it."

"What is this place?" I ask.

"One of the guys lent it to me."

"Good. We'll have to use it again sometime."

"Thank you for letting me fuck you ... I've wanted to do that for a long time," he says, as we dress. "What are you going to do to top this? Maybe you should wear a uniform next time."

"I'll think about it," I say.

MEDICAL STUDENT'S EXPERIMENT

Although my first homosexual experience took place many years ago, I can still remember it as though it were yesterday. My first year of medical school was about to end, but it had been a tough grind with very little free time. During the year, my roommate, Marshall, and I became close friends. We had discovered very early during our studies that it was much better to study together, so we spent a lot of our time with one another. At the beginning of our course we had been encouraged to practice physical examinations on each other, so my hands had examined and probed his hard masculine body from end to end, with the exception of that area covered by his briefs. The exploration of our bodies had always been very scientifically based, until that fateful day.

We started a class where the topic was examination of the male genitalia. The professor used a young well-hung model to demonstrate the technique. Since our class consisted of both male and female students the professor felt it was necessary to be very specific. He talked about the guy's penis, having him demonstrate how his foreskin could be retracted, then had the female students check the model's testicles. The class ended after the professor demonstrated how to examine the prostate gland. I found the presentation very arousing, and was confused when my dick stretched out in my briefs.

Following the class, Marshall and I decided to practice examining the prostate gland. Yeah, we were both a little nervous, but we were used to examining each other by that time, and we thought we'd be adults about the whole thing. After all, we were going to be doctors one day ... weren't we?

We stripped down to our briefs, both realizing that we were about to explore areas of our bodies that had until then been hidden. Marshall volunteered to be the patient first, so he pulled off his briefs and kneeled on the bed. As soon as I saw his moist crevice my dick began to expand. Confused, I tried to ignore it.

His muscular asscheeks were spread wide apart, exposing his hairy perineum and tiny pink anus. We didn't have any gloves in our room, so I put some lubricant on my index finger, then slowly pushed into his tight orifice, amazed at how hot and silky his rectum felt. As my finger moved around attempting to locate the hard gland I could feel his buttocks quivering.

"I think you have to go in further," Marshall suddenly said, at the same time dropping his head to the bed.

I withdrew my index finger, then after lubricating my middle finger, pushed both fingers in right to the base. His tight sphincter seemed more relaxed as I resumed my examination. My fingers rotated in his hole, probing for the elusive prostate gland without much success.

"Maybe it'll be easier if I lay on my back," he suggested.

I watched as he rolled over onto his broad back and pulled his muscular legs up to his chest, holding them in place by placing his elbows behind his knees and gripping his ankles in his big fists. As my fingers slipped back inside his rectum, my eyes focused on his huge testicles and big uncut dick, which had expanded considerably during the examination.

We both realized at the same time when I hit pay-dirt. As my fingers felt the hard gland he let out a sudden groan, making me stop.

"Did that hurt?" I asked.

"No, it just feels strange."

My fingers returned to their examination of his tender prostate, causing him once again to groan. As I probed his rear-end. I was surprised to feel his backside push up against my hand, as though he was trying to get more of my fingers in his hole.

"Sorry about that," he muttered. "It just happened when you touched my prostate. Like some natural reflex action."

"No problem," I assured him, as I valiantly tried to maintain a purely clinical interest.

"Can you see any semen yet?" he asked, trying to get a glimpse of his dickhead which was partially covered by his foreskin. "Pull my skin back so we can see."

I had seen many dicks before, but this was the first time I had seen anyone – other than myself, with a hard-on ... and I certainly had never touched one, but my own. My trembling hand slowly reached out for his dick and encircled his hefty shaft. As I gripped his throbbing manhood, he once again groaned, then pushed the steely shaft through my hand, uncovering the mushroom-shaped head. The fingers probing his hole were obviously having an intensely sexual effect, because the large meatus in his dickhead was oozing a copious amount of precum.

As we stared at his dick, Marshall began to shamelessly fuck himself on my fingers, moving his asshole up and down, at the same time slipping his pole in and out of my fist. I glanced at his face in shock as I realized we had moved into a totally different relationship. Suddenly this big muscular stud, who had been my roommate for a year, was behaving in ways unheard of, ways I had never conceived. His piercing, sexually aroused eyes stared back at me as he continued to move his hips.

"Oh, fuck, Lee," he exclaimed. "I can't tell you how good that feels. Have you ever had anyone probe your ass?"

I shook my head, not daring to speak, since I too was more sexually aroused than I'd ever been before.

He lowered his feet to the bed, closed his eyes, then resumed fucking himself on my fingers, trying to get more and more of them into his asshole. "I need something bigger up there," he suddenly said, as he looked at me. "Shove your cock up my ass, Lee. I want to see what it feels like."

"Oh ... okay," I heard myself say. I was into this, but surely not as much as Marshall seemed to be at that point. I was worried, I was afraid. It felt weird looking down at his hard familiar body, glistening with sweat, pumping on my hand. I was hard as a rock, but it made me feel like such a ... well, fag. All of this was new for me then, remember. Marshall looked up at me with a pleading look on his face, a new Marshall with a willingness to please and be pleasured, and began to stroke his own cock, never taking his eyes off mine. And that did it. Watching him masturbate, with my fingers still up his ass, put me over the edge.

My throbbing cock further persuaded me, so I stepped back from the bed and dropped my briefs. My dick stuck straight out from my abdomen, dripping precum in anticipation of fucking the spread-eagle butch stud reclining on the bed. Marshall stared at my dick. "You'd better take it easy," he said as I kneeled on the bed. "I didn't know you were that well-hung."

Marshall once again lifted his legs up to his chest while I covered my dick with lubricant. I placed the broad head at his manhole. My finger probing had obviously prepared him well, because all it took was one steady push and I was balls deep in his silky rectum. We both moaned when I came to rest on his washboard abdomen, and began rhythmically humping my sizeable tool in and out of his wet hole.

He groaned. "Oh, yes, Lee. Fuck my ass."

I was so turned on that I was soon pounding his hole like a jackhammer, giving his prostate its first real massage. The smooth folds of his chute clung to my shaft like a second skin, milking the cum from my heavy nuts. It was the tightest fuck I'd ever experienced and within minutes of penetrating him, I was seeding him. I cried out as Marshall grabbed my asscheeks in his hands and held me tight against his upturned ass, his inner muscles milking me dry. After a pause, I slowly got to my knees and watched as my wet dick slipped from his clinging sphincter. Marshall's pole seemed to have lengthened even more during the ass pounding and was oozing semen like a leaking faucet.

"Okay," he said, coming to his feet, "it's my turn now."

I kneeled on the bed and spread my asscheeks wide, trying to relax so he could probe my virgin hole. His long lubricated finger quickly located my sensitive gland, making me squirm with pleasure. Marshall probed for a while, then withdrew his finger.

"Roll over, Lee," he said.

When I was on my back with my legs up to my chest, Marshall lay on his side then, with the weight of his body, he held my legs in place. Then he really went to work on my hole, his long fingers twirled around in my chute, massaging my prostate and relaxing my assring. He knew when I was ready for him, because he came to his knees and placed his dickhead at my dilated hole.

I was practically panting with passion and sweating like a pig when I felt his huge knob broach my virgin hole, then held my breath as his thick shaft followed the head into my inner core. My asshole felt as though it was on fire, crammed full of man-meat for the first time. Marshall slowly started fucked my tight passage, withdrawing until just the head was still encased, then sinking it back to the hilt. Each time he hit bottom my asscheeks quivered with the force of the plunge. My eyes were closed tight in ecstasy when I felt his tongue slip into my mouth.

Wow, I thought as we kissed each other, my eyes shut, my butt clenching, I'm gay, I'm gay, and it's wonderful.

He slowly increased his hip movement until the speed of his battering-ram moving in and out of my tender chute became almost unreal. I had suspected he was a good lover, but had no idea just how good until that moment.

"Yeah, yeah, here it cums," he cried.

And suddenly I was there again, shooting the greatest orgasm, even better than the first, because this time I had a cock up my ass. Cum blasted from my cock, splattering all over my chest, just as Marshall soothed my inner tissues with salvo after salvo of hot cum. He continued to thrust into my ass, driving slow and hard as I clenched my muscles to jerk him off, pulling my own shaft to drain it. We both collapsed, panting and sweating, until Marshall finally got up and got us some water.

"I've never done anything like that before," he whispered, unable to look at me. "Did you like it?"

I began to laugh. "Are you kidding? That was the most amazing sex I've ever had. I was scared at first, but I'm not ashamed."

And I wasn't. As I recall, it was only a few months later that I gave up women completely, not even finding them sexually attractive anymore.

"Do you, um ... want to do it again sometime?" Marshall asked.

"Try and stop me," I said.

It was amazing how often we found it necessary to check one another's prostate, and we soon realized we had just the right equipment for examining the mouth and throat.

THE JOGGER BUMPS INTO SOMETHING HARD

After Tim finished his workout in the basement gymnasium of his condominium, he showered then, with his towel and bathing suit rolled-up under his arm, he headed for the elevators. He felt refreshed and invigorated. His cock and balls were swinging free in a baggy pair of silk gym shorts, and his sports shirt was unbuttoned exposing his hairy chest.

His mind was on the great sex he'd had the night before so, by the time the elevator arrived, his dick had begun to expand and tent out his shorts. On the way up, the elevator stopped at the parking level to admit a large group of people. The first person to enter was a young guy dressed in running shorts with slits up the sides, using the T-shirt, in his hand, to wipe the sweat from his brow. Tim's glance wandered over the smooth chest and muscular legs of the blond. After he punched the button for the twentieth floor, the blond jogger moved back toward Tim to make way for the crowd to squeeze onto the elevator. The group, headed for the tenth floor, laughed and talked about a surprise party they were attending. The jogger stood quietly directly in front of Tim.

Tim slowly became aware of the erotic aroma of masculine sweat rising from the jogger. His unruly endowment, already tumescent, stiffened out more, like it was reaching out for the jogger's asscheeks. When the elevator stopped at the first floor, to admit more people going to the same party, the group already in the elevator moved back, pushing the jogger's tight rear-end against Tim's protruding basket. There was nowhere for the jogger to go, so his ass pressed tightly against Tim, and Tim, always cruising, never budged. He watched the guy's neck flush red, the color spreading up to his blond hairline.

Tim's stiff tool lodged between the cheeks of the jogger's ass, and his hairy exposed chest pressed against the young guy's bare back. Rather than move Tim tilted his pelvis, pushed his flesh even harder into the hot cleft, and blew hot air onto the blond's shoulders. The young jogger, who seemed about to faint from the closeness in the elevator, leaned heavily against Tim, so he gripped

179

the guy's hipbones, to support him, and pull him even closer. Sweat running freely down the jogger's back moistened Tim's chest.

The jogger and Tim were alone after the elevator passed the tenth floor, with Tim slowly pumping his hard rod between the jogger's muscular asscheeks.

"You look like you could do with a drink," Tim said. "Why don't you come up to my place to cool down?"

The jogger, seeming suddenly to come to his senses, holding his T-shirt in front of his groin to hide his erection, moved away from Tim. "I should go home and ... um ... take a shower," he stammered. "I'm kind of sweaty."

"You're just fine the way you are. We can sit out on the deck and cool down."

It was clear to Tim that the jogger was innocent. Tim had aroused him, and he was having trouble dealing with it. His eyes gazed at Tim's body, from the handsome face to the obvious hard-on, and back to Tim's piercing eyes. He was still undecided when the elevator door opened at his floor, so Tim made the decision for him by leaning over and pressing the close button.

"My name's Tim. What's yours?"

"Christopher, but my friends call me Chris."

"Glad to meet you, Chris." Tim shook hands with him. "I haven't seen you around before. You lived here long?"

"We just moved in last month, so I'm still finding my way around."

The elevator stopped at the penthouse floor. Tim led the shy young jogger down the hallway to his suite.

"What a great place," Chris said as they entered the suite. "I love the way you've furnished it."

Tim led Chris out onto the sunny deck. "I don't know about you, but I'm ready for a cold beer."

"Great. I'm dying of thirst," Chris said.

Chris was standing at the railing when Tim came out with the beers. "You've got a fantastic view," he said. "The sea looks so calm and blue. Our suite faces the mountains."

Tim stared at Chris. The view's much better from here, he was thinking as he stared at Chris's bubble butt. "Yeah, it's great. I guess I'm getting so used to it that I hardly notice it anymore."

They settled down on a settee in the shade of a big umbrella, and sipped their ice-cold beers. Tim lifted Chris's feet up from the floor and swiveled Chris's legs around until his feet rested on his lap. When Chris lay back against the end of the settee, Tim removed Chris's sneakers and white ankle socks, massaged his feet, and dug into the pressure points with his thumbs. He lifted one of Chris's feet to his face, rubbed the sole over his cheek, and kissed the instep.

Chris squirmed on the settee, trying to get his foot away from Tim. "My feet must be all sweaty and smelly," he said.

"They smell just great," Tim said as he sucked Chris's big toe into his mouth. "And they taste delicious."

Tim took his time. He sucked Chris's toes, holding on tightly when Chris tried to get away. He looked deeply into Chris's eyes. "Have you ever been with a man before?"

Chris shook his head. His face became a bright pink. "No, but ... I ... always wanted to."

Tim's hands moved to Chris's well-formed calf muscles. "Well, just relax and enjoy yourself."

As Tim massaged Chris's long, smooth legs, he could see the mound moving in Chris's shorts. He took Chris's foot in his hand, and rubbed it against his hard-on. "Look what you're doing to me. I'm hard as-a-rock."

Chris took over and rubbed the sole of his foot over Tim's hefty bulge. Tim leaned back and took a swig of beer, then he held Chris's foot against his crotch. "I bet you're dying to see what I've got hidden in there, aren't you?"

Chris nodded, a smile crossing his face. "Yeah, it feels big. How big is it?"

"Tell you what," Tim said. "Since this is your first time, I'll let you take the lead. You can do anything you want to me. I'm just gonna sit back and enjoy myself."

He stared at Tim for a few moments, and then in a low quavering voice said, "Why don't you ... um ... why not ... um ... take off your clothes."

Tim smiled and then complied with Chris's wish. Things are moving along just fine, Tim thought as he removed his shorts and shirt and then leaned back spreading his legs wide apart. His dick, fully erect, lay flat against his washboard abdomen.

Chris knelt on the floor between Tim's legs, ran his hands along Tim's muscular thighs toward the throbbing pole and low hanging nuts, and stared at Tim's groin. Chris's hand shook when took hold of Tim's hard-on, and ran his hand up and down the length of the shaft, slowly pumping Tim's precum to the surface. Chris seemed to be in a daze, and unsure of what to do with the dick in his hand.

He jumped when Tim suddenly spoke. "Why don't you put it in your mouth? I'm sure you'd like to try, wouldn't you?"

Chris looked into Tim's eyes, as though he was looking for confirmation. Tim nodded, spread his legs farther apart, moved his asscheeks to the edge of the settee, lay back and closed his eyes.

Encouraged by Tim's words and actions, Chris slowly leaned forward and tentatively ran his tongue over Tim's cock-head and spread Tim's piss slit apart with his thumbs. He ran his tongue through the meatus, and slurped up the free-flowing semen.

"Yeah, that's the way, you've got it," Tim said placing his hands on Chris's shoulders.

Chris's electric blue eyes gazed at Tim for a few moments, and then he said, "I've dreamt about doing this, but I guess I never really imagined that it would actually happen."

He leaned forward, circled the plum shaped head of Tim's cock with his tongue, licked the shaft, gently squeezed Tim's nuts in his hand, and then licked the tender sac. One at a time, he sucked the nuts into his mouth, rolling his tongue around their circumference. When he's had his fill of nuts, his tongue moved back up the shaft until he was once again at the head of Tim's rod.

Chris's mouth opened wide, his lips, stretched to their maximum, slowly sank down Tim's shaft until his gag reflex objected, and then he backed off and concentrated on the top half of the long rod.

Tim lifted Chris's head off his cock and said, "Take your shorts off. I want to suck your dick."

He moved over to a padded chaise-lounge, lay flat on his back, motioned Chris over, and placed him on his knees, so that they were positioned crotch to face. When Chris was in position, Tim gazed up at Chris's smooth rod and tight balls. He pulled Chris down and rubbed his face against the moist, hairless, perineum. Chris groaned loudly when Tim's tongue licked his nuts, and then he slurped on Tim's joint. Tim pulled Chris's dick down to his lips, licked the crown, and then he lifted his head and sank the shaft into his throat.

Chris released Tim's dick and said, "Oh, God, that's fantastic. No one's ever done that to me."

Tim continued to deep-throat Chris until his jaw ached, and then he moved his head, sucked both moist nuts into his mouth, and chewed on them.

Lifting his mouth from Tim's dick, Chris said, "That feels good. I like playing with my nuts."

He sat back on Tim's face and stroked his own rod as Tim continued to chew on his swollen nuts. Tim didn't want Chris to shoot his load – he had other things planned, so he pried Chris's hand from his dick, and pulled Chris's moist valley to his mouth, gradually moving his tongue to Chris's smooth rear-end.

When Tim's tongue began to rim his virgin hole, a long drawn out whimper escaped his mouth. "Oh yes, you're eating my ass." Then he bent forward and sucked Tim's cock, managing to sink it into his tight throat. Tim had enough of the foreplay; what he wanted now was Chris's ass. He laid Chris on his back, pushed Chris's legs up to his chest, straddled the lounge, and sank his mouth once again to the tiny hole. He probed the quivering pucker, pushing his tongue into the tight channel.

After pigging out on Chris's tasty hole for a few minutes, Tim straightened up and moved so that his cock and balls were pressed tightly against Chris's perineum. "You know what I want, don't you?" Tim said.

Chris nodded and gazed into Tim's eyes. "Yes. I want you to fuck me ... but I'm scared it'll hurt."

"There's always a bit of pain the first time, but I'll take it easy."

Tim went inside and returned with condoms and lube. He straddled the lounge, applied plenty of lube to Chris's tight hole, and his sheathed boner, then he pushed it down and lodged the head at the entrance to Chris's chute. He sat dead still and stared into Chris's eyes as his cock imperceptibly spread apart the tissues of the jogger's tight manhole.

"Oh no," Chris said with a gasp. "It's too big. I can't take it."

"Relax, Chris, you can do it. Take some deep breaths and push down on me," Tim said.

Chris took a few deep breaths, and then he moved his hole around Tim's knob until it dilated and gave way, to the thick-bodied piston that was determined to enter. When Tim's dickhead suddenly breached Chris's virgin hole, and sank into his love-channel, Chris's eyed opened wide.

"That's it. The worse is over now," Tim said.

Chris moved his hand to his rear end where he encountered the thick rod surrounded by his tight sphincter. He gasped. "Oh, God ... it's really in me."

Tim lowered Chris's legs onto his thighs, pulled Chris up into a sitting position, and lay back on the lounge. When Chris came to an upright position, he impaled himself on Tim's dick. He hesitantly moved his backside and repeatedly raised and lowered himself on Tim's thighs so that Tim's dick could move in and out of his clenched sheath. He lifted his nuts out of the way and leant forward so that he could watch.

When Chris appeared to be fully dilated, Tim took over, grabbing Chris's hips and pile-droving his dick in and out of the clenched asshole. Chris lay forward on Tim's chest and sucked Tim's tongue into his mouth as Tim's battering ram pounded his rear-end into oblivion. His newly opened chute clung to Tim's rod, as though it were an elastic sheath, stretched to its limit.

Chris sat back and rested on Tim's thighs, stroked his cock, closed his eyed and smiled. When he climaxed his asshole clutched Tim's tool like a vise. He threw his head back, and let out a long screech. His cum flew high into the air, and landed in thick gobs over Tim's face and chest.

The added stimulation on his rod, and the sight of Chris ejaculating, brought Tim to a quick orgasm, his cock throbbing as he spewed his seed deep into Chris's chute.

Sweating and trembling, gasping for air, as though he had just run the marathon, Chris collapsed on top of Tim. They lay in each other's arms, letting their body processes return to normal. Chris eyes opened wide when he suddenly expelled Tim's deflated dick from his manhole. "I'm glad I bumped into you in the elevator today."

Tim rubbed Chris's rear-end. "I'm glad the elevator was packed, or we might never have connected ... literally. That was beautiful, Chris."

"You're not kidding. I can't believe what just happened to me. I've never had such good sex."

Tim went into the bathroom and cleaned himself. He returned to the deck with a wet cloth and towel, and then he gently wiped Chris clean and lay down next to him. Chris's hand wandered over Tim's backside, and slipped into the moist crevice between Tim's muscular cheeks. "Do you like to get fucked?" he asked.

"Sorry, Chris. I don't go that way, but maybe we can do something about it later."

The intercom buzzed, rudely interrupting their lethargic state. Tim stood up and went over to the intercom. He knew that it would be Jay, who was coming over for dinner. He buzzed him in. Chris quickly slipped into his shorts.

"I better get going," Chris said, moving toward the door.

"Take it easy. It's only a friend of mine," Tim assured him, "and he knows the score."

Tim pulled on his shorts and went to the door to let Jay into the suite. When Jay followed Tim onto the deck, Chris nervously stood next to the settee. Jay's left eyebrow rose and he gave Chris a knowing leer. Chris's face turned scarlet when Jay said, "Well, well, what have we here? A new trick I presume?"

Tim laughed. He introduced them, and watched Jay, with his friendly personality, calm Chris. Tim went inside for beers. When he returned, Chris and Jay were sitting together on the settee. They chatted like long lost friends. It was obvious, to Tim, that they had formed an immediate friendship.

Tim passed the beers around. "How would you like to join us for dinner, Chris? We're gonna order pizza in, and we'd like your company."

"I'd like that, but are you sure I won't be in the way?"

"Of course you won't be in the way," Jay said. "We weren't going to do anything but eat. Food that is," he added with a smirk.

"Great. I'll go downstairs and change, and let my mom know that I won't be home for dinner."

"You don't need to change for dinner, Chris," Tim said. "Just give her call and let her know you won't be home."

Jay licked his lips and winked at Tim when Chris went inside to use the phone. "I'm glad you asked him to stay. It should be fun. I hope you're not going to be greedy and keep him all to yourself?"

They spent the rest of the afternoon out on the deck, lounging around in the sun, drinking beer and exchanging life stories. Chris told them that he was graduating with an arts degree that year; however, he hadn't yet decided what to do with his life. "What kind of work do you do?" he asked.

"We're PIs," Tim said.

"What kind of training do you need to become a PI?" Chris asked.

"I was in law enforcement before I decided to go private," Tim answered. "Of course I had to get licensed by the state, which took a while. Jay's a whiz on the computer – which is a great help, and I've taught him how to investigate."

"He's taught me more than that," Jay interrupted. "Before I met him I was young and innocent – just like you. You've probably got all the right credentials."

They watched the sun sink into the ocean. Tim felt a chill in the air, so they moved into his den. Tim sat on a reclining chair and Jay and Chris made themselves comfortable on the big sofa. Tim watched Jay putting the make on Chris. It's more fun then a porno movie, Tim was thinking. I'll sit back and enjoy.

When Jay's hand gently massaged the tender skin of Chris's inner thigh, Chris looked at Tim, as though checking to see Tim's reaction.

"Don't let me stop you," Tim said. "I like watching a couple of cuties making out."

Chris pulled Jay to him. His mouth covered Jay's mouth as he ran his hand over the smooth expanse of Jay's chest. Jay's hand moved slowly up Chris's inner thigh not stopping until it rested on the bulge in his shorts. Jay went to his knees between Chris's thighs, pulled Chris's shorts off, and rubbed his face in the silky blond bush surrounding Chris's manhood.

Tim removed his own shorts and sat back. He spread his legs wide and draped them over the arms of the chair. His one hand played with his nuts. His other hand stroked his upright shaft.

Chris lay against the back of the sofa, his hands holding Jay's head against his groin. He fixed his gaze on Tim as Jay licked the head of his throbbing pole then sank the hard rod into his throat, right down to the root.

"Fuck," Chris said. "You suck cock just as good as Tim."

186

Donald Webb

"I should do. He taught me how."

Jay stood up, moved the coffee table out of the way, and then pulled Chris onto the rug with him. Tim watched the two studs at his feet, admiring their bodies. They assumed a sixty-nine position, Jay on his back with Chris on his knees above him.

Tim's one hand played with his own exposed asshole. He wet his finger with saliva and slipped it into his hole. He loved the feeling of his finger in his hole. He wondered if he'd ever let anyone fuck him. Maybe in the right circumstances he'd submit. He slowly massaged his dick with his free hand and pushed down onto his finger. He slipped a second finger into his chute and probed deeply. Precum oozed freely from the thick tube of his shaft, so he pulled his fingers out of his hole, caught the clear substance on his finger, and transferred it to his mouth. As he licked his finger clean, he was turned on by the smell and taste of his own ass-juice.

Jay played with Chris's asshole. As he slowly slipped his finger in and out of the tight orifice, he moved his head and licked Chris's sweet young hole, sinking his tongue all the way into the moist chute.

"You taste real good, Chris," Jay said. He looked over at Tim. "Have you been in here already? It tastes like you."

Tim nodded, "I sure have, and I was the first."

Chris took his mouth off Jay's cock and stammered, "Can I ... um ... fuck you?"

"I thought you'd never ask," Jay said.

Tim tossed a condom, and lube, over to Chris, moved onto the floor for a closer look, and then he helped Chris sheath up. Chris raised Jay's legs, and positioned his cock at the entrance to Jay's channel. From Tim's position, behind the kneeling Chris, he could see the head of Chris's cock push into Jay's pliable sphincter, moving all the way in, in one lunge.

"Fuck, dude," Chris said as he got into a rhythm, "you've got a tight hole."

Chris's asscheeks clenched, and unclenched as his shaft drove in and out of Jay's chute. His newly breached asshole winked at Tim, so Tim moved closer to the pair and crawled between Chris's legs. He placed his hands on Chris's asscheeks, spread them apart, and licked his crack, from balls to backbone.

187

Chris lay still on top of Jay, with his root buried to the hilt. He reached back and spread his cheeks for the man who had taken his virginity. "Fuck me. I want you inside me again," he said.

Tim rolled a safe down his rod, applied plenty of lube to Chris's tight hole, then he placed the bulbous head of his dick at the tight orifice and said, "Are you ready for me, Chris?"

"Give it to me," he said, then let out a long groan when Tim slowly bored into him.

Jay rubbed Chris's rear-end. "Relax, Chris. Relax," he said. "Take some deep breaths. He's all the way in."

When Tim rested on Chris's back, Chris wiggled his ass. Tim held still for a while then he slowly withdrew his shaft, until just the head buried.

"Don't take it out," Chris pleaded. "Please ... leave it in."

Tim pushed his rod back home. "Oh yes ... so tight," he said.

Tim sat on his haunches, with his dick-head buried in Chris's asshole, and then he pulled Chris back onto his reamer, his cock sliding all the way into the tight sheath. Chris began to move under his own power, fucking Jay with his cock, and Tim with his ass.

"Fuck me, Chris," Jay said. "Fuck my ass."

Chris was the first to climax. He squealed out loudly as his cock spurted deep in Jay's hole. "I'm coming, I'm coming."

Tim wasn't far behind; letting out a long wail when he climaxed. Jay grabbed his own boner, and with only a few strokes, spewed his load all over his chest and neck.

They chatted for a while, and then Jay and Chris left. After he'd cleaned up Tim dropped into bed exhausted. He had to be up early in the morning, so he set his alarm, and then drifted off to dreamland.

TIM LOSES HIS VIRGINITY

Tim had been driving for hours across the desert when he pulled into a small rundown looking gas station. He wasn't sure about buying gas from the rusty old pumps, but he did need a fill-up, and didn't know how far it was to the next station, so he took a chance. He had just turned off the motor when a young guy of about eighteen or nineteen years of age came ambling out of the garage. His naked, sweat and grease covered muscular arms and smooth chest, sprouted from his baggy coveralls. The obligatory baseball cap, with the visor toward the back, covered a mop of curly blond hair. As he walked over to the car, Tim could see his white hips through the gaping slits down the sides of the coveralls.

"You're just in time, mister," he said as he brought the nozzle over to the car. "I was just getting ready to close. You want me to fill 'er up?"

"Please," Tim said, yawning and stretching his aching muscles as he exited the car. He stood next to the car for a few moments exercising and watching the kid bending over the hood as he cleaned the windshield. Tim's eyes ran over the muscular buttocks, their shape now clearly visible through the taut material. "You have a restroom?"

"Yeah. Round back. Door's open."

Tim walked around the garage to the detached restroom. The outside door squeaked on its rusty hinges as he shoved it open. There were two doorless stalls, in the small room. They were separated by a thin plywood wall and there were no other amenities available to the weary traveler. As Tim entered the stall furthest from the door, he immediately saw the large gloryhole in the partition. Even out in the sticks Tim thought as he pushed his jeans and briefs down his thighs. He had just finished pissing and was scratching his sweaty balls, when the outside door squeaked. He heard movement in the next stall and was amazed to see two knees, concealed in baggy coveralls, resting on the floor.

His dick expanded rapidly when he thought about the rosy lips on the other side of the partition. Not waiting for an invitation, he moved over and shoved his long shaft through the hole, where it was immediately engulfed by a hot moist mouth. He stood with his hips pressed tightly against the partition as the kid worked on his rod. He must get a lot of practice in here; Tim thought as the kid deep-throated his monster, the slurping sounds clearly audible in the small room. The cock sucking kid grabbed his balls and hung on for life as he mouthed Tim's formidable piece of meat. When he felt his orgasm approaching, Tim held onto the top of the partition and fucked the wide-open throat. His balls tightened up in his sac as he blasted his load into the gas-jockey's mouth.

Tim pulled his shaft from the slimy mouth and was busy wiping up with toilet paper when he heard the door squeak as the kid left the room. Talk about wham-bang; thank-you-ma'am. It must've taken the kid all of two minutes to suck him bone-dry. When he got back to the car, the kid was leaning against the trunk, nonchalantly chewing on a piece of straw.

"That'll be fifty bucks, mister." Then he added with a smile, "For the gas. Anything else you need?"

After paying the kid and giving him a good tip, Tim climbed into his car and took-off. It was beginning to get dark and he still had two hundred miles to do before reaching his destination. He had just got back on the highway when he spotted a young guy standing at the side of the road with his thumb stuck out. Tim pulled over and opened the passenger door. He watched through the rear window as the chunky young blond, wearing a backpack, came bounding up to the car, his tight faded jeans molded to his muscular thighs. The material over his bulging crotch was worn white from the constant movement and pressure beneath.

"Thanks a lot," he said as he climbed into the car. "I really appreciate you picking me up. There aren't too many rides available out here."

"Where're you headed?" Tim asked as he pulled back onto the highway.

"Jamestown ... and you?"

"Me too," Tim said.

The young guy's name was Nathan. He chatted constantly about baseball and football for the next hour, practically wearing Tim out. Tim had been up late, the night before, so his eyes were beginning to droop with exhaustion, when he saw a sign advertising a motel one mile up ahead.

"I don't know about you," Tim said, "but I'm getting kind of sleepy and shouldn't really drive much more. I think I'll get a room at that motel and then head into Jamestown in the morning."

"Well, that sounds like a good idea, but I can't afford a room. I'll just have to try and hitch another ride."

Tim thought about this response for a while and then he said, "If you don't mind sharing a room with me, I'd be glad to put you up."

The young guy stared at Tim, mulling things over. "Are you sure I won't be in the way?"

"I wouldn't have asked you if I wasn't sure," Tim said.

"That's great. I could do with a good night's sleep. I was wondering what I was going to do in Jamestown."

Tim pulled into the motel and entered the office making sure he took a room with one double bed. When they entered the room, Tim was glad to see that Nathan didn't seem perturbed by the fact that he would be sharing a bed with him. Tim was really tired and was not in the mood for sex after his recent excellent blow-job. He decided that he would wait until morning before trying to make Nathan.

"I'm bushed. I think I'll hit the sack. Nothing bothers me; I could sleep through an earthquake," he said to Nathan. "If you want you can watch TV ... you can."

"I don't want to watch TV, but I'd like to take a shower if you don't mind."

"Go ahead."

The shower was running when Tim stripped off his clothes then climbed into bed in the nude and immediately fell asleep. He knew he'd been sleeping for a long time, when he suddenly awoke to feel a hand on his butt. At first he was confused, not remembering where he was, but as comprehension occurred he realized that it was Nathan feeling his ass. Tim lay dead-still on his abdomen and feigned sleep, maintaining his steady breathing as Nathan continued to fondle his buns. If this was Nathan's fantasy then he would let him have it. Besides, it felt good.

The hot hand slowly moved over Tim's muscular butt, gently stroking the smooth skin. Nathan slowly lowered the sheet until Tim was lying stark naked on the bed. Tim's head was turned away from Nathan so he partially opened his eyes. The room was quite bright from the outside lights, so Tim could see both himself and Nathan in the wall mirror. Nathan was up on his elbow staring at Tim. His hand reached out and once again caressed Tim's mounds of ass-flesh, his fingers trailing through the moist crevice. Not encountering any resistance, Nathan became bolder. Tim watched in fascination as his legs were slowly spread wide. It was a strange feeling to placidly watch someone doing to him, what he usually did to others

Nathan moved between Tim's spread-eagle legs. He watched as Nathan leaned over toward his rear-end. He could feel the hot breath on his ass as Nathan sniffed the valley between his cheeks. Tim's aching organ was pressed firmly into the mattress when he felt the first tentative touch of Nathan's wet tongue on his hole. He had difficulty maintaining his pose and wondered how far he would let Nathan go before pretending to awaken. The young stud was holding Tim's cheeks wide apart with his strong hands, so that his tongue could dig deeply into the virgin hole. Tim's mind went back to a recent experience he'd had with Ray, a country singer. Ray had pretended to be unconscious, allowing Tim to molest him. Now that the tables were turned, Tim realized how turned on Ray had been.

Tim felt one of Nathan's fingers breach his manhole, probing deeply into his tight chute. It felt so good that he decided to let the stud continue for a while longer. He'd been thinking about letting it happen for some time, so why not tonight? he thought. And it did feel good. Soon he could feel two fingers in his hole twirling around inside his chute. When the fingers brushed against his prostate he nearly let out a cry of pleasure. Still not wanting to give the game away, he restrained himself from pushing back against the invading digits. He could feel nothing but pleasure, and there was no pain associated with Nathan's deep probing, so he relaxed and let it happen.

When Nathan climbed off the bed, Tim thought, oh, fuck he's giving up. I was starting to enjoy it. But Nathan wasn't giving up. He reached for his backpack and retrieved some items. Tim watched as he rolled a safe down his shaft and then smeared lube into Tim's chute. When he rose to his knees between Tim's widely spread legs, Tim realized that now was the time to stop pretending, but he just couldn't move. His feelings were ambivalent. He wanted to see what it felt like to have a cock in his hole, but at the same time he didn't. I'll let him put the head in me and then I'll stop him Tim thought.

Tim could feel his sphincter dilating as the head of Nathan's dick entered his virgin manhole. Nathan must've prepared him well because all he felt was pleasure. He was just about to move when he felt Nathan's long shaft sink into his channel, right to the hilt. It was too late. The deed was done. There was no point in stopping Nathan now that he had been deflowered. He watched in awe as Nathan's hips rose and fell, pumping his rod in and out of his now fully dilated hole. The physically fit young stud pounded his ass like a battering-ram, and yet all Tim felt was pleasure. Nathan groaned loudly as he lost his load up Tim's newly breached ass. He lay on Tim's back forcing his rod in as far as it would go, holding still while he filled the safe with his thick jism.

Tim couldn't believe what had happened. He had lost his cherry to the young stud and he had enjoyed every minute of it. He lay quietly as Nathan, after slipping out of his hole, and removing the safe, pulled up the sheet and fell asleep. Tim lay awake for a long time, trying to come to grips with his feelings. His ass was still on fire and his big cock was throbbing and oozing precum. He was hoping Nathan would remount him and fuck the daylights out of him, but that didn't happen.

When he awoke the next morning, he could hear the shower running. Tim had his first look at Nathan's body when he came into the room with a towel wrapped around his waist. His masculine chest was covered in blond hair and his long legs were lean and muscular, the kind that runners have.

"How'd you sleep?" Nathan asked.

"Great. How about you? Nothing seems to wake me once I'm asleep."

Nathan seemed relieved as he watched Tim getting up. Tim putting on an act rubbed his backside and groaned as he stood up, "Fuck my ass feels sore. I feel as though I sat on a red-hot poker. I must've pulled a muscle or something."

Nathan's face blushed a deep red, as Tim limped into the bathroom. After a quick shower they were back on the road. Tim dropped Nathan off downtown and then he went on to the courthouse to give a deposition. It was late afternoon by the time Tim was back in his car heading for home. He couldn't believe his eyes when he saw Nathan once again hitching a ride. He pulled over and smiled when Nathan jumped in.

"Where the hell are you off to now?" Tim asked.

"Thanks again, man. I'm on my way home. Can you drop me off where you picked me up yesterday?"

"You live out there?" Tim asked in surprise.

"Yeah. My brother and I run a small gas station out there in the desert."

Tim couldn't believe it. Don't tell me I've had sex with two brothers. What a small world. The trip back seemed to go much faster. As they passed the motel, Nathan looked over at Tim, but Tim ignored him. He would like to have stopped but he was in a hurry to get home. It was dark by the time they arrived at the gas station.

When he pulled up in front of the pumps the blond kid called out from the door, "Sorry, we're closed."

When his brother got out of the car he said, "Oh, it's only you Nathan." Then looking over at Tim, he did a double take. "Aren't you the guy who was here yesterday?"

Tim nodded then said, "I sure was and I need to use the facilities again."

"Sure, go ahead. But be careful ... the lights don't work."

As Tim walked around the building he could see the brothers deep in conversation. He entered the dark restroom and felt his way to the far stall, then he pushed his jeans and briefs down to his boot-tops. He had barely finished pissing when the squeaking door announced the arrival of company. His meat had been hard on-and-off ever since he had lost his cherry early that morning and was now once again demanding attention. He moved over to the gloryhole and shoved it through, groaning when the hot mouth captured him. The kid's doing an even better job this time, he thought. He's spending more time on my dick-head and using his hand on my shaft.

Tim jumped when he heard the door once again squeak on its rusty hinges. He tried to get away from the gloryhole but the kid held him tightly by the balls. He relaxed when he felt a hand run down the small of his back and over his buttocks. Good, Nathan's coming back for seconds, Tim thought. When he felt the tongue on his ass he gave himself up completely. It was very hard to pretend that he was asleep now, so he might as well enjoy. His cheeks were spread apart and his hole attacked with gusto. This time there was no holding back. His asshole was being chewed by an expert and his cock was being sucked by another.

He tensed briefly as he felt the hot body press against his back. What the fuck, he thought. I enjoyed it last night so I might as well give the guy a second chance. He spread his own asscheeks with his hands to let the sheathed cock in. He gasped as the big knob entered his tight hole, spreading the tissues apart with ease. Before he knew it, his chute was packed with man-meat and he was getting lifted from his feet by the savage fucking. His hole opened wide to permit the pounding, while his massive shaft was getting the sucking of its life. He could feel the whole partition moving as he was pile-driven by the humpy blond.

He was totally absorbed when he heard a voice in his ear, "Oh, mister, what a great ass. This is the first time I ever fucked anybody."

Tim gasped with surprise when he realized that it was the young kid fucking him.

"Oh fuck, mister," the kid said. "I'm shooting up your ass."

Tim could feel lube and spit dripping from his hole when the panting kid pulled out. He was aching to cum, but Nathan was concentrating on his balls, as though trying to hold him back. He could feel another mouth on his joint and realized that the young kid had gone around to join his brother. His balls were gripped tightly, pulling him to the partition, while his cock was deep-throated.

He was just getting into the blow-job when he felt a cock touch his hole. This time it was definitely Nathan coming back for seconds. He was totally prepared when the thick shaft sunk deeply into his well-lubricated chute. Oh fuck he thought. Yesterday when I came in here I was a virgin and here I am, getting fucked for the third time. Nathan was fucking him like a rabbit, pounding in and out of the channel lubricated by his younger brother. Tim's jism flew out of his cock into the young blond's throat, while Nathan's cum erupted deep in his bowels. He hung onto the partition for support when Nathan slipped out of his hole.

After hearing the door squeak he pulled up his jeans and headed for his car. The two smiling brothers were waiting for him.

"I hope you'll be out this way again sometime," Nathan said. "We don't get to meet many people out here in the sticks, so we have to depend on each other for excitement."

Tim smiled at them as he got into his car. "You can be sure I'll be back. Maybe next time I'll spend the night."

As he drove off into the night, with lube oozing from his ravished hole, he could see the two gorgeous blond brothers walking arm-in-arm to the door. Funny he thought, they've both sucked and fucked me and yet I've got no idea what their cocks look like. Maybe next time?

TIM GETS TAKEN DOWN

Tim wanted to increase his muscle mass, but his job kept him busy during the day, so he phoned a gym and made arrangements for some after hour instruction. It was after ten p.m. when he arrived at the gym for the arranged workout and introduced himself to Jorgen, the instructor. He could tell right away that Jorgen was gay. Jorgen was a perfect specimen of Scandinavian maleness. His smooth muscular body bulged in all the right places. The closely cropped blond hair, green eyes, dark tan and the mound in his gym shorts, all added up to one gorgeous hunk.

For the first half-hour of his session Tim concentrated on his exercises and followed Jorgen's instructions. After Jorgen had locked up the gym and it was clear that they were the only two remaining in the building, Tim couldn't stop himself. He had to have Jorgen. At first Jorgen seemed confused, like he didn't know what was happening. He probably thinks I'm straight, Tim thought. I'll have to be more aggressive.

Jorgen stood at the head of the bench and spotted for Tim. From his vantage point, Tim could see up the wide-open legs of Jorgen's shorts. The jock-encased mound had grown considerably since the beginning of the set and tented out the thin material. Tim placed the weights on the stand and ran his hands up Jorgen's smooth muscular legs. He pulled Jorgen toward him, slid up on the bench, so that his head was between Jorgen's thighs, and breathed in the heady scent of Jorgen's heated up perineum.

Tim ran his hands up into Jorgen's shorts, grabbed hold of his moist asscheeks, and pulled him tightly down to his face. Jorgen allowed Tim to eat him through his shorts for a short time and then he stepped back and removed the weights from the stand. He removed his shorts and jockstrap, moved back over Tim's face, and spread his cheeks wide so that Tim could get into his deep crack. Tim gazed up at the smooth white globes of ass-flesh covered in a light moist sheen. He had never seen such a gorgeous butt. It was as though he was in a trance when he ran his hands over the mounds, before pulling Jorgen to his mouth. The gym instructor's asshole, surrounded by a light sprinkling of soft blond hair, had that clean sweaty athletic taste that Tim adored. He dived right in, chewed on the sensitive pucker, and then ran his tongue around the crater, into the hole itself.

Jorgen gasped with pleasure. "Oh, yeah, dude. Eat my ass," he said and then leaned over, ran his hands into Tim's shorts and jockstrap and pushed them down his thighs. He took Tim's throbbing dick in his hand, lapped at the free flowing semen, and then sank the knob into his mouth.

Tim groaned into Jorgen's crevice when he was buried, balls-deep, in the gym instructor's throat. Jorgen removed Tim's shorts and jock and ran his hands down Tim's legs. He pulled them up, and locked them behind his arms, took Tim's ass-mounds in his hands and pulled Tim's asshole to his mouth.

They attacked each other with relish, as only two experts can do. Tim, who had only just recently lost his virginity to a couple of brothers, wasn't sure if he was ready to go that route again, tried to clamp his asshole, but it was no use. He knew his hole was widely dilated when Jorgen's tongue slipped deeply into his chute, and touched areas that had so recently been aroused by the brothers. The muscular gym instructor held Tim so tightly he couldn't even back away when he felt a finger in his hole, and teeth on his nuts.

Tim realized he might have bitten off more than he could chew by taking on the muscular dude. It was one thing to be fucked by a couple of strangers, he thought, but I'm not about to let anyone I know fuck me. Who knows who he'll tell? He tried desperately to get out of the clutches of the gym instructor. In his effort to get free his rear-end wiggled around the probing finger, which only served to facilitate the probing. But when Jorgen touched his prostate, he began to relax and enjoy the sensation. Tim moved his mouth to the gym instructor's balls and sucked them into his mouth. He began to finger Jorgen's tight hole, digging in deeply, until he too was able to massage Jorgen's prostate.

Jorgen suddenly stood up and pulled Tim over onto a wrestling mat. Before Tim could move Jorgen was all over him. He rolled Tim around, and slapped his ass, as though Tim was a cheap hooker he had just picked up on the street. Jorgen pulled him into a sixty-nine position and sank Tim's hard-on down his throat in one fast move.

Tim grabbed Jorgen's ivory-like dong in his hand and chewed on Jorgen's foreskin. He slipped his tongue between the skin and the shiny dick-head to lick up the free-flowing precum, and then his mouth covered the head and pushed the skin back. The two muscular studs held tightly onto each other, as they deep-throated the rods in their mouths, and probed each other's asshole.

198

Jorgen, once again, assumed the dominant role. He spun Tim around and clamped his mouth to Tim's mouth and sank his tongue in as far as it would go. Tim could taste his own asshole on Jorgen's lips when they kissed. Jorgen rolled Tim over onto his abdomen, held him in a tight wrestling hold, and nestled his rammer between Tim's sweaty asscheeks. Tim was in a panic. Jorgen was an expert wrestler and he was unable to get out of the wrestler's grip, no matter how hard he tried.

They sweated like pigs, and fought for control. Jorgen's hard dick-head started to breach Tim's hole when he said, "Please! Stop! I don't want to get fucked."

But it was too late Jorgen's thick cock was already deeply imbedded. Jorgen slowly pumped his naked dick in and out of Tim's chute. "You don't like it?" he asked. "I thought this is what you wanted?"

"I don't know. It feels good, but I'm not sure if I want to be a bottom."

"What's wrong with being a bottom? That way you get double stimulation."

"How would you know? I bet you've never been fucked?"

"You wrong. I like it. When I finish fucking you, you fuck me."

Tim wanted to yell, "Pull it out, pull it out, but he couldn't, it felt too good, so he relaxed and let Jorgen have his way. Jorgen must've felt the fight go out of Tim, because he raised Tim's hips and fucked him like a dog. His long fat dick, with an extra large head, was giving him more pleasure than the brothers had given him, and he wanted it to continue for ever. He pushed back on Jorgen, and said, "Fuck me. I want it."

Jorgen pulled out his dick, rolled Tim onto his back, then threw it back into Tim's wide open chute. Tim grabbed his own dick and fisted himself in time to the fucking. "I cum, I cum," Jorgen said, and Tim came too.

Jorgen rolled onto his back. Tim looked at Jorgen's dick. He couldn't believe it had been up his ass. His own dick had wilted.

"We shower now," Jorgen said.

"Tomorrow I'm going to fuck you," Tim said.

"I don't get fucked," Jorgen said.

"You said you did," Tim said.

"I lied."

Disciples of Priapus

Tim pulled on his shorts and then left the gym knowing he'd never be back.

THE AUTHOR

Donald Webb has had numerous short stories published in gay magazines and STARbooks Press anthologies. *Death Came Calling*, his debut mystery novel, is slated for release in fall 2013. He lives with his partner of forty-five years in Victoria, BC, and may be reached at <u>andon402@shaw.ca</u>.

; any underwear. "Excuse me," I said, having a hard time looking
d by that bulge in his crotch, "but don't I know you?" "Maybe," h
f to   bout a me
Ray   God, you
r?   in?" he as
Lik   s stronges
dy   e on Gree
e l   I ever sa
o t   any ideas?
ng   he same
ul   ery long t
ac   me swell.
ith   e in store
o c   behind so
e u   in public
ne   vent to the
y.   grabbed
I
ci   t, so firm
ha
m   bing dick
I   n cock, be
nd of unzipping filled the small space. I don't know who's hand
efore I knew it, I had his rod in my hand, and mine was in his. "
o?" he asked, his tone challenging. I knew exactly, and sank to m